THE COMPLETE ADVENTURES OF CORDIE, SOLDIER OF FORTUNE, VOLUME 4

OTHER BOOKS IN THE ARGOSY LIBRARY:

Tarantula Tower: The Adventures of Scarlet and Bradshaw, Volume 4

BY THEODORE ROSCOE

Henry Plays a Hunch: The Complete Tales of Sheriff Henry, Volume 5

W.C. TUTTLE

King of the Dead: The Saga of Monella, Volume 3

FRANK AUBREY

Cave of the Blue Scorpion: The Adventures of Peter the Brazen, Volume 5

LORING BRENT

The Monster of the Lagoon: The Complete Adventures of Singapore Sammy, Volume 3

GEORGE F. WORTS

The Fourteen Points

ARTHUR B. REEVE

Shark Trail: The Complete Adventures of Bellow Bill Williams, Volume 3

RALPH R. PERRY

Minions of the Shadow

WILLIAM GRAY BEYER

Rats of the Harbor: The Complete Cases of Dirk and Baker

RAY CUMMINGS

WAR DRAGONS

THE COMPLETE ADVENTURES OF CORDIE, SOLDIER OF FORTUNE, VOLUME 4

W. WIRT

ILLUSTRATED BY

JOHN R. NEILL & SAMUEL CAHAN

COVER BY

PAUL STAHR

STEEGER BOOKS • 2021

© 2021 Steeger Properties, LLC, under license • First Edition—2021

PUBLISHING HISTORY

"War Dragons" originally appeared in the August 6, 1932 issue of *Argosy* magazine (Vol. 231, No. 5). Copyright © 1932 by The Frank A. Munsey Company. Copyright renewed © 1959 and assigned to Steeger Properties, LLC. All rights reserved.

"The Devil's Tattoo" originally appeared in the November 12, 1932 issue of *Argosy* magazine (Vol. 234, No. 1). Copyright © 1932 by The Frank A. Munsey Company. Copyright renewed © 1959 and assigned to Steeger Properties, LLC. All rights reserved.

"A Manchu Robin Hood" originally appeared in the January 21 & 28, 1933 issues of *Argosy* magazine (Vol. 235, Nos. 5-6). Copyright © 1933 by The Frank A. Munsey Company. Copyright renewed © 1960 and assigned to Steeger Properties, LLC. All rights reserved.

"The Face in the Rock" originally appeared in the April 29, 1933 issue of *Argosy* magazine (Vol. 238, No. 1). Copyright © 1933 by The Frank A. Munsey Company. Copyright renewed © 1960 and assigned to Steeger Properties, LLC. All rights reserved.

"About the Author" originally appeared in the September 8, 1928 issue of *Argosy All-Story Weekly* magazine (Vol. 197, No. 5). Copyright © 1928 by The Frank A. Munsey Company. Copyright renewed © 1955 and assigned to Steeger Properties, LLC. All rights reserved.

ALL RIGHTS RESERVED

No part of this book may be reproduced or utilized in any form or by any means without permission in writing from the publisher.

Visit argosymagazine.com for more books like this.

TABLE OF CONTENTS

WAR DRAGONS

Two Japanese officers in Manchuria drank a toast—a toast that was to send adventurer Jimmie Cordie deep into China on a secret and dangerous mission

CHAPTER I

"WE WILL CONQUER!"

A COLONEL IN the Japanese army sat at a well lighted, heated house in Mukden, Manchuria. There was need for the heat because of a blizzard outside. The colonel, when a particularly vicious gust of wind shook the old wooden house, looked up from the maps he was studying. He thought for a moment of his regiment and other regiments that a few months ago had been garrisoned in Japan among the flowers, and shook his head. He did not like the cold, he did not like Mukden, or Manchuria or active campaigning.

The door opened and another Japanese officer came in. "I told your orderly that I would announce myself, Colonel Iyeharu," the newcomer said with a smile.

"You are welcome, Major Mito. At the moment you look like a snow man. The night is a bad one."

"Very," answered Major Mito, as he took off his coat and hat, shaking the snow from them into a corner of the room. "But I bring news that is not bad, comrade of my youth. And see what else I have brought." He took a bottle of brandy from his coat pocket, then tossed the coat on a chair. "So that we may drink a toast."

"You are more than welcome. You come with what you say is good news and also with a bottle of brandy. Mine was all gone and I was about to send my orderly for some. What is the good news?"

Red Dolan fought with every trick he knew

"First I will open the bottle and pour out the brandy into the glasses so that we may lose no time in drinking the toast."

Two minutes later, Major Mito said, "I drink to the day which will soon be here when our troops will hold all Shantung, Honan, Kiangsu, Anhwei, Chehkiang and Hupeh—in China!"

Long before he had finished naming these provinces held by the Nationalist government of China, Colonel Iyeharu was on his feet, his eyes shining, his body at attention.

"I drink the toast with you," he said formally. As he put his glass down, he went on, "But, Mito, are you sure? How do you know? It does not seem possible that the time has come to do as we have planned for so—"

"Always the doubter," interrupted Mito with a laugh. "I do know, and I—you know I have very strong friends at home and very little goes on that—"

"I know that your wife is the sister of the wife of the general staff chief," Iyeharu answered with a smile. "That is why you are so well informed, my friend. Sit down, please."

"No matter how. I wrote asking that I be transferred back to Tokyo and as you are my friend that you be transferred with me. I have received word that the transfer will be made soon and also the news about China. In sixty days, Nippon troops will land at Shanghai and take China, from Shanghai to the border of—"

A noise like the creaking of a board was heard. It came from the wall to the right of where the two Japanese were sitting. It did not sound like the wind had made it. It sounded as if some one had trod on a loose board that had turned a little.

Both officers were on their feet before the sound died away, both with their heavy service revolvers out. Instantly they emptied the revolvers into the board wall, spreading the shots from a foot up from the floor to the height of a man.

A shrill cry of *"Aie!"* was heard above the detonations and then, as they lowered their revolvers, silence.

The orderly ran in, his rifle at the ready. "Break down that wall," commanded Colonel Iyeharu.

The orderly reversed his rifle and with the butt easily smashed the flimsy wall boards out. Some fell out on the ground, but three of them fell across a body to another wall.

"Drag it out here," commanded Iyeharu, his face pale. The orderly dragged the body out into the room and both Iyeharu and Mito stepped up to the wall. "A passageway," Mito said grimly, "leading to that hole. Our engineers certainly did not examine this house before it was given you as headquarters."

"That explains why so many of our moves against the bandits

have been blocked or met with force," Iyeharu answered. "Much was discussed in this room."

"Too much," Mito answered. "If what we have just spoken of becomes known, it will—"

"How could it? The one who heard lies there dead. He was going when we heard him." Colonel Iyeharu turned to the orderly. "Bring Captain Saime to me at once. He will be at the headquarters of General Osaka. You know Captain Saime. Do not tell him anything about what has happened and—do not tell any one else. Your life depends upon your tongue, Komura. You have served me faithfully for many years—see that you continue to do so. This is a matter that involves my honor."

The orderly, who had come to attention when Iyeharu spoke, saluted and went out.

MITO WENT to the body which was face down and turned it over with his foot. "He was Manchu and was very young. See, Iyeharu, we hit him five times. Do not look so woebegone. He heard what we said, it is true, but now the only ones he can tell are his ancestors. Take a drink and you will feel better."

The two officers sat and drank brandy until the orderly opened the door and announced loudly, "Captain Saime."

The Japanese military intelligence officer who came in was a middle aged man, with cruel looking eyes and thick sensual lips and nose. His manner was brisk and efficient.

He saluted and after the salute was returned Colonel Iyeharu said, "Major Mito and I were talking. We heard a noise in the wall, fired at the place it seemed to come from and this—" he pointed meaningly to the body, "is the result."

Captain Saime went over to the body and looked down at it. "I know him," he announced. "He is, or rather was, Hsai Lao Chang, eldest son of the Mandarin Yang Hui Chieh. So—this is where the leaks have been coming from. I thought that the old mandarin was acting as a connecting link. I will send for him and his family. We will soon know all about it."

But they did not soon know all about it. The detachment sent to the house of the old mandarin came back and reported that there was no one there and that there were evidences of a hasty flight out into the blizzard.

"Your shots were heard," Captain Saime said, "and some one outside who knew of this youth being here gave warning. What matters were spoken of?"

"Routine matters," answered Colonel Iyeharu. "The expedition against the bandit Tsinghai principally."

"I will soon find the Mandarin Yang Hui Chieh," Captain Saime said, "and' when I do he will pay with his life for what he has done. His son has already paid. It may be that once he talks, we can plug other leaks. There are many Manchus here that are not to be trusted. I will take charge of the matter, Colonel Iyeharu. I speak for the military intelligence."

After he had gone, Iyeharu asked Mito, "You—but how could he? The one that heard is dead. If it were known that you and I openly discussed—what you spoke of—we would both be disgraced."

"And now we will be decorated for having discovered a spy," answered Mito with a smile. "Do not think any more of it. Can the dead talk to the living?"

YEN YUAN, old, fat, placid looking, with finger nails encased in golden sheaths, sat in the beautiful flower gardens of his palace in Hongkong. He looked more like some kindly, scholarly old grandfather than the head of the most powerful, dreaded secret society in the Orient. The T'aip'ing numbered some three million members and ranged from the highest official to the lowest coolie. Yen Yuan had the power of the high, the middle and the low justice and his orders were obeyed to the letter, without question or hesitation.

With him sat an old man, a Manchu, and a slim, black-eyed American.

"I asked that you do me the honor of coming here to my gardens, honorable elder brother," Yen Yuan said, "to hear a tale that I thought best told here where there is no chance of eavesdropping." His English was perfect—nor was there any reason why it should not have been. Yen Yuan had been educated at Oxford and at one time had been ambassador for China to England.

"The one who sits beside me," he went on, "cannot speak English. Therefore I will translate. O mighty mandarin of the fifth military class, I present to you Captain James Cordie, an American and my honorable elder brother. Captain Cordie is the one of whom I have spoken. You may speak freely to him. Captain Cordie, the Mandarin Yang Hui Chieh."

Jimmie Cordie, ex-adjutant, Foreign Legion, captain of machine gun company, A.E.F. and since the war fighter in the far places smiled as he answered, "I am honored by being presented to the Mandarin Yang Hui Chieh."

Yang Hui Chieh spoke, Yen Yuan translated and Jimmie Cordie listened. Finally Jimmie said, "Wait a minute, I don't get it. You said that your son was killed there in the house by the Japanese officers. Now you say that your son told you what the officers said."

The mandarin said something after Yen Yuan had translated and then Yen Yuan said, "His eldest son was killed. That night, his other son, a boy of fourteen, begged so hard to go with his brother that he was allowed to go without Yang Hui Chieh's permission. He went into the passageway with his brother and stood there.

"It was very cold, and after the officer said, 'In sixty days Nippon troops will land and take China, from Shanghai to the border,' the boy signed to his brother that he was going. The brother nodded and the boy started. It was his foot that turned the board that made the noise. The shots did not reach him, as he was some feet away from the place the noise was made when they came through the wall. They did reach his brother. The boy got out and ran home. There he told his father, and immediately the entire household fled."

"I see. Tell him to go ahead with the story, resplendent one."

"There is no more story to tell, Captain Cordie. That is all. The Mandarin Yang Hui Chieh left his wife and little son in a safe place and won his way to me. His work is done and now he must rest. Pardon me for a moment while I tell him so."

Yen Yuan spoke in Chinese, the mandarin answered, Yen Yuan, spoke again, and this time when the mandarin answered he shook his head. Yen Yuan smiled and clapped his hands twice. A palace official standing some twenty feet away came forward and bowed. Yen Yuan gave an order and as he did the old mandarin rose from his chair.

He bowed to Yen Yuan and then to Jimmie Cordie and walked away with the official.

"**HE IS** very obstinate," Yen Yuan said with a smile. "He will not stay here, he will not accept a guard of honor; all that he will accept is an escort to my gates. He goes to the house of a Manchu noble. Truly these Manchus are stiff-necked. He has his own people to guard him if necessary." Yen Yuan looked away from Jimmie at the flowers and the little artificial lake.

Jimmie Cordie sat still and waited for Yen Yuan to speak.

Finally Yen Yuan said, "The little men of Nippon must be stopped, honorable elder brother. I know their strength and also—I know the weakness of China. There are many generals—with as many armies—but they are fighting only among themselves for what they can loot. It may be that they would combine against a common enemy."

"Some of them would sell out to Japan and turn their guns on the others," Jimmie answered, "and if they did not, they are not equipped or trained well enough to withstand Japan. There is only one man that I know of who could even hinder Japan, and even he could not once the Japs began landing divisions."

"You refer to General Tsai-Ting-Kai?" asked Yen Yuan.

"Yes. His Nineteenth Route army is fully equipped and he has many German and Russian officers, to say nothing of several Yanks and Johnny Bulls. His men have been taught discipline, trench construction and warfare. But he cannot whip Japan by himself; that is too big a job, O second father to me."

"Yet he might, as you say, hinder them?"

"There is no question about that, given that they only land a few thousand troops, thinking all they have to do is to kick a few Chinese out of the way in taking a walk across country. Once the Japs got mad at him, they'd mop up on his Nineteenth Route army. They'd have to, to save their face."

"Do you think that General Tsai-Ting-Kai could do what you call hinder them for—thirty days, clever one?"

"Depends on how many men they land and where they land them. If they land bluejackets and marines at Shanghai to take the native city and then push on to Nanking, General Tsai-Ting-Kai could stop them right there. And it would take time to bring a division over from Japan. I know the Japs well enough to know that they think they are invincible because they mopped up on Russia and have been able to chase the Chinese—up to date. So they think that they can do it this time just the same way. They'll start off with a few thousand men, and if General Tsai-Ting-Kai will move his army up back of Shanghai there is no question in my mind that he can make the Japs think they started out hunting rabbits with a shotgun and ran into a grizzly bear. How long he can hold them is another question, ruler of millions."

"Much can happen in thirty days, honorable elder brother. It may be that the men of Nippon will be withdrawn in that time."

"That's right," Jimmie agreed with a grin, "much can happen. There is an old saying in my country, 'First catch your rabbit before you start cooking him.' Applying it here, first get General Tsai-Ting-Kai to bring his army up to do the hindering. He'd get it shot to pieces and then the other generals would eliminate him and what was left."

"And yet it may be that he can be persuaded," Yen Yuan answered blandly.

THE ORIENTAL looked over at the flowers, and again Jimmie sat silent, his eyes on the impassive old face of Yen Yuan. One minute went by, two minutes, three minutes, and then Yen Yuan looked back at Jimmie.

"Once you told me, honorable elder brother, that you knew Sahet Khan of the Uryankhes Tartars."

"I do, very well."

"He is in your debt?"

Jimmie smiled. "Why—I suppose he is, resplendent one. In a raid too close to the border of India he was taken by the English. They put him in a stockade at Akola. Without going into a long story, I helped get him out. He said that he was in my debt, but you know Tartars, mighty one, better than I do."

"Will you go to him, O second son to me, and deliver a message from me?"

"I'll try to get to him," Jimmie answered promptly, "but it's a long, rocky road between here and the Lower Mountain in the Thian Shan range, all-powerful one."

"That is true, peerless one. I cannot send Chinese or Manchus to him. His riders slay all who approach without waiting to ask questions. But you can go and ask him one. I mean, honorable elder brother, that you can reach him and deliver a message."

"I probably can," Jimmie answered, "given I can get within asking distance. What shall I ask him, ruler of men?"

"Say to him this: Hold the Thian Shan for General Tsai-Ting-Kai against all who come from the west, and the jade hilted sword of Genghis Khan is yours. Yen Yuan, head of the T'aip'ing promises it."

Jimmie Cordie shook his head. "I doubt very much if he will do it. The Tartars think the Chinese far below them and to ask a Tartar khan to hold for a Chinaman—not so good. It might be possible that Sahet Khan would, to get the jade hilted sword."

"As you say, it might be possible that he would," Yen Yuan agreed blandly. "Will you go and ask him?"

"Why, yes. What connection has General Tsai-Ting-Kai with the holding of the Thian Shan?"

"This, elder brother. He wishes to become war lord of the

North above all else. Always and ever he is working towards it. If he reaches finally to where he can proclaim himself war lord of the North, his army must be ready to fight the Soviet back if they attempt the passes of the Thian Shan. That is why, for the past two years, he has not joined in the fighting among the generals.

"If he is told that the Tartars will hold the Thian Shan range for him and he is offered other things such as unlimited money and support in the North, it may be that he will see his way clear to resist the little men of Nippon when they land."

"I see," Jimmie answered. "If you offer to replace his army in addition, he would probably fall for it. Will you detail Shih Fu to me, shining one?"

"Yes, and whoever else you wish. May the gods make your way smooth."

"We'll see what we can do towards that end ourselves," Jimmie answered with a smile. "Looks like the dragons of war may soon be lashing their tails and breathing fire."

CHAPTER II

TORTURE

MANDARIN YANG HUI CHIEH had come to Yen Yuan in a hired ricksha and had commanded the bearers to wait for him. Now, as he was being carried along the Street of Ten Thousand Delights back to where he was staying, he smiled a little. He did not know what the powerful T'aip'ing could do to stop Japan, but he knew that his part was ended, once Yen Yuan had been told what had been overheard.

A fight suddenly started up in the street and the ricksha seemed caught in the middle of it. The bearers put it down and fled. Yang Hui Chieh sat still for a moment, then as men brushed against it, almost overturning it, he got out. Two Chinamen near called, "This way, lord of the world! To the shop of Li Chang!"

Yang Hui Chieh looked over and saw a shop entrance at which the two Chinamen were pointing. He was old and his fighting days were over; also, he was Manchu and did not like to have milling coolies so close to him. He walked to the shop and entered. A Chinaman came up and bowed. "If you will deign to walk to the rear of my unworthy, miserable shop, resplendent one, there you will find peace and quiet until the mongrels have stopped killing each other."

Yang Hui Chieh bowed curtly and started back. As he passed a piece of velvet hanging on the wall it fell on him. Something hit him on the head and he went down, unconscious.

When he came back to life he was seated in a chair in a room far underground. That he knew by the dampness and the stone walls. His legs were tied to the chair and his arms pulled back of him and also tied at the wrists. His head ached and he could feel that there was dried blood on his head and left side of his face.

Yang Hui Chieh said to himself as he opened his eyes, "I am in a trap."

The first thing he saw was the face of Captain Saime of the Japanese military intelligence. And then his eyes saw, back of Captain Saime, two Chinamen, and on the floor close to his feet, a tray of knives.

"You have come back to the land of the living, Chinese dog?" asked Saime, a cruel smile on his full lips.

"I am Manchu, not Chinese—little mongrel cur of Nippon," answered Yang Hui Chieh calmly.

"For that you die much more slowly, old water buffalo. Take off his right shoe and stocking," he said to the two Chinamen. One of them stepped forward and bared Yang Hui Chieh's right foot. "Cut a strip from the sole," Saime commanded. "A small strip. He is to be flayed very slowly."

The Chinaman stooped and picked up one of the knives. As he did, Yang Hui Chieh said to himself, "I must be careful, very, very careful. May the gods grant me strength to endure the pain until the right moment comes."

A strip of flesh fell away from his foot and his lips set in a tight line. The pain was almost unbearable.

"Before the next," Saime said, "how long did you have a listener in the house of Colonel Iyeharu?"

"For two months," answered Yang Hui Chieh.

"To whom did you repeat what was heard?"

"To Tsinghai, the bandit leader and to other bandits."

Saime laughed. "You are ready enough to talk, Manchu jackal. I thought that Manchus would endure to the death the torture without speaking."

"I am old," answered Yang Hui Chieh, closing his eyes so that the Japanese captain might not see the gleam in them. His right hand was coming loose. "Old and weak, little one of Nippon. If I can save myself torture, why should I not?"

"I am here to ask questions, not answer them, old fool. The night your son was killed, what did you hear?"

"My son was killed, as you say. How then could he report to me?"

"How were you warned so that you could flee?"

"One was on guard outside and heard the shots. He came to me."

"Now—what did you tell Yen Yuan of the T'aip'ing?"

"That I will not answer."

"Cut him again."

THIS TIME Yang Hui Chieh screamed in agony. He could have held it in, but he wanted Captain Saime to think that he was breaking.

Again Saime laughed. "You do not like that, Manchu war lord? Answer my question or there will be three more strips cut from your foot before I ask it again. What did you tell Yen Yuan of the T'aip'ing?"

Yang Hui Chieh moaned and twisted in his chair, "I—I—I cannot bear it. Yet I—I am Manchu and should—I told him what my son had repeated to me about the movements of Nippon troops and of the bandit Tsinghai."

"That is not all. What else?"

Yang Hui Chieh moaned and quivered as if cold. Inside, he was offering up a prayer that the chieftains of his House of Chieh who sat watching him from on high would also pray to the gods that he, Yang Hui Chieh, could play a Manchu trick on this pariah cur. The time was coming close when he must play it.

"Nothing else," he answered.

"Cut another strip," ordered Saime, his eyes showing the pleasure he was getting from the torture of an old man.

"Wait," yelled Yang Hui Chieh. "Wait, I will tell you. Spare me further torture!" His right hand was loose now. "I—I told him that the war lord of Szechuan would join Tsinghai if the T'aip'ing would assist him."

"So, that was it? I thought that there was more to it than the repeating of tales of what has already happened. What has the American, Captain Cordie, to do with it? He was also present."

"Nothing. I did not see him. He was not present while I was with Yen Yuan."

"You entered and then, a little later, he came. I think you are lying. Cut another strip, deeper this time. Then take off his other shoe and stocking."

Yang Hui Chieh swayed forward, upsetting the chair. His right hand and arm came around in front of him as he fell across the tray of knives. His hand grasped one and as it did, he laughed. A happy laugh, full of scorn.

"O little fool of Nippon," he said—and drove the knife deep into his heart. His lips were still smiling as the two Chinese turned the body over and as his spirit winged its way on high to be greeted with honor by the chieftains of the House of Chieh. The Manchu trick had worked.

That night, Captain Saime wrote to Colonel Iyeharu: "I have seen and questioned the Mandarin Yang Hui Chieh. He was receiving the reports from his son and relaying them to the bandit Tsinghai. He fled here to Hongkong to tell the T'aip'ing that the war lord of Szechuan would join the bandit, if backed by the T'aip'ing society. The matter is closed except for the questioning of an American soldier of fortune who may represent the war lord of Szechuan in some way. I will have him brought before me and find out what connection he has with the matter, if any. It is well to unravel all strings. I will then return to Mukden."

Yang Hui Chieh had died happy, believing that he had thrown Captain Saime completely off the trail. He had, but in giving the name of the war lord of Szechuan, which was the first name to come into his mind, he had, without knowing it, put the Japanese across Jimmie Cordie's trail to the Uryankhes

Tartars. The way to the Lower Mountain was through the war lord of Szechuan's territory.

So, when Captain Saime and the men working for him saw Jimmie Cordie and some other white men leave in two T'aip'ing war junks loaded with men and equipment and head north, Captain Saime smiled as he said, "My guess was right. He goes to tell the war lord of Szechuan that the T'aip'ing will back him against Nippon. I will see to it that Captain Cordie and his friends do not reach Szechuan."

CHAPTER III

COUNCIL OF WAR

A COMPACT COLUMN marched north and west from Ningyuen, on the Gulf of Fuchan, where the T'aip'ing war junks had unloaded it. Six white men, one hundred bearers who were T'aip'ing swordsmen and one hundred riflemen, also T'aip'ings and all Manchus. The bearers carried more ammunition than anything else and sixteen of them—eight in the van and eight in the rear—carried four Browning machine guns, set up and ready to operate.

From the start at Ningyuen, the column had been looked over by several ambitious war lords and bandit chiefs. But in a very few moments the war lords and bandit chiefs had decided that they did not want a thing to do with the column—and did want the column to get past their particular stamping grounds as fast as possible.

The six hard bitten white men who wore belts heavy with cartridges from which swung holstered revolvers, the grim, scarred faces of the bearers and riflemen and most of all the ready machine guns, all helped what Jimmie Cordie called "the local talent" to reach the decision that the column was a good thing to let alone.

So, as far as Tsin-pong, on the west side of the Siramurin River, the march had been in the nature of a parade.

Red Dolan sat down beside the Fighting Yid and the Boston Bean, who were stretched out beside a fire. Camp had been made near the river, the stars were out and the weather was just cool enough to make a camp fire a luxury, not a necessity. The Yid had just said to the Boston Bean, "Vot could it be sveeter, I esk you? Ve are full of grub, de stars are out, dare is plenty of good vater, dare is cigarettes und dare is nothing to do till to-morrow. All de comforts of a home, ain't it, Codfisher?"

"Evidently Red doesn't think so," the Boston Bean answered lazily as Red sat down. "From the expression on our dear Mr. Dolan's face one would think he had been tasting sour pickles. What is the matter, Terrence Aloysius, me good man?"

"Yes, tell it to poppa—Irish loafer. Has any one been talking mit de harshness to—"

"Go to hell, ye Yid chimpanzee," Red Dolan, ex-Foreign Legion and lieutenant of military police, A.E.F. interrupted, "and that goes for ye also, ye long legged piece av Bosting tripe."

"Oi, vot a vay to talk mit friends," protested the Yid. "Ve only vant to know vhat is it de trouble."

"I know what it is, Mr. Cohen," the Bean said. "Mr. Dolan is mad because up to date there has been no fighting to do. Mr. Dolan craves action, Mr. Cohen."

"And who wouldn't?" demanded Red bitterly. "Here we are half way there and not wan teeny bit av a fight have we had. Bad luck to the dogs who take wan look at us and run away."

The Boston Bean laughed. "Stick around, Terrence, old kid. We're not there yet. I have a feeling that you'll get all the fight you're looking for very soon now."

The Boston Bean was tall and lanky and his face always looked sad and sorrowful. He carried himself as if there were nothing much left to do but go to sleep and he intended to start doing that at any moment. In the Massachusetts social register he was listed as John Cabot Winthrop, but in the Orient, wherever soldiers of fortune gathered, he was known as the Boston Bean or the Codfish Duke or any other name that even remotely suggested Boston.

The sad look and the sleepy manner were both misleading. The Bean was absolutely reckless and happy-go-lucky and, unless he were really asleep, never missed a note of the band. He had served in the Foreign Legion with Jimmie Cordie and Red Dolan and in the A.E.F. as a captain, attached to G-2-B, the secret service division of American Army Intelligence. The Boston Bean fought against any odds with a bored "you be damned" expression in his eyes.

"I hope so," Red answered. "All Jimmie will do when I ask him what the hell 'tis all about is to laugh and begin some damn stuff about the wild men up in the—"

A Manchu came up and bowed. "Captain Coldie's compliments and will you gentlemen join him in his tent."

"We will," answered Red, "wid pleasure. Ye needn't tell him, me bucko. We'll tell him ourselves."

JIMMIE CORDIE looked up and grinned as Red, the Bean and the Yid entered the tent. "Light and sit, gents. The board of strategy is about to start."

" 'Tis about time something was doing," Red said as he sat down beside a slim, boyish looking man, who with another man, was with Jimmie.

"Red is mad because dare has been no chance for him to do it any fighting," explained the Yid sociably.

"Stick around, Red," Jimmie answered. "I'll see if I can scare up a little fight for you pretty soon. Here it is for you birds. Up to the minute we've come through darn easy. But from now on, it's no man's land. The game is to get to the Uryankhes Tartars as fast as possible, deliver a message and then get home, also as fast as possible."

"Is that all?" demanded Red. "What the hell sense is there in our getting all hooked up to—"

"Keep quiet, Irishman," interrupted the Yid, "und maybeso Jimmie vill tell you. Pipe it down or Jimmie und me vill kick from you de slats, ain't it, Jimmie?"

"Let's have it a little later," the man sitting beside Jimmie Cordie interrupted. "Get down to it, Jimmie." He was George Grigsby, ex-Legionnaire and major of infantry, A.E.F., born in Breathitt County, Kentucky. Fully as big and as strong as Red, who weighed two hundred and thirty-odd pounds, he was known in the Orient as "a damn good man to have alongside" at any time. To the other reckless, devil may care soldiers of fortune, Grigsby was as a sheet anchor to windward. Mostly a silent man, he fought with a little cold smile in his eyes and on his lips.

"The children must play, George," Jimmie answered with a grin. "Listen, Red. What may seem darn foolishness to you may be darn important to some one else. This message to Sahet Khan must be delivered, come hell or high water. I've told it to you all. The whys and wherefores I do not know. If I did I'd tell you. Now, no matter what happens, as long as there is one man left, he must go on with it. Never mind any of that 'we'll all die together' stuff. There is too much at stake. Is that plain and agreed upon?"

"Sure 'tis plain, Jimmie darlin'," Red answered, still puzzled, "but what the hell can happen to us? Many's the time we have gone—"

"I know, Red. Maybe nothing will happen to us, but if it does, we're set. One man can deliver the—"

"Wait a minute, Jeems," the Boston Bean said. "I see that you've been reading 'Twenty Years After' which is quite all right. But what you didn't read in—"

"Been doing what?" demanded Red. "What the hell is Boston Bean talkin' about, Jimmie?"

EVER SINCE the day when Red Dolan had met Jimmie Cordie in the Foreign Legion, he would ask, "What now, Jimmie?" or, "How about that, ye small sized shrimp av the world?" The answer always satisfied Red. And if anything puzzled him, he would come to Jimmie, sure of a satisfactory explanation. Mr. Terrence Aloysius Dolan, born Cork, Ireland, would fight anything, at any time or place and he had only one remark to make when confronted by the foe: "Aw, slap 'em to hell outta the way." He loved the slim, black-eyed Jimmie Cordie far better than he did his patron saint and as Jimmie said, "hung around closer than nine hundred dollars in bad money."

"The Codfish Duke of Massachusetts means a book, Red," Jimmie answered, smiling at the big Irishman. "A man named Dumas wrote a book called 'The Three Musketeers.' It was about three soldiers who took another soldier into the party. Then later Dumas wrote another book, a continuation of the first and called it 'Twenty Years After.'

"In that book, the four soldiers were sent from France to England after something for the Queen of France. When they started, they agreed that no matter what happened, one was to go on. The Bean is insinuating that I copped the idea of one of us going on, from that book. And just between you and me and the bright North Star, I did. And it's a darn good one, also."

"I was going on to say," the Bean said, "that it would not work in this case because Jimmie is the only one that Sahet Khan will believe. What good would it do any of us to come staggering up to Sahet Khan and deliver a message about the jade hilted sword of Genghis Khan?

"Not a damn bit," went on the Bean, answering his own question. "He would think the one that did it was goofy and probably stick him in a pot of boiling oil. I've heard that he considers that a good cure for almost anything."

"I think the Bean is right, Jimmie," Grigsby said. "You are the one to reach Sahet Khan."

The boyish looking man, who had sat with a smile on his face, listening, spoke. He was John Cecil Carewe, once a flight commander of an air squadron in the British service. He flew for war lord or potentate whenever a flyer was needed who could fight as well as fly. No two men could look more different in every respect than Red Dolan and the slight, blond Englishman who bore a proud English name. Yet, inside, he and Red were as alike as two peas in a pod as far as their love of a fight went against anything at any time.

"I say, Jimmie, old thing, George is jolly well right, you know."

"Und how!" the Yid agreed. "Ve all smooth it de path for you, Jimmie. You do de gettin' dare thing und ve do de dying, how's dot?"

The Fighting Yid was about as broad as he was tall and his blue eyes seemed always to be about to pop out of his head with surprise at such naughty doings in a sad old world. He had been a first sergeant in a machine gun company, A.E.F., and since France had fought in the Orient for whoever needed his services.

Born on Hester Street, New York, and named Abraham Cohen, the Yid's surprised look was as misleading as the Bean's sorrowful one. The Yid was never surprised at anything. Wherever Jimmie Cordie and the rest were, there the Yid tried to be. If he was fighting for a war lord and found that they were on the other side, the Yid would promptly desert and cheerfully turn a machine gun on his former employer. Jimmie Cordie had once said, "The Yid is a soldier of fortune, neither pure nor simple," and that about sized the Yid up. He was born without ethics of any kind and never acquired any. Beyond that, if he had any nerves, no one ever saw him display them.

"Well," Jimmie Cordie answered, "you gents may be right, at that. Sahet Khan is darn apt to skin a stranger first and then think about asking him why he was up in the hills. We'll put 'er this way. I've got the ball and you birds are my interference, and Sahet Khan is the goal line."

"That's it, Jimmie," Grigsby answered. "Let's get some sleep."

CHAPTER IV

TO THE RESCUE

ABOUT NOON THE next day a Manchu patrol came in to the column which was entering a pass leading to the higher hills. "Three run towards the pass. Two youths and a maiden. Far behind, pursuing them, comes a small party of Chinese." He spoke in Pushtu, the universal language of the border.

"Let the maiden and the youths pass you," Jimmie ordered, "then capture the pursuing party or drive them back."

Ten minutes later a Chinese girl and two Chinese boys ran into the pass from the side of a hill. They saw the white men halted in front of the column, and the girl cried out shrilly, "Lescue! Lescue! Save us! Save us! We ale Chlistians!"

There is no "r" in the Chinese language and very few Chinese can make a sound like it. If it comes at the end of a word they can manage it, but if at the beginning or surrounded by other letters, an "l" is substituted.

As she was crying out, she was running towards Jimmie Cordie. The Chinese boys kept right up with her, and all three threw themselves at Jimmie Cordie's feet.

Jimmie stooped and raised the girl, who was about fifteen. "You're all right," he soothed. "Saved and everything. Calm down, little lotus bud. Nothing can hurt you now. See, here are many elder brothers to protect you."

"Vely bad men after me," the girl answered. "No let them hult me?"

"Hurt ye?" demanded Red, whom any woman could twist

around her finger. "Let them try to do it, mavour-neen. 'Tis us that will learn the black hearted dogs better."

The two boys got to their feet as the leader of the Manchu patrol came up.

"They resisted captule, lold, and we slew them," he reported in English of which he was very proud.

"Who were they?" asked Jimmie.

"That I do not know, black-eyed, smiling one. They wele Chinese, dlessed as soldiels. We allanged an ambush and they walked into it. Befole they could file, we wele on them, demanding sullender. They lefused—and we slew them all."

Jimmie smiled inwardly at the report. He knew how much time a Manchu would give an armed Chinaman in the hills to surrender.

"Send the patrols farther out until we get under way again," he ordered. "It may be that there is a larger body close."

The girl had been listening and now said, "Vely close, vely close! At Tsinan. Hully, hully, lescue Levelend Palker and wife and Missee Dola Palker and Missee Edith Palker and native Chlistians and—"

"Wait a minute," Jimmie interrupted; "take another breath, little golden one. Start at the beginning. First, who are you?"

"I am Wie-tze-fu-jen, Chlistian, and these youths ale Yo Fei and Hu-tahai, also Chlistians."

"Where did you run from?"

"Flom mission house near Tsinan. Please hully and lescue—"

"Come on, Jimmie," Red interrupted. "What the hell are ye standin' there for? 'Tis some missionary that's—"

"Hold it a minute, Red. Let's find out what we're going into."

THE GIRL, who had a pretty, intelligent looking face, answered, "The Levelend Palker and family ale at mission house near Tsinan. Vely bad war lold want Missee Dola Palker. Levelend Palker say no can have, and vely bad war lold say will take and kill Levelend Palker and lest of family. All native Chlistians vely much aflaid but me. All Palkers my family since I was baby. I say I lun to get good war lold to come to lescue. These youths say they come with me. We stalt out flom hole in back wall and bad war lold's men see. We lun and they chase us. You come lescue Levelend Palker light away?"

"Was the bad war lord attacking when you left for help?"

"Yes, plenty. In flont and along little liver. Not in back, vely steep hill go up."

"How many men has the bad war lord got?"

"Vely many. Hundleds, thousands—I do not know."

"That's definite. Well, the—"

"Jimmie, what are you thinkin' of?" demanded Red. "Wid a white woman and kiddies in danger are ye standing here askin' questions?"

"I've heard Chinese stories before, Red. Five minutes won't make much difference, old kid. How far is the mission from here?" to the girl.

"We lun down hill, along liver, up hill, down hill, then up hill to pass. I do not know how far. The sun has not moved much since we stalted."

"All right, we'll go over and take a look-see. It can't very far. These kids would have played out. Get a little ahead, peach blossom, and show us the way."

An hour later the soldiers of fortune looked down at a little valley, through their glasses, from the top of a hill. At one end of the valley, close to the hills, there was a square stone house. A stone wall about five feet high ran around the house about fifty yards away from it.

Gunfire could be heard, and little puffs of white smoke could be seen floating up from the wall. In front of the house, about two hundred yards away from it, were a number of Chinese soldiers, lying flat on the ground or kneeling down, firing at the house. Over by a little river were two or three companies, lined up in company front.

"The Reverend Parker is holding the fort," Jimmie said with

a grin, "and doing 'er with black powder at that. Let's go down to the 'lescue.' And what the heck we are going to do with a missionary family along with us, the good Lord only knows. Shih Fu, take your swords to the right and come through the timber. Yid, you and Boston Bean take two of the Brownings and fifty riflemen. Ease down and come around the wall to the left. George and Carewe and I will stare straight down. We'll wait until you get down. We'll see that the girl and the— Where is she?"

"Over there on the right with the Manchus," the Bean answered as he and the Yid started.

"All right, she's as safe with them as she would be with us. Make it snappy, gents."

The Chinese made no attempt to fight. They took one look at what was coming around the wall at them, another at what was coming down the hill and then they ran. The companies lined up near the river did not get much of a chance to run. The Manchus had taken advantage of cover offered and got very close before they charged. The deadly swords were among the Chinese, slashing in and upward in the Manchu death cut, before the Chinese recovered from the surprise of seeing swordsmen suddenly rise up from the ground. Very few of the Chinese reached the river to swim to safety.

"Some more av the cowardly dogs," Red said scornfully as he, the Yid and the Bean came up to where Jimmie and Carewe and Grigsby were standing in front of the house. " 'Tis a fine piece av—"

"Darn funny that no one comes to—"

"Take a look over by the river and up on the hills, Teems," the Boston Bean said, "and tell us how funny what you see is."

They all looked and Jimmie Cordie laughed. "Will you walk into my parlor, said the spider to the fly. We did."

"We can't hold them here, Jimmie," Grigsby interrupted. "More chance back of the wall. Here comes Shih Fu. They are evidently behind him as well."

The hills on both sides had suddenly become alive with soldiers and along the river there was marching a full regiment. As George spoke, a mountain battery opened fire. The shells went far overhead, but all of the men knew that range and elevation were easy to correct. The Manchus came up on the run and Shih Fu, leader of the T'aip'ing, a war captain who had been with Jimmie Cordie before several times, announced calmly, "There are two legiments of the monglels closing in flom the nolth, honolable elder Mother. Shall I destloy them?"

"Not at the minute, little brother. We take the house and hold there—until we see what we are up against," he added. "It's probably mined, but what do suckers like us care? *Allons, enfants perdus!*"

UP TO the wall and over it they charged, the soldiers of fortune leading with .45 Colts out and ready. Through the yard and into the house which was vacant and unfurnished in any way.

"Darn considerate of them to leave us a fort," Jimmie said with a grin.

"Maybeso pretty soon she go boom und up ve go," answered the Yid. "I hope it dot you've led it de good life, Irisher. I vould hate to be up dare playin' mit a harp und listening to the yells of a Irish gonif coming up from below."

"Ye are not there yet, ye Yid flat faced duck. What now, Jimmie, darlin'?"

"Stand 'em off. That's all I know at the minute. Get out to the wall, gents, and welcome our new boy friends who are coming to call. George and I will take a look for mines or whatnot. That little devil sure did play Delilah to the queen's taste. She ought to be on the stage and—"

A shell hit the house high up near the roof on the left side. The stone wall resisted it, but it was warning that the range had been corrected.

The Chinese tried out a direct charge from the direction of the river only to have it stopped by a withering fire of machine guns and rifles. They tried it again with the same results. Then, a little later, they tried to keep up a rain of shells on the wall and advance. But the mountain battery could not place the shells on the wall or very near it and after that try, the Chinese gave up attempting to take the house. The battery continued to shell the structure, but the walls were thick and the shells two pounders, so little harm was done.

The war lord, Wuting, turned to Captain Saime who stood beside him under cover of a windfall on one of the hills. "Many of my little brothers have fallen, O man of Nippon, and yet the foreign devils are not taken."

"They will be paid for as agreed," answered Saime, "and for every shell you fire, five shall be given you, also other ammunition and equipment. If your soldiers had been more prompt and had cut off the foreign devils from the house as was planned, mighty ruler of the North, the matter would be closed by now."

"My little brothers did not know that the foreign devils would come down from the hills so swiftly or that they would face Manchu swords. As you say, Nippon will pay."

"Is there water in the house?"

"Yes, water, but no food."

"We will starve them out. There is no hurry, peerless one."

"Then we await their surrender?"

"Yes. Draw the lines close and see that they do not break through. Order the battery to cease firing. They are doing no damage and wasting shells. The ones in the house cannot be frightened by noise. They are veteran fighters. Order that the regiments be moved so that they may quickly support each other. The foreign devils may attempt a sortie."

Captain Saime had followed the T'aip'ing war junks in a fast ship secured from a Chinaman in the pay of the Japanese and then had followed the column for a chance to cut Jimmie Cordie out of it or to destroy the whole column, he did not care much which. Saime was fully convinced that Jimmie was on his way to see the war lord of Szechuan, and had been sent by the T'aip'ing.

He would have liked to have questioned Jimmie the same

way he had questioned the old mandarin, but he had despaired of getting Jimmie away from the column. So when the column got into the territory of a war lord friendly to Japan, Saime had arranged the trap. He, Saime, would get to the war lord of Szechuan later and arrange with him, which would help teach the T'aip'ing not to interfere with Nippon business.

The Japanese captain had a firm belief that any Chinese general or war lord could be bribed. Now, as he looked at the house, he smiled. The Americans had walked into a trap—and would stay there forever.

CHAPTER V

OUT AND AWAY

"WELL," DEMANDED RED Dolan, as the sun went behind the hills, "are ye plannin' to stay all summer, Jimmie?"

Jimmie Cordie laughed. "As soon as it gets a little darker, we'll start, Mr. Dolan. If you are in a hurry, you may start now. We'll catch up to you."

Red looked around at the hills, where innumerable camp fires were being lighted, and grinned. "I'll wait for ye, Jimmie darlin'."

"That's nice of you, Red. I'm beginning to think I need some one to hold my hand. The way I fell into that trap was sure a—"

"Any one would have fallen into it, Jimmie," Grigsby interrupted. "A trap baited with women and children in trouble is a hard one to avoid. It's water under the bridge, Jeems. Let's plan from where we stand."

"Only thing I can see to do is to shoot our way out. I'd like to know who set the trap. Darn few war lords up in this neck of the woods have brains enough to set the stage."

"Let's go," Red said. " 'Tis plenty dark right now."

"Don't be in such a hurry, Red," Grigsby answered. "They will wait for you. Jimmie, this bird, whoever he is, has got at least a thousand men and a mountain battery. We saw and heard that much. He knows the hills and we don't. Let's say we start in the dark—what then? It's a cinch that whoever set the trap wants us—or you. We will get a fight—"

"Have I lived to see the day that ye hesitate at a fight, George Grigsby?" demanded Red. "Do ye mean to sit there and tell us that we can't slap all the Chinks in China outta the way? Jimmie and me will take ye by the hand and—"

"Put a jaw tackle on," Jimmie said. "Never mind that slapping thing for a minute. Go ahead, George."

"The hills between here and the pass are full of blind cañons and gorges, and given that we get to the pass we'd be stopped in any narrow place where the hills come close. If it were just an attack by bandits or tribesmen I'd say do what Red wants to do, slap 'em out of the way and go on about our business.

"But this bird has at least two organized regiments and some big guns. That shows that he is no footloose gent rambling around to see what he can pick up. If it were in the open and they jumped us, it might be different. But here, they know where we are, and we don't know where they are or will be. If we get caught in a blind cañon or in a place where the Brownings can't operate to advantage, they will hold us, Jimmie."

It was a long speech for the taciturn Grigsby, and all of the men listening sat quietly, their eyes on his face.

"All of which means?" Jimmie asked.

"This, Jimmie. Whoever it is has presented us with a stone fort. There is water here and we have plenty of iron rations. We will make a sortie towards the river and while we are doing it you leave by the rear for Sahet Khan. It's the interference you spoke of, old kid. We can last here for a long time—and once you are in the clear, can start for home any time we get ready. If we don't make it there is nothing lost."

Jimmie Cordie studied for a moment. He knew that during a fight he was just as liable to get killed as any one else. And he felt that George Grigsby was right as far as the outfit they were up against was concerned. If the expedition was wanted bad enough to elaborately trap, it would not be allowed to fight its way to the pass and then be left alone. The three charges showed that.

"All right," he finally said. "Here, I'm boxed up. In the hills I've got a running chance to make it. I'll take Red and ten of the Manchu swords, commanded by Shih Fu."

"That is traveling pretty light, Jeems," the Boston Bean said.

"The lighter the better. Especially in getting through the lines this gent has established according to the fires."

"Vy not split it up?" asked the Yid. "I go mit Jimmie und Red und—"

"Red and I will go," Jimmie said. "It's dark enough, George. Let's get started off. If we don't see you apes again we've had a nice time at your party, haven't we, Red?"

"We have," answered Red as he rose. "What will we take wid us, Jimmie?"

"Our Colts and 30-30 rifles. In this case, Mr. Dolan, a good run is much better than a poor stand."

The sortie was started off by a burst of machine gun fire in the direction of the river, followed by the long drawn out war cry of the charging Manchu swordsman. Out of gates came a column, machine guns in front.

"LOOK! THEY are going to try to win clear," Captain Saime cried as he rose from where he was sitting with the war lord Wuting in front of a tent. "We will destroy them this time. I thought they would try for the river. Are the regiments in place?"

"Yes. Listen! You can hear the ones coming up from the rear to cut the foreign devils off from the house. This time they will be in time."

The regiment at the rear did get around in front of the house, but instead of having the backs of men to fire at, suddenly found themselves right in the path of a charge.

The column had gone some three hundred yards towards the river, then whirled about and started back to the house. The regiment, that had been on time, melted away under merciless machine gun and rifle fire and those who escaped bullets met Manchu swords.

"More of my little brothers die," Wuting said coldly. "Truly, this is an expensive matter for Nippon."

"Nippon will replace your little brothers and also will pay in gold so that your sorrow for those who have died will be eased. The foreign devils will not try again. They did not even dare to try the crossing of the river. Now we can wait them out."

"Is the matter so important, then?"

"As I told you, ruler of the North. If the war lord of Szechuan combines with the bandit chief, Tsinghai, it would mean that a Nippon division must be sent to the West. Separated, Nippon can handle them all, but to allow one combination to be made means that others will also be made. So, I stop the—"

A wounded Chinese officer staggered up to Wuting. "Two of the foreign devils," he gasped, "and a small unit of the Manchus, O Lord of Tsinan. They came through like devils and the guard left could not stop them. *Aie!* The sharp swords that—"

"Two of them?" questioned Captain Saime. "Describe them."

"One—was—slight and dark. The—other—was—a great—man with—with—I go into the coldness to—"

"Not yet," rasped Saime. "Hold yourself here. Was one—"

"One said—in the language of the foreign devils that I was taught in—in—what does it matter where? I am about to ascend the—"

"Not yet. What was said?"

" 'That's the boy, Jimmie,' and then, 'Come on, Led. Quit your foolin' alound.' "

As the Chinese officer finished, he fell at Saime's feet.

The war lord Wuting looked at the Japanese captain and said blandly, "Speaking of waiting them out, what now, O man of Nippon?"

"This," answered Captain Saime coldly. "All that has been promised you, you will receive. More if you hold the rest of the foreign devils and their Manchus here until I return. I wish to see them die."

"You are going somewhere?"

"Yes. Order that men who know the hills make ready to go with me."

"In which direction are you going?"

"North and west. The game has just started, mighty one."

CHAPTER VI

TWO PLOTTERS

TIENSUNG, WAR LORD of Szechuan, sat on a dais in one of the smaller audience rooms of his palace at Szechuan. In front of him stood the nervy Captain Saime.

He needed nerve to make a fast trip across country with only a few men furnished by Wuting, knowing as he did that the chances of his reaching Szechuan were a hundred to one in the face of the roving bands of killers of all kinds that swarmed through the hills, making them a madhouse of fighting. And it took cold nerve to demand an audience with the war lord of Szechuan, known for his almost insane cruelty and merciless treatment of any in his power, no matter who they were.

Tiensung looked down at the Japanese captain, who stood at attention. The little pig-like eyes of the Chinese war lord seemed to be fully closed.

"You have my permission to speak, captain of Nippon," he finally said.

"That of which I wish to speak, mighty war lord whose fame rings around the world, is best spoken where other ears than ours cannot hear. It is a matter between my Emperor and you—of whom the stars have said—will rule the North."

"Under Nippon's supervision," Tiensung answered smoothly. "It may amuse me to hear you—as will your screams under the torture amuse me if the matter does not interest me." He raised his right hand a little, and the officers that stood behind him and the rifle guard that stood on either side of the dais left the audience chamber.

"You may proceed, Captain Saime. First, bring that chair from the wall and place it here beside me."

To tell Captain Saime to bring a chair instead of clapping his hands and ordering that the chair be brought was in itself an insult. Captain Saime obeyed, his face impassive. But he was saying to himself, "Some day you will pay of that, Chinese dog."

"Now start your tale," Tiensung said as Saime sat down, "and make it an interesting one, little soldier of Nippon who is far away from the guns of his Emperor—and close to the knives of Lingeh'ih." By Lingeh'ih he meant the "lingering process," the slicing to death.

CAPTAIN SAIME felt that Tiensung was playing with him as a cat plays with a mouse, but did not show it on his face or in his eyes.

"This, then, is my tale, O war lord of Szechuan. One is on his way to you with the following message from the T'aip'ing society: Join with the bandit chief Tsinghai against the forces of Nippon and you will receive the backing of the T'aip'ing in all that you wish to undertake. This I say: Refuse to do so and you will be paid what you wish to ask by Nippon and once the bandits and foolish generals who are now offering resistance to Nippon are destroyed, you will be given the North to rule over, backed by our guns. The T'aip'ing cannot withstand us, powerful one."

Tiensung sat still, his eyes still two-thirds closed, his thin lips tight, his face as impassive as that of a stone idol. Was this little soldier of Nippon crazy? Or was it a trap? If a trap, who was setting it? He, Tiensung, to be offered the support of the T'aip'ing? He, who was of the Chao Ho society that even now was at warfare with the T'aip'ing? And the combining with the bandit Tsinghai with whom all men knew he had a blood feud. All men but these men of Nippon who were truly fools. He would walk softly in the matter until he found out the truth.

"The T'aip'ing is very powerful," he answered smoothly, "and here in China. The Emperor of Nippon is far away. And Tsing-hai is a war brother of mine. Together we have fought in many battles." This last to see if Captain Saime knew anything about Tsinghai.

"The T'aip'ing will not be powerful, once we have taken—once we have taken over Manchuria, commander of countless armies. This I offer you, gold enough to make you the most powerful war lord in the North, the backing of Nippon with which the backing of the T'aip'ing cannot be mentioned in the same breath, and the overlordship of the hills."

"You say that one comes?"

"Yes. He should arrive at any time now. He left Tsinan just before I did. May I suggest something?"

"You may."

"This: Await his coming. Then, after he has told you what the T'aip'ing will do for you, compare it with what I have offered or will offer after hearing what he has offered."

Tiensung opened his eyes a little and looked at the Japanese captain who spoke Chinese so fluently. "I will do as you suggest, Captain Saime. It may be that the one who comes has got lost in the hills. I will send out searching parties. It will be arranged so that you may hear his offer. You have my permission to depart."

"May I stay a moment longer, mighty one? I crave a boon."

"Men seldom crave boons when in my presence," answered Tiensung coldly, "except for release by death from torture. What is it?"

"That if, after hearing the one that comes, you decide to join with Nippon, that he be given me for questioning."

"First I will do some questioning myself," Tiensung answered. "After I do, if I join Nippon, you may have him." He added to himself, "You will also answer some questions, little soldier of Nippon."

After which he again gave Captain Saime permission to

depart. The Japanese captain saluted and backed out of the room, his bearing very military and confident.

"IS YOUR leg hurting very much, Red?" Jimmie asked. He and Red, with four of the Manchus were sitting on the ground, just outside the mouth of a little cave, far up in the hills. Below them and on both sides, under cover of rocks and trees, were Uzbeg tribesmen. And on the rock ledge that led to the cave were quite a few bodies, mostly tribesmen, the other bodies being those of T'aip'ing swordsmen. Shih Fu, wounded in the right arm, sat with Jimmie and Red.

"Not so bad, Jimmie. Me head hurts more. How is the wrist av ye?"

"Pretty stiff, Red. That cut paralyzed the muscles, I guess. Your wounds, little brother," to Shih Fu, "are they deep?"

"No, honolable elder blother. Alleady the blood has ceased to flow. Shall we again lesson these jackals?"

Jimmie Cordie grinned. "Our lessons don't seem to stick. I'm afraid they are very stupid scholars, Shih Fu. We'll wait until night and then see if we can get through them."

The first night out from the stone house they had successfully avoided several parties of armed men of various races. The day that followed had been spent holed up. The second night had been as the first, but as it broke dawn the second day, they had run into a mounted band of Uzbeg tribesmen. And in a place where there was no chance to get away on either side. It was a case of retreat or fight through.

They went through, but in doing it Jimmie took a slash across the wrist from a sword, Red got a kick in the leg from a horse and as he staggered to one side, an Uzbeg sword just barely reached the side of his head. Shih Fu had a bad cut in his right arm and two or three more light ones in his shoulder and leg. Two of the swordsmen went down, dead before they hit the ground.

" 'Tis only swords they have," Red said, "and us wid Colts. I'm going to get me wan av those swords. Wid it I will slap all the wild men from here to hell outta the way. I see wan wid a pretty hilt, Jimmie. I'll get it and—"

"Heads up!" Jimmie warned. "They are coming up! Use your rifle, Red. Shih Fu, take your swords over to the left. We will—"

"Get goin' wid the highbinder friends av ye," Red said quietly. "I'll hold 'em, Jimmie darlin'."

"I couldn't get a mile, Red," Jimmie answered with a grin. "I've lost too much blood. The interference is disbanded. We'll take 'er right here, together."

UP CAME the Uzbegs, disdaining all cover. It was as if they had decided to wipe out the little party up at the cave without counting losses.

The two 30-30 rifles began an unhurried and methodical bang... bang... bang—and at each report an Uzbeg fell.

"It won't be long now," Jimmie said with a smile as he reloaded.

" 'Tis the way I wished to go," answered Red, "wid ye beside me and—"

"Chinese come!" called Shih Fu. "Many of them, with lifles!"

The Uzbegs evidently saw the Chinese as Shih Fu did. They stopped climbing the ledge and ran for their horses.

Five minutes later a Chinese officer bowed to Jimmie Cordie.

"You Captain Coldie?"

"Yes, I am Captain Cordie—and you?"

"I am Major Ch'ienlung, Thild Lifle Legiment of the war lord of Szechuan. I was sent into the hills to escolt you to Szechuan, Captain Coldie. While sealching for you, the sound of filing came to us."

"You were sent to escort me to Szechuan? Then my presence was—may I present Lieutenant Dolan. Red, this is Major Ch'ienlung."

Jimmie had switched to the introduction when it had suddenly dawned on him that it might be possible that Yen Yuan had asked the war lord of Szechuan to ease him, Jimmie Cordie, on his way to Sahet Khan. Like Captain Saime, Jimmie knew nothing of a war between the T'aip'ing and the Chao Ho society.

Red looked at the dapper young Chinese officer and grunted, "H'r'ye." Mr. Dolan never cared much for the Chinese.

Major Ch'ienlung smiled and bowed to Red, then said to Jimmie, "I will have litters made to cally you and Lieutenant Dolan, Captain Coldie."

"I think that there will be another litter necessary," Jimmie answered, then as he looked around and saw that Shih Fu had disappeared, went on, "but I see that he is able to stand, so the litter may not be needed."

Why Shih Fu had disappeared, Jimmie did not know; but if he had, there was some reason for it.

Major Ch'ienlung had been looking at Jimmie and Red, and while he had noticed a little group of Manchus standing near he had not counted them and did not miss one when he glanced over at them as Jimmie spoke.

"We will be in Szechuan in five hours, Captain Coldie," he said. "Thele you will find doctols to tleat your wounds."

CHAPTER VII

A SWORD IN HAND

TIENSUNG HAD NO intention of letting Captain Saime be present at any conference he, Tiensung, had with Captain Cordie. At least, not the first one. Like all Chinese, Tiensung held audiences very early in the morning, around four o'clock or earlier. The Japanese captain was sound asleep when Tiensung entered the room where Jimmie Cordie had just been awakened by an official.

On the way to Szechuan, Jimmie's wrist had become infected and he had developed a high fever. So high that he had become delirious and had to be tied to the litter. On arrival, he was taken to one room and Red Dolan to another. It was a week before Jimmie became sane once more, and now, as he sat up on the couch, he was still very weak. The treatment by the Chinese doctors had cured the infection, but the cure had almost sent Jimmie on the one-way trail.

"You ale well enough to talk, Captain Coldie?" asked Tiensung. He had waved his escort and a doctor out of the room and ordered that no one be allowed to approach within fifty feet and that all rooms on either side be vacated. Tiensung did not want any one to hear what the T'aip'ing had to offer. The mere fact that it was offered might lead the head of the Chao Ho society, if it were overheard, to think that Tiensung was flirting with the T'aip'ing, and the thinking would be fatal to Tiensung.

"I think so," answered Jimmie. "Enough to thank you for the

rescue, O war lord of Szechuan, and the courteous treatment we have received here in your magnificent city."

"My unwolthy effolts to make you comfoltable hele in my miselable de-gladed collection of huts is not to be mentioned in the same bleath as the honor of having you hele. I have heald much about you, Captain Coldie, and of the othels who fight at your side. You fought the machine guns for Genelal Kwang Tung at Yangchow?"

"Yes, mighty one. You were there?"

"On the other side," answered Tiensung smoothly. "My little blothels chalged many times against the guns only to be dliven back. Befole we come to the matter of your coming, Captain Coldie, will you, in the gleatness of your condescension, explain to me something that I have often wondeled about?"

"I will if I can, ruler of the North."

"It is your connection with the powelful T'aip'ing Head, Yen Yuan."

That puzzled Jimmie Cordie. If Tiensung had a message for him or had been ordered to further him on his way to Sahet Khan, he, Tiensung, would know the answer. But there was no mystery about his connection, and he answered promptly.

"Once, many years ago, I was a student at one of the institutions of learning in America. There was a young Chinese student there with whom I became friendly. He was in a strange and, to him, hostile land. He spent as much time with me as he could and seemed to like me very much. One day I missed him from classes, and after making inquiry, found him to be sick with a virulent fever. He had been taken to a hospital, and I found him there. He was in the shadow of the valley of death, O commander of armies.

"All that money could buy, he had, but he lacked a friend. I stayed there with him for a month, and did what we call in America, 'kidded' him away from the valley of death. Later, after the World War, I met him by chance in China. He took me to his father, Yen Yuan. I could not persuade either Yen Yuan or

Shanhai Li that I had not saved Shanhai Li's life. Yen Yuan announced that I was his honorable elder brother. I know that an order went out through the T'aip'ing that I was that, and that I was to be treated as such by all who wished to keep on living. Does that explain, war lord of Szechuan?"

"Yes, vely fully, Captain Coldie. You ale not, then, a member of the T'aip'ing?"

"No, I am not a member, resplendent one."

"The matter is plain to me. Now, what is the message flom Yen Yuan to me, Captain Coldie?"

"I have no message for you, lord of Szechuan. I thought that you had received one to relay to me or that you had been requested to further me on my way. There has evidently been a mistake made by some one."

"On your way to whele?" asked Tiensung.

JIMMIE CORDIE was on guard now. The trap at Tsinan and now this war lord asking that a message be delivered. He answered readily, "On my way to the shrine of the Mings. There are some jades up there in the hands of one of the old priests which are of interest to the T'aip'ing. Jades that were carved by the first head of the mighty society."

"I see," answered Tiensung. "As you say, thele has evidently been a mistake made by some one." He rose as he continued, "Lest and get stlong, Captain Coldie. When you ale able to tlavel, I will fulther you on your way."

"He doesn't say to where," Jimmie said to himself. Aloud he asked, "The one who was carried here with me? I would like to have him here. And the Manchus who were also brought to your famous walled city?"

"The one that was callied hele will be blought to you. The Manchus ale the honoled guests of my soldiels. You ale sule you have no message for me?"

"Very sure," answered Jimmie with a smile. "Who told you that I had, illustrious one?" He did not expect to have the question answered, knowing the Chinese—and it was not answered.

"An idle tale was told me," Tiensung said as he turned toward the door. "Lest and get stlong, Captain Coldie."

Jimmie, after Tiensung had gone, settled back against the pillows that propped him up. "No so good," he murmured as he closed his eyes. "That bird has something up his sleeve. Looks like—I—jumped out of—the frying—pan, right smack—into the fire." As he finished, he went to sleep.

Tiensung went back to his palace, his face as impassive as ever. He believed what Jimmie had told him and his brain was as active as his face was still, planning just what to tell Captain Saime the T'aip'ing offer was. He would make the Japanese captain top the offer and then let him have Captain Cordie to do with as he saw fit.

It might be that under torture the foreign devil would reveal interesting things. If he died still denying that the T'aip'ing had sent him, Captain Saime would put it down to the obstinacy of the American and the chances were that Captain Cordie would admit anything to gain respite from pain.

All in all, as Tiensung went to his gardens he was very well pleased with the turn of affairs. To have Japan bidding against, or thinking she was bidding against, the T'aip'ing for his support, was a very good thing as far as he went.

He was sitting in the gardens when Captain Saime was brought in front of him. Behind Tiensung there stood several officers of his staff. There was a chair placed a little to the right of him.

"YOU HAVE my permission to sit down," he said as Captain Saime saluted. As the Japanese captain sat down, Tiensung held up his right hand and bent it backwards. The staff officers dropped back out of hearing.

"The messenger from the T'aip'ing sent for me early this morning," Tiensung went on blandly. "He thought that he was about to go howling out into the cold darkness where all spirits which have inhabited the bodies of foreign devils go when released. He wished to deliver the message before, therefore I went to him. I regret that there was not time to have you aroused so that you could accompany me."

That did not fool Captain Saime at all. He knew just what Tiensung had done and why he did it. But he did not show the knowledge as he asked, "Did the spirit of the foreign devil go howling out into the cold darkness, mighty war lord?"

"No. It was a fainting fit. The doctors brought him out of it. He is better than ever, now. You may have him for questioning— as soon as our matter is settled."

"May I ask what the T'aip'ing offer is, ruler of the North?"

"You may," purred Tiensung. "If I will at once march to join Tsinghai and help him resist the forces of Nippon, I will receive one million taels, a division fully equipped and later, when Nippon has been driven from Manchuria, control of the North from the Khinghan Mountains to the Siberian railroad."

Captain Saime smiled, "Too little, mighty one. Nippon offers two million taels, all the divisions you need to control your territory which will be from the Khinghan Mountains to the Amur River and south to the Siramuren River. Also the Thian Shan range."

"The Thian Shan is held by the Uryankhes and Altai Tartars. It would take many divisions to unseat them."

"The divisions will be furnished, O ruler of the North. The passes of the Thian Shan must be fortified against the Soviet dogs."

"How will the money be paid me?"

"I will send for it, resplendent one, and remain here until it comes. Now—may I have this Captain Cordie to question?"

"Yes. The matter is closed. Let Nippon live up to the agreement and I will hold the North for her. I know of this American Captain Cordie. He will be a hard man to make admit anything."

"I will make him talk," answered Captain Saime, his full lips taking on a cruel twist, "if you will detail your torturers to me."

"I will. First, I will send for him and the one who came with him. Question both of them. The big man with the flaming hair may also know things. If they do not answer quickly, I will have them taken to a place where they will answer—and only you and I and the torturers may hear."

RED DOLAN'S wounds had been light ones and as he stood by Jimmie Cordie's side in front of Tiensung and Captain Saime he was as good as ever, save in one respect. His temper was rapidly becoming unleashed.

Jimmie was so weak that he could hardly stand and Red knew it. He saw the Chinese war lord and the Japanese captain sitting down and Jimmie standing in front of them, trying hard not to sway back and forth.

"Captain Coldie," Tiensung said blandly, "the one sitting beside me is Captain Saime of the folces of Nippon. He also undelstands English so I will speak in that language."

"Oh, ye will?" snarled Red, glaring at Tiensung. "And who the hell do ye think ye are, leavin' Jimmie Cordie to stand while ye and that little monkey-face sit in chairs? Have a chair brought for Jimmie Cordie and be quick about it, ye flat-faced scut."

It was plain to be seen that Red's temper was entirely gone—and with it what sense of discretion he had. To call a war lord a "flat-faced scut" when the war lord sat in his walled city, was something few men would do, even if backed by a couple of regiments. But Red Dolan did it, standing there without a thing on him except his clothes. Their rifles and Colts had disappeared right after they got to Szeehuan.

"Steady, Red," Jimmie said calmly. "Let him make the play."

"I do not know what a flat-faced scut is," Tiensung said velvetly. "I will ask you to explain it to me, later. At the moment, Captain Saime wishes to ask Captain Coldie some questions."

"What ye will do first is to have a chair brought for Jimmie Cordie," Red said. "Are ye to be sittin' there fannin' the mug av ye and Jimmie, who is sick, to be standin'? Wan av him is worth wan hundred and wan av ye half-baked tin war lords."

"For Pete's sake, Red," Jimmie interrupted, "you are doing your best to get us both killed. Please—let me handle it, old kid."

Tiensung's own temper was none too good at any time and he never had to hold it—unless he was with other war lords stronger than he in men.

"You dale, you monglel of a foleign devil? You dale? You will die vely slowly in—"

"Aw, go on back to the laundry," Red interrupted scornfully. "Ye wear a sword, don't ye? Put wan in the hands av me and stand in front av me, man to man, ye yellow faced gibboon. I'll show ye whether I dale or not, what the hell ever that is."

The air felt cold and rare to Jimmie's nostrils and eyes, seemed shimmering and dancing in little waves of light that would turn to darkness every so often. For some unknown reason, Red's defiance began to seem very funny to Jimmie. As Red finished, Jimmie laughed again, and said, "That's the boy, Red. If that 'yellow faced gibboon' doesn't start him off—put the black curse of Cru'mel on him. I'm with you, old kid Dolan."

Tiensung paid no attention to what Jimmie said. He was looking straight at Red with eyes that were like those of a king cobra.

"You ale a swoldsman?" he asked smoothly.

"Good enough for the likes av ye," Red answered contemptuously.

"I cannot closs swolds with you," Tiensung went on, "because it would be beneath me, vely far beneath me. But—" he turned and called to the line of officers, "Kwang Liu, come forward,"—the last in Chinese.

ONE OF the officers came up and saluted. "Give your sword to the foreign devil with the flaming hair. I will honor you by giving you mine with which to give him the death of the thousand cuts. Afterwards, you may keep my sword and the one he has defiled will be destroyed. See how many cuts you can make before he dies." Then Tiensung turned to Captain Saime, "The one who has defied me, dies now. You may have the other to question. This one dies to wipe out the insults he has offered." This in Chinese.

"As you wish, lord of Szechuan," answered Captain Saime indifferently. "Captain Coldie will tell me all I wish to know."

"What are the monkey faces sayin', Jimmie?" asked Red.

"I don't know, Red. Evidently you are going to be given a sword and—"

" 'Tis right ye are! Here comes the lad that come up to the cross between a—"

"Save your breath, old-timer," Jimmie interrupted, and he swayed a little. "You'll need it. The time's gone by to be calling names."

"I'll get ye his sword in a minute, Jimmie," Red answered, "and then we'll run these scuts from here to hell."

"If we can't, who can?" asked Jimmie, smiling at Red. "Make it snappy though, Mr. Dolan." What Jimmy really thought was that he and Red were as close to the angel of death as they ever had been and this time they had no chance of avoiding the meeting. But he smiled at Red, the old reckless, happy smile.

" 'Tis a good sword," Red announced as he balanced the sword that Kwang Liu had handed him. "It won't take me but a minute, Jimmie darlin'. Then ye will have wan."

"Fair enough. Get me one and we'll go home."

Kwang Liu, a master swordsman, stepped up to Red, fully confident of his ability to do as ordered. He advanced his blade a little, contacting Red's to feel out the strength of Red's wrist. He found out in less time than a split second. Red was as fast as he was strong and absolutely ignored what the other man might be doing to him once swords were up.

During the time that Kwang Liu had to think or see anything further on this earth, he thought that he saw a bolt of lightning flash down and strike his blade, tearing it from his hand. Then he thought he saw another bolt go up. He did not even see it come down to his head. Kwang Liu, master swordsman, fell dead, almost cut in two.

Red let out a wild Irish yell and stooped for Kwang Liu's sword. As he straightened up with it he shouted, "Here it is for ye, Jimmie! Now we'll—Mary Mother!" Jimmie Cordie was lying face down on the ground.

"Jimmie! Jimmie! Are ye dead?" He dropped the sword and ran over and knelt beside Jimmie Cordie, all else forgotten.

"Seize him!" shouted Tiensung, rising from his chair. "Take him alive! He dies in the boiling oil!"

As the officers ran towards Red, Jimmie opened his eyes. He saw Red's woebegone face and smiled. "I'm back, Red. I must have— Heads up!" Jimmie was facing so that he could see the oncoming officers.

CHAPTER VIII

SAHET KHAN

THE FIGHTING YID sat down beside the Boston Bean on the wall of the stone house. "You know it something, Codfisher?"

"One or two things," answered the Boston Bean lazily. "Not more I will admit, Mr. Cohen, but I'll stand on the fact that I know at least two things—and both of them are that I am getting tired of this house party. Let's go home."

The Yid grinned. "Von of de Manchus sneaked it out last night und vent all over de city of dis var lord dot thinks he is holding us here. He says dot it vould be duck soup mit gravy to smack him in de pants. Dot battery has been moved down from de hill und parked by de var lord's palace. Und de regiments is all playing pinochle und drinking—"

"Playing what?" the Bean demanded. He had not been listening closely to the Yid. The sun was warm and the Bean was about half asleep.

"Vell, he didn't say it pinochle," admitted the Yid. "Anyvay, dey is all mit de belts loose."

"Does George know it?"

"Yes. De Manchu vas telling it to him und I vas dare. George says dot Jimmie und Red know dot ve are here und dot dey vill come back dis vay to see if ve are still here, so ve might as vell stay put."

"Well, George is probably right at—" The Boston Bean stopped talking. Both he and the Yid had seen Shih Fu, with Grigsby and Carewe, coming towards the wall.

"Here it is for you birds," Grigsby said, "Jimmie and Red ran into some Uzbegs and got some of that fight Red was looking for. They both were wounded and about to pull that Custer's last stand thing when a Chinese officer showed up with a company. He announced, after the Uzbegs ran, that he had been sent to escort Jimmie to Szechuan."

"Dot he had been sent? Vot de hell? How did it any von know dot Jimmie—"

"Ask some crystal gazer," the Bean interrupted. "Go on, George."

"Shih Fu tells me that the war lord of Szechuan, whose name is Tiensung, is a member of the Chao Ho society which is at war with the T'aip'ing. What that has to do with sending an officer out for Jimmie, and how they knew that Jimmie was in the hills, is—as the Yid says—'vot de hell.'" Grigsby smiled at the Fighting Yid.

"Didn't you tell it to Jimmie?" asked the Yid of Shih Fu.

"My honolable elder blother was wounded and so was the lord of the flaming hair, honolable Yid. Thele wele five of the T'aip'ing left, including me. The officer of Tiensung had with him some fifty liflemen. If I had told my honolable elder blother and he had leflused to go, we would have died thele or been taken captive and callied to Szechuan. I could do nothing dead or as a plisoner in Szechuan. So I disappealed and came to lepolt. The lines that this dog of Tsinan ale maintaining alound the stone house have many holes in them."

"You did right, Shih Fu," Grigsby answered. "I think that we may as well call it a day here and take a little walk over to Szechuan. With Jimmie here, it was all right to hole up and push him along towards Sahet Khan the way he wanted to be pushed. I don't think we could have made it if we had started with him that night. This war lord was hooked up for us then. Now it is a horse of another color. Let's see what this gent can offer to stop us going to Szechuan. We haven't any one along now to watch over."

"O.K. mit me," the Yid said.

The Boston Bean stretched lazily. "I think a little walk would do me good."

"Right old dears," Carewe announced. "We'll go to Szechuan and ask the jolly old war lord why he sent for Jimmie and Red, what, what, what?"

Grigsby laughed. "All right. Let's go."

The column almost reached the hills before Wuting, war lord of Tsinan, was able to offer any resistance that amounted to anything. He had heard that another war lord was getting ready to attack him and had brought the battery down from the hills to help defend his city, also one of his regiments.

By the time he got his battery in position and a regiment started to get between the hills and the foreign devils, the column had brushed aside the few companies that stood in the way.

Wuting, seeing that the column would make the hills, and not wishing to lose any more of his "little brothers" who would be needed in the coming fight with the other war lord, did not order an advance in the hills. From what he had seen, he was quite content to have the foreign devils get as far away from him as they wished.

A FEW minutes later, in the hills, Carewe, who was walking beside Grigsby, said, "I say, I've heard of this war lord of Szechuan, George, old thing. We can't take his city with the men we have. He has a jolly old standing army that from all I've heard is a—what is it Jimmie calls it—oh, yes, a bearcat. And his city is walled. There is a chap I know who fought for him once. This chap isn't given to drawin' the long bow and he told me that this war lord of Szechuan's army was fully equipped and whatnot. If he is holding Jimmie and Red, what's the giddy old plan?"

Grigsby smiled. "Up to the minute, there isn't one, Carewe. At least I haven't one. I know that Szechuan is a good deal different than Tsinan. There they had got over the tension of watching us and the regiments had been moved away from the stone house.

That bird evidently thought that we were afraid to come out. All I can think of is to send Shih Fu or one of the other T'aip'ing into Szechuan and find out whether Jimmie and Red are there and still alive or what has happened. Then try and plan a rescue if, as I said, they are there and alive."

"Right," answered Carewe. "Once we find out that Jimmie and Red are there, we may be able to seep enough men through the gates one by one to cut them out, what, what?"

"We may," Grigsby agreed, "and in the meantime, let's speed up a little. If we make a forced march, Shih Fu tells me that we can be close to Szechuan in three days."

The third day, about noon, the Yid was telling the Boston Bean about a brilliant idea of how to take Szechuan, which the Yid claimed he dreamed the night before. "I go in as de ambassador of Cheeseslovakia all dressed up mit feathers und var paint und everything und you come mit as my chief foot varmer mit—"

The Bean had just begun to interrupt with, "You are still asleep, Mr. Cohen. I will be the ambassador from—" when a T'aip'ing patrol ran up to Grigsby and Carewe. The Yid and the Bean stopped discussing dreams and ran up to see what was being reported.

"Mounted men," the leader of the patrol was saying when they arrived. "Many of them. One thousand, thlee thousand, fifty thousand! They cover the hills."

"Which way are they heading?" asked Grigsby.

"This way. Stlaight for us. Shih Fu stay to watch them for a few minutes. He say tell you, honolable major, be vely quick take position to defend. He say no can lun or no can fight them in open."

"All right, Taokwang, Get back to Shih Fu and tell him I say for him to fall back to the column." As the T'aip'ing turned and ran, Grigsby looked up at the hills on either side.

"Up there on the left," he said curtly. "We'll see what we can do for them."

"You didn't dream anything about this, did you, Mr. Cohen?" asked the Bean, as he and the Yid climbed.

"No, Codfisher," answered the Yid with a grin, "dis don't need it no dream, old kid. If dey are riders und anyvare as near as strong as Taokwang says, de dreamin' days is over."

THE FIRST riders to appear around the sharp turn of the pass spotted what was up on the hill to their right instantly. They let out wild yells of glee. Here was some fighting for them to do. There was some open ground on their left, and they rode into it, as other riders came around the turn. More and more until the pass and the open space was filled with big men on stocky, shaggy ponies.

"Look," Carewe said, pointing up at the hill to his right.

"Und ven you get it through looking dare," the Yid said, "Take it a look over by the left und up back of us. Also dey are climbing."

Shih Fu, who had arrived as the column reached the place it was going to make a stand, turned to Grigsby. "They ale Ulyankhes Taltals," he announced. "I did not lecognize them befole."

"Uryankhes Tartars? If Sahet Khan is with them, I may be able to—" He stopped talking as he took out a white handkerchief. "Get me a rifle," he ordered. A rifle was brought him and he tied the handkerchief to the muzzle. Then he stepped out of the rock barricade that had been hastily thrown up and waved the rifle.

The flag of truce was greeted with yells of scorn from the Tartars below who were just starting a charge on foot. That they were going to pay no attention to it was evident. But as the charge advanced, a few more yards, a rider came around the turn, followed by two more. They forced their horses through the press without regard for any in the way.

The charge stopped as if every man in it were frozen. The first rider pulled his horse to a plunging halt and looked up at Grigsby, who was still holding the flag of truce. When the rider appeared, Grigsby had just commenced to lower the rifle.

Finally the rider turned his head and said something. The other two riders dismounted and walked up the hill to where Grigsby stood.

"What is it, English dog?" one of them snarled in Pushtu.

"Not English," corrected Grigsby courteously. "American."

"You start with a lie," the other rider grunted. "You are English. I have slain too many of you not to know."

"America where Americans live is a country that was once owned by the English, and the Americans are—"

"Well, what do you want, English dog?"

"This. Is Sahet Khan with his riders?"

"There sits Sahet Khan on his horse—Englishman."

"Take me to him."

"What? Take you to Sahet Khan? Fool, you had much better die here than on the sharpened stake or in the hot oil, as you will if you come within his reach."

The Tartar who spoke wanted a fight, not to see a surrender or terms made with Sahet Khan.

"There is a matter I wish to discuss with Sahet Khan," Grigsby answered calmly. "It may be that he will not thank you if you prevent his hearing about—the jade hilted sword of Genghis Khan."

"What? You rave, English dog! What do you know about—"

"I will tell what I know to Sahet Khan—not to you. Take me to him."

"Come, then."

Sahet Khan, of the Uryankhes Tartars, looked down at George Grigsby and said coldly, "Well, what do you want of me?"

"I want to tell you this. Captain James Cordie, who rescued you from an English prison, is in the hands of the war lord of Szechuan, a prisoner, as you were once. He was on his way to you with a message concerning the jade hilted sword of Genghis Khan, your mighty ancestor." Grigsby spoke slowly and distinctly.

"Captain Cordie in the hands of the mongrel of Szechuan! He with whom I swore blood brotherhood a prisoner, as you say truly, I once was! What is this about the jade hilted sword of the Great Wolf of whom I am a direct descendant? You dare lie to me, Sahet Khan, Englishman?"

"I am not English. I am American, as is Captain Cordie. He bears the message for you about the sword, not I."

"He has it?"

"That I do not know, Sahet Khan. This I know—he is a prisoner in the hands of the war lord of Szechuan. We are on our way to the rescue. And you?"

"Who are you?"

"I am George Grigsby, one of the men with whom Captain Cordie has been for years. The others on the hill are also men with whom he has shared his bread and salt. One other he has with him. We started with him to you."

"Come with us, friends of my blood brother. There is peace between us—unless you have lied. If you have, you die on the sharpened stake."

CHAPTER IX

IN THE TORTURE CHAMBER

RED TURNED HIS head as Jimmie Cordie said, "Heads up," and saw the officers of Tiensung closing in. "I'll smack 'em out from under their hats," he announced. "Rest easy, Jimmie darlin'."

Red had dropped the sword as he ran to Jimmie, and before he could get back to it the officers were on him, striking at him with the hilts of their swords and the butts of their revolvers. Red Dolan went berserk and became as deadly as a wounded grizzly bear.

The Chinese officers were lighter, much smaller men, and they were also trying to obey Tiensung's command to take Red alive. One of them kicked the sword Red was after out of the way, but that did not prevent Red's getting a sword. He tore one from the hand of an officer, breaking the officer's wrist as he did it. He swung the sword up, only to have his arm grasped by two assailants and pulled further back. He fought with every trick he had learned in street fights in Cork and in the Foreign Legion and finally broke the holds on his sword arm.

Jimmie Cordie, as the officers closed with Red, tried to get on his feet and would have made it if Captain Saime, who had run up, had not pushed him back to the ground by placing a foot against Jimmie's chest.

"Stay right there, Captain Cordie," he said mockingly, "and rest easy, as the red-headed fool advised." Then Saime, after seeing Jimmie go down, turned a little to watch the fight.

A Chinese officer staggered past, his face a smear of blood. A little past Jimmie he wavered, then fell. Red had got him in the face with a full left swing, caving it in as far as cheekbone, nose and jaw went. As the officer fell, he dropped his heavy service revolver.

Jimmie Cordie began inching over to it, very slowly. Finally he reached it and took it in his right hand. Captain Saime's push had been far from gentle and it had almost sent Jimmie back into the shadows. It seemed to Jimmie that he spent a million years in cocking the gun. Finally he made it. Then, with an effort that took all of his remaining will power and strength, he sat up, just behind Captain Saime.

"Turn around, Captain Saime," Jimmie Cordie said.

The Japanese captain whirled around at the sound of Jimmie's voice, his hand going to his revolver butt.

"I thought that you might like to have the hole in front," Jimmie went on calmly. As he finished the sentence he shot Captain Saime dead.

Red heard the shot, and thinking that some one had shot Jimmie, broke through the circle that inclosed him. He was blood from head to foot and his sword was dripping blood. He looked like some great prehistoric caveman as he charged in Jimmie's direction.

He saw Jimmie with the gun in his hand, saw the body of Captain Saime, and he saw Jimmie get up on his knee to rise. Red let out the yell that the Dolans had charged to on many an Irish battlefield for more than a thousand years, and then, as he reached Jimmie's side, shouted, "Jimmie! Ye scut! Now we'll give 'em hell! Back to back, Jimmie! 'Tis us—"

Jimmie, from his knee, shot and killed an officer who had run at Red, his sword hilt raised for a downward blow.

And the echo of the shot seemed to suddenly multiply a thousand times in the hills. Then it changed into the staccato, snarling, *Tat-Tat-Tatatat* of machine gun fire.

"An attack! From the hills! To your war stations!" Tiensung

shouted. An officer, who had been running through the gardens, reached him.

"The Uryankhes Tartars attack, lord. With them are foreign devils who have machine guns. The Second Regiment in the hills hold them back, but cannot do so long against the Tartar charges and the machine guns."

"Report to Colonel Wang that reinforcements are on the way to him and he is to hold to the last man."

"What's coming off, Jimmie?" Red asked.

"I don't know, Red. I got two words. They were 'Uryankhes Tartars.' It may be that—"

Tiensung, in passing three or four of the officers who had been trying to pull Red down, gave an order. They advanced on Jimmie and Red with drawn revolvers, halting well out of Red's reach.

"Sullender or die," one of them called.

"Go to hell, ye—" Red started.

"That's plenty, Red," Jimmie interrupted. "Why die now? Let's stick around a little while. Drop that sword and put your hands up." As Jimmie spoke, he dropped the revolver.

"Come with us," the officer who had spoken ordered.

"I'll carry ye, Jimmie."

"Nothing doing. I can walk, old kid. Are you badly hurt?"

"Who, me? 'Tis mostly Chink blood on me. If ye say so, Jimmie, I'll slap 'em to hell outta the way and we'll go over the wall."

"I couldn't even walk to the wall, let alone help in that slapping thing. Come on, Mr. Dolan."

IT WAS not far to the House of Punishment to which Tiensung had ordered them taken, and Jimmie made it on his feet. It was a one-story wooden building with no windows, to the left of the palace in a space where there were no other buildings.

"Take care of these foreign devils for Lord Tiensung," the

officer said to the tall gaunt Chinaman who had been called to the door by a guard who stood outside.

"I will, resplendent one," he answered grimly. "Very good care. They will be here when my lord comes."

Jimmie and Red were led to a cell at the rear of the building and locked in it. There was no furniture of any kind in the cell, and the air was foul.

"What now, Jimmie?" Red demanded as he sat down, back to the wall.

"That's easy," Jimmie answered as he leaned against the cell door. "We rest here in peace and quiet until the Uryankhes come for us. What could be sweeter?"

"Hell of a lot of things," Red said promptly. "For wan—what's that?"

It sounded like a cross between the long drawn out scream of a mountain lion and the wail of a lost soul in the darkness. It came from somewhere beneath them.

"May the good Saints, Matthew, Mark, Luke and John, protect the wan who yelled," Red said, crossing himself. "Where are we, Jimmie?"

"I don't know, Red. If you want a guess, we're right over the place where Tiensung does his inquisition stuff."

For three or four minutes Red prowled around like a caged animal, treading softly so as not to awaken Jimmie Cordie, who had dozed off. He tried the door to see how firm it was, and found that it was too firm to be even shaken. He sat down again, this time with his back to the wall on the left side. As he settled his weight against it he felt it give a little.

"What the hell now?" he muttered. "Is the damn' buildin' fallin' down under the weight av me?" and as he spoke, he turned and pressed his hands on the boards of the wall.

Two minutes later Red knelt beside the half conscious Jimmie Cordie. "Wake up, Jimmie darlin'! Wake up! Jimmie, wake up!"

Jimmie's eyes opened. "Get away from me, you big ape. I was sound—"

"Jimmie, come awake. I pushed the wall open and there's a trapdoor and steps leadin' down to the divil knows where."

"You did what? You're dreaming, Red. Get away from—"

"I am not, Jimmie. Wake up and be the old self av ye. 'Tis a way out of this dump, maybe. Wance out and wid—"

Jimmie Cordie laughed. "I'm all right, Red. That nap cleared my brain, anyway. Tell me again."

"Turn the head av ye and see the hole in the wall. I sat down and rested the back av me against it and she gave on me. I pushed wid me hands and away she went. The boards was rotten and like paper, Jimmie. In the next room there is a trapdoor in the corner av the floor. I lifted it up and there is steps going down."

"Yeah? Get away so I can get up. That nap opened up a reserve strength tap I had in me somewhere. I'm me old self wance more, Terrence Aloysius. Let's see where the steps lead to."

THE STEPS led down to a tunnel which was perfectly dry, paved with stone and pitch dark.

"What now, Jimmie?" Red asked, as Jimmie reached the bottom of the steps, Red having gone down first.

"Forward, Mr. Dolan. Let me go first. This—"

"What? I will not. 'Tis sick ye still are. I'll go—"

"Listen, Red. The Chinese have a pleasing habit of letting prisoners think they are escaping. This tunnel may lead up into the middle of the warden's office for all we know. Or there may be a hole in the middle that will drop us a few thousand feet. I'm lighter on my feet than you are and can—"

"Go on ahead then. Wait till I get hold av the belt av ye."

The tunnel curved a lot and several times pitched either up or down. Jimmie felt cautiously with his foot before he put it down. After five minutes' walking he said, "One thing is dead open and shut; we won't come up in the warden's office, anyway. Maybe this is a private way to the palace."

"Whatever it is," Red answered, "we are on our way, Jimmie

darlin', and that's better than bein' in that room. I hope she leads to where I can get the hands av me on a sword."

"If hopes are being passed out, I hope that she leads beyond the walls right smack into the middle of—"

"What happened?" Red demanded as he bumped into Jimmie's back.

"I tried to push some steps down with my nose," Jimmie answered. "Stay put for a minute until I feel around and—here's the end, Red."

"Let me go up first. No tellin'—"

"It's a cinch there'll be another trap-door or whatnot. I couldn't push a mouse up or over. Go ahead, Red, and don't make any more noise than you can help. We're inside the walls yet."

Red climbed the steps, a few more than were at the torture house end of the tunnel. His head hit against wood and he ducked. "I hit the top," he announced. "If this damn thing don't give way on me, I'll push the buildin' off us, Jimmie."

"Go ahead and push and don't talk so much," Jimmie answered from the darkness below.

Red put his hands against the wood he had hit with his head and slowly straightened up. The steps creaked as his brawn went into the push, then something gave above and light came streaming into the tunnel.

" 'Tis done, Jimmie," he said. "Up wid ye." As he spoke, he was on his way up.

When Jimmie got halfway up, Red's face, shoulders and arms appeared. "Gimme the hands av ye. No wan is here. 'Tis a temple near the wall. No wan can see us from the—up ye come."

The trapdoor that Red had pushed up had been secured by an old rust eaten chain and padlock. Red's strength had torn the screws from the rotting wood.

The room they were in was one that was evidently used or had been used as a storeroom for temple and priestly paraphernalia. It was crowded with images of the gods, bases for them, urns, temple banners and chests containing the robes of priests.

There were two windows, both overlooking the wall of the city, about a thousand feet away.

Jimmie eased over along the side to where he could look on an angle out one of the windows. "Heck, they can't see us," he said. "I see them. Holy cats! The whole army is there. There goes another battery up the runway to—to—" he left the window and sat down on the base of an idol.

"What the hell are ye doin' now?" demanded Red. "Takin' another nap? Come on, Jimmie, let's go and find us—"

"Pipe down," Jimmie interrupted, absently. "There must be—"

A MINUTE passed, then another, and the third was half gone before Jimmie spoke again.

"Red," he began quietly, "get it out of that brick-top head of yours that we can fight our way out to the hills. No two men or fifty-two alive could do it. If we can't frame something and put it over, we are as much sunk here as we were at the other end of the tunnel. First, do you know what temple we are in?"

"I do not. All Chink temples look alike to me, Jimmie darlin'."

"I don't doubt it. Well, we are in the Temple of the War Dragon."

"How the hell do ye know that?"

"I know by the banners on the walls and the images of the Dragon's servants, nitwit. Why do you suppose we've been let alone here for so long, in a temple where there are fifty or sixty priests?"

"I dunno. Why?"

"Because they are probably up on the walls with the Dragons of War."

"And a hell av a lot av good it will do them to—"

"Darn right it will do a lot of good. Red, get this. The Chinese are the most superstitious race of people on earth. They know that the War Dragons are made and manipulated by the priests and yet, to the Chinese, the dragons are real. You sabe that?"

"I do not. Go on wid it if ye do."

"Let me put it this way. They kid themselves into believing that the imitation dragon they see is the real thing. You remember the boy and the rope trick in India? You know, where a rope is thrown up in the air and a boy climbs it? People really think they see—"

"I got you, Jimmie darlin'. The Chinks want to think it is a real dragon and so they do."

"That's the boy, Red. They can even see the priests' legs, but that doesn't make any difference. When the soldiers see the War Dragons paraded in front of them, facing the enemy, they honestly believe that real War Dragons are there to help them. The psychological effect gives verisimilitude to—"

"Whatever that is. I believe ye, Jimmie darlin'. What do we do?"

"Wait a minute. Believe this also, old kid Dolan. One slip and we're done. You used to play parts in the Cork theater, you tell me. Can you play one now—for our lives?"

"I can. Come on wid it. What wid the big words and all, I'm sunk. Tell me what the part is and I'll play it to the end."

"Fair enough. Now, there are all sizes of War Dragons, big, little and middle sized. We'll hunt around and find a two-man size. Get in it or under it or what the heck ever the priests do and start for the wall where the runway is they've been using to get the big guns up.

"Now, if there are any priests around outside they may know that it isn't according to rule for a small sized dragon to show. If there are and they see us, it's good night and good-by, Mr. Dolan. If there aren't any of the said priests around, we've got a fighting chance to make the wall and get in front of the soldiers. Once there—let nature take its course. That's the best I can do for us at the moment."

"And a damn fine best it is, ye shrimp av the world," Red answered joyfully. "Come on!"

CHAPTER X

THE DRAGON

THEY WENT SILENTLY and cautiously through to the next room, then the next and the next—like a big grizzly and a lithe wolverine stalking their kill. There was no sign of life around the temple and no sound except the gunfire from the walls and answering fire from the hills. Through a big hall and then into another wing of the temple.

All of a sudden they heard voices that came from a room to their left. The door of the room was open and Jimmie and Red side-stepped along the wall until they came close to it.

"Two talking," Jimmie said softly, knowing that a whisper carries farther than a low natural tone. "Maybe more, listening. I'll take a look-see." He was on the side of the door and by gently pulling it towards him could look through the crack.

"Four old men," he announced as he turned to Red, "working on a dragon. It's the workshop, Red. Three or four dragons in there. No killing if we can help it. Knock 'em out."

One of the old men saw the two foreign devils as they came through the doorway on the run and let out a feeble squeak of terror. The others looked up and as they did Red slapped with his open hand the one who had squeaked. It was like the cuff of a bear's paw and the old man fell from his stool, out before he hit the floor.

Jimmie, as the man nearest him rose, uppercut him. The man folded up like an accordion and joined the first on the floor. Red reached out and got a third man by the collar of the blouse and drew him in. As he did, the heel of his left hand connected with the man's chin. The fourth man drew a knife and thrust at Jimmie, who sidestepped the thrust and knocked him out with a clean right to the point of the jaw.

"And that's that," Red announced, looking down at the four unconscious Chinamen. "What now, Jimmie?"

"Pick out a dragon to fit us," Jimmie answered with a grin. "That one over by the wall looks about a two-man size, Red. Wait a minute. They'd spot our legs. Pull the pants off a couple of the sleepers while I go and look the dragon over."

TIENSUNG WAS not afraid of the Uryankhes Tartars as long as he was inside his walled city. In the hills it would be a different story. He manned his walls with his regiments and his big guns, even though it cost him the Second regiment to do it.

The Tartars had ignored Grigsby's suggestion that the outposts of the regiment be silently destroyed by the Manchus, one after the other, and the regiment cut off from the walls. To Sahet Khan and the rest of the Uryankhes, the Chinese were like so many rabbits to be rounded up and slain. But this time the Tartars went up against a veteran, fighting regiment, well armed and disciplined. After the first recoil, the Second regiment of Tiensung dug in across the passes and little valleys that led to the walls and put up a fight.

"Oi, such a business," the Yid complained to the Boston Bean who was on the next machine gun, during a lull. The Tartars had charged directly across the line of fire and the Yid and the Bean had to stop shooting. "Instead of sneaking it up on dem und den over de walls, de Tartars see some von to fight und dey did it. In the meantime, vot becomes of Jimmie und Red, I esk you?"

"If I answer that question I'd open an office as fortune teller, Mr. Cohen. Maybe this war lord won't hook up the attack with them and will lay off until—there the Tartars go over the rocks! That's the finish of the right of the line."

"Vot good vill it did us?" asked the Yid peevishly. "By now dis var lord has got it everything on de valls but de mortgage."

"Look on the bright side of things, my distinguished friend from Hester Street," the Bean answered with a grin. "It may be that right now the War Lord of Szechuan is shivering in his shoes, waiting to give up his city."

George Grigsby came up with Carewe. "You birds feel like a little forlorn hoping?"

"Sure ve do," answered the Yid promptly. "We are svell forlorn hopers, ain't it, Codfisher?"

"As forlorn hopers we are in a class by ourselves, Mr. Cohen," answered the Bean gravely. "What brands of forlorn hoping have you to offer, gentlemen?"

"How does this one suit you?" Grigsby said. "Shih Fu and his men just brought in a wounded Chinese officer they went out to get. The officer knows all about Szechuan, and he told Shih Fu all he knew. There is a place on the north wall that is being repaired and about half of it has been pulled down. Sahet Khan will fake an attack at the gates and at the east and west walls.

"We can get fairly close to the north wall by going up a hill and then down through the timber. The idea being to go over the low place and after asking the first persons we meet where Jimmie and Red are, go and get them and get out. Sahet Khan has too much sense to make a direct attack on the walls, and once this war lord knows that, he may take time to figure Jimmie and Red are hooked up with the attack in some way. If he does—"

"Good night for Jimmie und Red," finished the Yid for him. "Ve are mit, George, ain't ve, Beaneater?"

"We am. Let's go, gents."

A CHINESE regiment, coming up on the double to protect the wall, saw a small War Dragon come in stately fashion down the temple steps and start towards the wall.

The colonel shouted an order, and the regiment swung out to give the dragon plenty of room. The soldiers cheered as they passed the dragon and called encouragement to each other. "See! The War Dragons come to help us! They will breathe fire on the dogs who attack!"

If they could have heard what was being said inside the dragon, the cheers would have been changed to yells of rage at the profaning of a sacred thing by foreign devils.

"Jimmie! Steer the damn thing. I'm blind as the bat av Kilkenny. Walk straight. I'm stumbling all over hell."

"This dragon is supposed to wiggle, dumbbell. But if you stumble you'll be doing that little thing in hell right after. Stay with it, Red. Lift up a little if you can. It's pretty heavy on my shoulders."

"What? Sure will I lift, Jimmie darlin'. Is that better? Tell me when we get there."

"I will. Stick along. Not far now. When we get to the runway I'll stop a minute. Then, if we make it up and onto the wall, when I say, 'Now!' throw it off you and jump. That's all I can think of."

"I'm wid ye, Jimmie."

The dragon made the runway and then, after a pause, went up it. Chinese soldiers at the rapid fire guns and the heavy battery and the supporting infantry, those that saw the dragon coming, made way for it, cheering as the regiment had done. Jimmie Cordie could not see much on either side, but could see enough to steer the dragon through the spaces left by the guns. The wall was about fifteen feet wide, and he reached the edge.

Just as he was going to say "Now!" he heard a yell of rage almost beside him. A priest of the War Dragon's temple, one of those not being used to help carry a dragon, had come up. This priest knew that only the dragons that were already on the wall were to be used and had, as soon as he saw the unscheduled dragon, come up to find out why it was out of the temple.

The pants that Red had put on were far too small for him around the waist, and he had put his belt around them to hold them up. It had, for quite a little while, but in coming up the runway the pants had slipped down. The priest saw Red's legs and yelled.

"Now!" Jimmie said, throwing the dragon's head off. Red, at

the yell, had not waited for the signal. He threw off the hind end of the dragon and kicked his legs out of the pants.

To the soldiers it looked as if the dragon was falling apart at the yell of the priest. They all stared as if under a spell of suspended motion.

"Come on," Jimmie shouted.

Red kicked at the priest who was closing in, catching him in the stomach. The priest promptly lost all interest in dragons of any kind.

An officer, quicker witted than the men, drew his revolver and fired point blank at Red, hitting him in the chest. Red whirled around, then staggered to the edge and, with Jimmie, jumped from the wall.

CHAPTER XI

"THE WRECKING WAGON"

IN THE MAKING of the wall on that side of the city, or in the repairing, there had been quite a few heavy, large blocks of stone left on the ground close to the wall.

They both, in their jump, just barely cleared several of the blocks that were laid out on a line parallel to the wall. As Jimmie lit, his ankle turned under him. Red lit on his feet, but there was blood coming from his mouth. "Back against the stones," Jimmie ordered. "Red! Roll to the stones! They can't reach us there."

As Jimmie spoke, Red was already rolling over and over to the line of blocks. The angle to the top of the wall did not permit gunfire to reach any one lying flat on the ground against the stones.

"I'm done, Jimmie darlin'," Red said thickly. "Go on. Don't mind me. I'm—I always been wid ye, Jimmie. 'Tis only ye that—"

His voice was drowned out by machine gun fire from the nearest hill. It was long range, but the men at the Brownings had seen and recognized Jimmie and Red through their glasses.

The Boston Bean, the Fighting Yid, Carewe and Grigsby, with tight lips and cold eyes, strutted their stuff, all they had to strut.

The Yid and the Bean made the wall just above Jimmie and Red into a shambles. Grigsby and Carewe started from the middle and cleared the wall on either side for fifty yards. It was a sleet of steel jacketed bullets that nothing could live in.

"Stay with it, Red," Jimmie said, crawling along until he could get an arm under Red's head. "Here comes the wrecking wagon. Hang tough, old kid. It's all over but the shouting."

" 'Tis the Yid and the Bean," Red answered wearily. "I know the way them monkey-faced gibboons pull—" Red Dolan temporarily passed out of the picture.

The Yid and the Bean arrived at the same moment, both of them panting from the run. "How is dot for interference?" demanded the Yid as he halted.

"I esk you?" Jimmie answered. "Get to Red. He's badly hurt. Carry us. My ankle's gone south from the way it feels. Where did you get the Tartars?"

"They are the Uryankhes Tartars, Jeems, me good man," answered the Bean. "May I suggest less questioning and more carrying?"

"You may. Get the Tartars back from the wall. There's two or three regiments on the other side."

"They'll come back with us. Stick around until I get some of 'em to pack you and Red. You're too heavy for the Yid and me."

Shellfire was coming now from the parts of the wall beyond machine gun range and the Tartars had found out that they could not climb the wall, so were ready to go back to the hills. There was no attempt made to pursue the rescue party and with Jimmie and Red borne on crossed swords, the Yid, the Bean and the Tartars made the hills.

WHEN HIS officers reported what had happened, Tiensung waved them aside. He had other things more important to occupy his attention than the escape of foreign devils or the profaning of priestly War Dragons. While he was not afraid of the Uryankhes Tartars, he knew what it meant for his city and himself if they got over the walls.

"I will retake the prisoners later," he rather optimistically announced. "Get back to your regiment."

The promises of the Japanese captain who had died, the torture of the two foreign devils and all else but the keeping of the Tartars out of his city, had faded from his mind. But Sahet Khan, despite all his contempt for the Chinese, had too much sense to keep on attacking well-guarded walls.

It was not until later, when the Tartar charge did not materialize, that Tiensung realized that the feint had been made by the Tartars and not at the north wall. Even then he did not order his regiments out of the city. He knew what would happen to them.

That night, in the hills, Sahet Khan listened to the message Jimmie had brought to him. Jimmie had been with Red, who was badly hurt.

"I will hold the Thian Shan for no Chinaman," he said contemptuously. "Not even for the jade hilted sword of Genghis Khan, for which I would give much."

Jimmie, after receiving very efficient first aid from the Yid and the Bean, was feeling much better although still weak. Too weak to argue against a Tartar's absolute contempt for anything Chinese. So he said, "You swore once by the yak tail banner of Genghis Khan, your great ancestor whose fame still rings around the world, that I had released you from a trap, the jaws of which held you close. You swore that whatever I asked, that you would grant if it were in your power. You also went through the ceremony of blood brothership with me."

"I did," Sahet Khan answered. "But, as a blood brother you cannot ask me to hold the hills for a Chinese mongrel. I am a Tartar, blood brother, and so are you since the blooding."

"I know, Sahet Khan, blood brother. This I ask then—hold the hills against all who come from the west—for me, thy blood brother."

"Ho! That I will do gladly. I hold the hills for you against all that come from the west. I swear it on the yak tail banner of Genghis Khan. No matter who comes or what is offered me, I hold for you.

"I do this," Sahet Khan went on, "for you—and not in any way for the jade hilted sword."

Jimmie could see the longing in the fierce, eagle-like eyes

of the Tartar. He smiled and answered, "I know that you do it for me, blood brother. The matter is closed. Now—as my blood brother, will you accept a present from me, offered as a token of my love?"

"I will," answered Sahet Khan just as promptly. "What is the present?"

"The jade hilted sword that once your mighty ancestor wore at his side. It is in Hongkong, blood brother. Once I return there, it will be sent you."

IT WAS a month later when Jimmie Cordie sat once more in the gardens of Yen Yuan. His face was a little pale and he had lost a good deal of weight, but the smile on his lips and in his eyes was as ever. "And the doctors have reported that Red is well on the way to recovery, for which the Nine Red Gods be praised. The lord of the flaming hair is a hard man to nurse and keep in bed. So—the Japanese captain is dead, and Sahet Khan holds the Thian Shan for me. I hold for you, second father to me."

"And I," Yen Yuan said blandly, "hold for General Tsai-Ting-Kai. The jade hilted sword is ready for the Tartar, clever one."

"That's fine. He sent some of his sub-khans down with me—and his whole tribe is waiting at the border to escort it home. It's all over and there is no use talking about water under the bridge, but there's one thing that puzzles me. The only way I can figure a leak is through the Mandarin Yang Hui Chieh—and I've always thought that a Manchu noble could not be opened up."

"The Manchu noble was not, as you say, opened up, peerless one who is a son to me. He was trapped by the Nippon captain after leaving here that morning. I missed him and search was made by my little brothers. The Mandarin Yang Hui Chieh was traced easily to a shop in which he had been decoyed by an arranged street fight. The shopkeeper and all near were questioned and after a little persuasion told all they knew.

"Then," Yen Yuan went on, "two men were brought before me. Again, with persuasion, they also told. They were the men who had assisted the Nippon captain in the torture of the Mandarin

Yang Hui Chieh. He played a Manchu trick on the little Nippon captain. Resisting torture until the time came, he told a tale that led far away from the truth.

"But in telling it he selected the war lord of Szechuan to name. The gods must have wished to also play, putting that name in his mouth. The Mandarin Yang Hui Chieh did not know that your path neared the war lord of Szechuan."

"Well," Jimmie answered, "I'm glad to know that. Anything else wouldn't sound right to me. I told Red I'd be back in an hour." Jimmie rose and smiled at Yen Yuan. "Any time you have any more messages to deliver—one more thing, mighty one. You knew how the Tartars feel towards the Chinese. Why did you expect that Sahet Khan would hold for a Chinese general—even for the jade hilted sword?"

"I did not expect that he would, brilliant one," answered old Yen Yuan placidly. "That is why I asked you to go instead of sending a T'aip'ing column strong enough to brush all opposition out of their way.

"It came to my mind," Yen Yuan went on, a little smile on his own lips, "that if Sahet Khan would not hold for the Chinese—he might for you. I knew that you would ask him to do so."

Jimmie laughed. "I'll pass the question of how you knew that. I started to say that if you wanted any more messages delivered, don't hesitate to call on me, although I think that as a messenger I'm a darn good trap springer. All I hope is that General Tsai-Ting-Kai will see the light."

"General Tsai-Ting-Kai will see the light," Yen Yuan promised, smoothly.

Before Jimmie Cordie got back to Red, who was at George Grigsby's apartment on the Peak, General Tsai-Ting-Kai must have "seen the light," for his Nineteenth Route army was on the march towards Shanghai.

THE DEVIL'S TATTOO

"There's a rat which gnaws from within," Jimmie Cordie told the besieged Manchu war lord—and set out to do some ferreting

CHAPTER I

THE RAT WITHIN

THE WALLED CITY of Kitai, in the foothills of the Yabtono mountains, northwest China, had been and still was the stronghold of the Manchu House of Tzu. Behind the walls, there was nothing but a mass of ruins and debris. The heavy guns of the War Lord Chan-king, who was attacking, plus the bombs dropped from his planes, had reduced the city to piles of broken stone and rubbish. All houses of wood had long since gone up in flames, and the temples, the palaces of the Manchu nobles, and the beautiful flower gardens, were no more.

The city had had no defense against Chan-king's four bombing planes. No defense except the astonishing endurance of flesh and blood. The heavy guns mounted in the hills that commanded the city rained shells, then the planes had come roaring over to drop bombs. One or two hours of this, then the guns ceased firing and the planes withdrew. Silence for a brief space of time and then a hard, fast charge, delivered by uniformed, disciplined troops, supported by machine and rapid fire guns that swept the walls with a sleet of steel.

But ever and always, day and night for three days now, the charge was met by a defense equally hard and fast. Machine gun muzzles would appear out of what had looked a moment before to be solid wall and a merciless, accurate fire would destroy the charge.

Word of the attack had been received in time to send all women and children, with the old men who could not even hold swords, out of the city to a friendly War Lord far back in the hills. And the War Lord Chan-king was finding out, as other War Lords had found out before him, that to take a Manchu city when it was defended by veteran fighters was, as the Fighting Yid said, "No job for a boy, ain't it?"

From where he stood on top of one of the hills, Chan-king watched a charge being shot out of existence by the machine guns of the defense.

"My little brothers die fast," he said to the officer standing beside him. "Truly, this mongrel who promised much has failed. Once I take the city, if he is still alive, I will give him Lingeh'ih as a reward—not the gold he craved."

"It may be that as yet he has not had time to put his plans into effect, Ruler of the World. The Manchus are clever and—"

"The foreign devils still man the machine guns," interrupted Chan-king, grimly. "He was to have destroyed them. If it was not for them, my little brothers would have been over the walls long since, and I would have been in the city."

The officer did not reply, raising his glasses to his eyes as an excuse not to do so. Privately, he was not quite so sure as Chan-king that getting over the walls would mean the taking of the city. He knew that once over, there would be some five thousand Manchu swords to meet among the ruins; and he had had experience with Manchu swordplay, as a couple of long scars on his body testified. Personally, he had no desire to confront one of the swordsmen of the House of Tzu, even if he, the officer, had a gun in his hand. He knew that the Manchu swordsmen would keep right on coming, in spite of lead or steel tearing into their bodies, until they were within sword reach. And he knew that most of Chan-king's "little brothers" felt the same way about it.

The Manchus had cut their way through countless Chinese to the Peacock throne of China, and had ridden their horses over Chinese bodies while doing it.

No matter how much modern training, how much in the way of modern guns and equipment and discipline, how many modern ideas "Young China" might have, in every Chinese there is ingrained a dread of Manchu swords. In the North within the last year, for instance, the troops of a Chinese War Lord had

The passageway was suddenly as still as the two bodies on the floor

broken and fled when a Manchu sword charge had come from the hills against them. And those troops had been veterans of the fighting in the South; had been armed with machine guns and modern rifles, backed by artillery, officered by Chinese who had been trained in Germany and England. The sight of the long lines of grim-faced Manchu swordsmen, clad in the sleeveless silk fighting shirts and shorts of the Manchu graduate of the

School of Swords, led by the Master-Swordsmen, had been too much for the Chinese morale. The troops from the South forgot all about their modern training and ideas as they saw the flicker of the sun on the razor-sharp swords; and then they did as their ancestors had done since the fourteenth century, they raised a shrill cry of *"Aie! Aie!"* and fled, leaving all their modern equipment on the battlefield behind.

Hence the officer raised his glasses, knowing that anything he said might endanger his life.

"**HERE IT** is for you apes," Jimmie Cordie said. "And double-special for you two playboys." He looked at the Fighting Yid and the Boston Bean. "Any more waste of ammunition is out. When they break and run, lay off. No more speeding them on their way with fancy shots. The ammunition is getting darn good and all!"

Jimmie Cordie wore the uniform of a captain in Prince Tzu Yu's army. Ex-Foreign Legion sergeant, and captain of a machine gun company in the A.E.F., since the war he had fought in the far places. Among the Chinese he was known as "The Black-Eyed Smiling One—whom it is best to obey very promptly if one wishes to continue to live."

Jimmie was sitting on a box of cartridges, in a chamber dug out of the wall, underground. Sitting on other boxes, facing him, were five other men, the foreign devils referred to by Chan-king.

They were: the Fighting Yid, born Abraham Cohen on Hester Street, New York; the Boston Bean, who in the Massachusetts Social Register was listed as John Cabot Winthrop; Red Dolan, two hundred and thirty pounds of simon-pure fighting Irishman; George Grigsby, born in the Kentucky hills, once a major of infantry in the A.E.F., and like Jimmie Cordie, fighter in the places where any flag flew; and John Cecil Carewe, formerly Flight Commander, British service. Jimmie Cordie, Red Dolan, the Boston Bean and Grigsby had been in the Foreign Legion together. The Yid had been Jimmie's first sergeant in France. All of them made up what a Texas soldier of fortune once classified as "that durn Jimmie Cordie's outfit of damn regardless hombres."

"Oi, Jimmie," protested the Yid, "for vy don't it you bawl out de Irisher? Vy pick on me und be Codfish Duke? Bawl Red out, I esk you.—He shoots mit de eyes shut and points de gun up in de air."

The Yid was about as broad as he was long, and he had china blue eves that always seemed about to pop out of his head with surprise at such doings in a naughty old world. That look was misleading. The Yid was never surprised at anything; and if there was anything he was afraid of, no one had ever seen it.

"What!" yelled Red Dolan. "Ye Yid gibboon! If I get me two hands on ye, I'll take ye apart and see what makes ye tick—ye Hester Street cross between a flat-face duck and a black and white kitty."

"Outside of that," the Boston Bean announced, gravely, "Mr. Dolan thinks a lot of our dear Mr. Cohen."

The Bean was tall and lanky, with a sorrowful looking face that was as misleading as the Yid's surprised look. The Bean was absolutely reckless, and happy-go-lucky to the *n*th degree. A multimillionaire, thanks to his mother and father and three or four maiden aunts, he had left town and country houses, yachts and all that money brings in order to wildcat around in the Orient. His one idea of a perfect day was to be in a tight place, operating a machine gun, dirty with powder smoke, a cigarette hanging out of his lips.

"I do, do I?" Red shouted, thoroughly enjoying himself. "And who asked you to butt in, ye long-legged piece av tripe from Bosting? Wan Dolan can lick forty-nine Yids, wid nine Bosting Beans thrown in."

"Shut it up, Irish *gondif!*" the Yid answered, loftily, "me und Jimmie vill kick from you de slats—ain't it, Jimmie?"

"It ain't. Do your own fighting. You and the Bean ought to be able to take Mr. Dolan for a buggy ride."

"They ought, ought they?" Red, former lieutenant of military police in France, rose to the bait. "They ought? I'll take them, and eighty-wan Cordies besides, wid one hand tied behind me.—What the hell now?"

While Red was telling how many Yids and Beans and Cordies he could take, there had come three explosions. Immediately afterward there sounded a devastating one.

"Holy cats!" Jimmie Cordie said, rising. "That sounds like the reserve ammunition.—To your guns, you gents! Our boy friends will be coming to take a looksee."

THE MANCHU Prince Tzu Yu stood with some of his staff officers, looking down at a deep hole in the ground that covered almost a hundred yards in the center of the city—or what had once been the city. As Jimmie Cordie ran up, he looked at Jimmie, his face and eyes as impassive as ever. He was a young man, educated in England, dressed in natty khaki uniform; but he was a Manchu War Lord, from the top of his head to his toes.

"The pariah curs have reached the reserve ammunition, Captain Cordie," he said, smoothly.

"So I see," Jimmie answered, looking down at the blackened hole which contained but the charred remains of boxes, and the muzzles of some guns that had been blown from their carriages. "Not so good, Tzu Yu. We are blame near out of—"

A man, dressed in the uniform of a colonel of artillery, ran up. He was excited and he began to wave his arms above his head.

"Ah! *Mon Dieu!*—My guns! Sacred name of a name! Ah, species of a camel! You destroy my guns! See, Jimmie, *mon ami*, my—"

"Can you bring your guns back by wailing like a woman?" asked Tzu Yu, blandly. "Control yourself, Colonel de la Brive."

"But yes, *mon général! Mon Dieu!* This is *de trop! Sang de Dieu*—"

"Calm yourself, Pierre," Jimmie interrupted with a grin. "You're making a show of French tempera— Here she comes! Duck, everybody!"

The shrill *whee-eeeeee* of a shell got louder and louder.

Pierre de la Brive and the Manchu officers ran to the dugout entrance.

"Come with me, Captain Cordie," Tzu Yu said calmly.

He led the way through a ruined temple, to a flight of steps leading down; then down the steps to a passageway, and along it to a room. Once in the room, he sat down on a stone bench and motioned Jimmie to sit down beside him.

"You saw the attack by the planes?" he asked.

"No, I was down with the machine gunners."

"One came, then another and another. They circled as if to make sure of their target, then they dropped bombs, one after the other—all in the same place. At last another plane came and dropped a larger bomb. The last one reached the ammunition."

JIMMIE CORDIE sat still, whistling an old, old song—"I know a bank whereon the wild thyme grows; where cowslips and the modest violet—"

Tzu Yu sat as still as Cordie, his impassive eyes on the American whom he trusted fully. In England, Jimmie had been able to do one or two things for Tzu Yu; and in the South they had fought for a War Lord together. Then Tzu Yu, on the death of his father, had been called to Kitai to assume his duties as the Head of the House of Tzu. Shortly afterwards, he had sent to Hongkong an urgent message: "Come and help me hold against the dogs who snarl at my heels, War Brother."

Tzu Yu was a Manchu noble, reared according to the strict code of the Manchus, who firmly believe all other races to be inferior. Yet he had accepted the slim, deeply tanned young American captain as his equal, as had the other Manchu nobles of his House of Tzu.

Finally Jimmie Cordie stopped whistling. "They knew where the reserve ammunition was stored. There is a rat here—a rat which gnaws from the inside."

"That is true, War Brother. A rat is here—which gnaws from the inside."

"Whoever he is, he could draw a map plain enough to enable the flyers to drop their bombs in the right place. The ammunition was moved only day before yesterday. That means that the map was sent out of the city and—Tzu Yu, I know that in most Chinese and Manchu cities there are many rat holes leading in and out from the walls. Do you know those here?"

"Most of them, Captain Cordie. As you say, there are many in all cities."

"Have men lowered from the walls to-night. They can be pulled up in case of attack. Holes must have an outlet somewhere. It may be that holes you know nothing of exist here in Kitai. The rat must be found, Tzu Yu. Our food supply is limited, and now the reserve ammunition is gone. Soon it will be Manchu swords against the guns and bayonets of Chan-king."

"Men will be lowered, Captain Cordie. If we can hold for a week, it may be that the curs who snap at our heels will be whipped back to their kennels."

"Yeah? How come? I thought that we were playin' a lone hand."

"One came through the loosely held lines of the jackal Chan-king and told a tale to me. The Marshal Chang Hsueh-Liang was the War Brother of my resplendent father, who now sits with the Chieftains on High and watches me, his unworthy son, defend the city of the House of Tzu from the attack of mongrels. Marshal Chang Hsueh-Liang has left Nanking with his route army for Jehol, there to resist the further aggression of the little men of Nippon. He has sent word to me that he will come this way. If we can hold until he arrives, he will destroy this pariah cur who snarls before our gates."

"We better find the rat who gnaws from within, Tzu Yu. If he reaches the food and the water supplies—not so good. It may be longer than a week before Chang Hsueh-Liang gets here. I'll move the machine gun ammunition to a place where we can keep an eye on it. As soon the sun goes down behind the hills, get men over the wall."

CHAPTER II

RED AND BLUE SNAKE

THE TEMPLE GONGS that had been taken underground began to sound the warning: "An attack! An attack!—To your battle stations! To your battle stations!" Jimmie Cordie had got even half way to where the machine guns were when he heard them.

The passageway he was in wound around a good deal, joining other passages. Underground, Kitai was more or less like a labyrinth. A Chinese or Manchu city is more or less cut out for several stories or levels beneath the ground. It was a good thing for the defenders of Kitai that the city was that way. It gave protection against the shells and bombs, unless a concentrated effort against any one spot was made, as in the blowing up of the reserve ammunition.

As the gongs sounded, Jimmie heard the machine guns open fire. "One-two," he counted, aloud. "There goes the Yid. I can tell his gun out of— The Codfish is awake, too. One-two-three-four—Red is out of commission, now. I told that big ape not to—"

Jimmie's flash light picked up the body of a man lying in the passageway, some fifty feet ahead.

As he ran forward, his .45 Colt out of its holster, Jimmie knew the reason why Red Dolan's gun was not working. Red lay face down, a little pool of blood under his chin.

Jimmie Cordie was a veteran fighter, and he had seen many men with their faces to the ground, some of them sent there by himself. Yet as he saw in the split second his flash light picked out the body, he felt sicker to his stomach than he had ever felt before. As he ran forward, the years of action during which the big, red-headed Irishman had fought at his side came back to him with the clearness of a moving picture. He seemed to hear Red say, as always, "What now, Jimmie, ye shrimp?" The answer, no matter what it was, had always satisfied Red Dolan.

Jimmie was still sick when he reached Red, and yet his training of years made him do what he did before stooping over Red. He threw his flash light along the walls and up against the roof, his Colt ready to issue death to any living thing he saw.

In the wall to the right there was a long narrow slit, like the slits one sees in old castles in Europe, through which arrows were shot at those who attacked. Back about ten feet from the slit, the wall did not quite reach the roof. There was a space of two or three feet.

Jimmie saw the slit first, then the open space. Without a second's hesitation he ran to the open space, played his flash on it for a moment, put the light in his belt, and with his left hand muscled himself up. It was either a foolhardy—or a very brave thing to do. Jimmie had no way of knowing but that the one who had tried for Red was not lurking up there, or just behind; and Jimmie's head had to come into the clear before he could use the Colt in his right hand.

But Jimmie Cordie never even thought about it. Up he went, and when his flash light went on, he saw another passageway, running parallel with the one Red was in. As far as the beam of his flash would reach the second passageway was empty.

"He saw Red coming," Jimmie said aloud, as he dropped back. "And then he went to the slit and thrust at Red's throat when—Well, for the love of Pete!"

RED DOLAN, whom Jimmie had believed to be dead, was sitting up, his throat and uniform front smeared with blood. But there was a grin on his lips. Jimmie leaned back against the wall, faint from the reaction. Red put a finger to his lips.

And as he did that, Jimmie Cordie's clever brain snapped into action.

"My God!" he gasped audibly. "He's dead! Red Dolan is dead! I'll get the hellion that did it, if it's the last thing I do! His throat is cut from ear to ear!—Dead! Oh, my God! Red Dolan—dead!"

As he said this, he ran to Red and knelt beside him.

"Be dead, you big ape!" he muttered out of the corner of his mouth, knowing that a whisper carried further than a low tone of voice.

Red promptly lay dawn, face to the ground as before. Jimmie was still shaken, but his brain was working. He saw the blood on Red's throat and he knew it was real blood; and yet— Red had sat up and grinned, and if his throat was cut, how could he have put his finger to his lips? It was enough to shake any man; and Jimmie loved this red-headed devil.

Jimmie did not want to leave Red playing dead, because whoever had tried to put Red on the one-way trail might not have left the passageway yet. He might come back, if Jimmie left; and he might really finish Mr. Dolan then.

Jimmie knew that Manchu swordsmen were in a good many of the passageways, especially those that led quickly to the top of the ground.

"Keep on being dead," he ordered, softly. "I'm going to try to get the Manchus here."

He went to the open space and raised his Colt, then lowered it.

"Not so good," he told himself. "If Red is dead, why do I shoot?—Well, brainless, to get help to carry him. No—I'd go and do that myself," he thought.

He holstered his Colt and went back to Red, kneeling beside him once more.

"I'm going to try and pack you, Red," he muttered. "Where the hell did that blood come from?"

"From under me chin," Red answered softly, out of the corner of his mouth. "The edge ave the damn' sword cut me a hair's thickness; enough to—"

"Pipe down! Right now you're dead as the dickens. Go limp, you big redheaded gibboon.—But you damn near scared me to death."

"And damn near death I was meself," Red muttered as he obeyed.

Jimmie Cordie weighed around one hundred and sixty-five, and Red Dolan, some two hundred and thirty. But what there was of Jimmie Cordie was all steel; and the clean, hard life that he had always led enabled him to put Red Dolan across his shoulders and walk down the passageway.

He did not have to go far. As the passageway broadened out, a Manchu officer with a squad of swordsmen came along, on the way to the food supply, which was now guarded on all sides.

"You, Captain Cordie?" the officer said. "What has happened to—? It is Lieutenant Dolan."

"Someone reached him with a sword," Jimmie answered, distinctly. "I found him dead in the passageway. Help me carry the body to the machine guns."

FIVE MINUTES later, Red Dolan sat with his back to the wall in a little space hollowed out of the wall, where spare parts for the guns were kept. He wore a bandage that went under his chin and up over his head. The Manchu officer had sent for other swordsmen, and they were searching all passageways and holes much as a snake searches a rabbit warren. Other swords were on guard at every entrance to the machine guns.

"Let's have it, Red," Jimmie said. "If you feel strong enough to do a little talking. You must have lost a heck of a lot of blood, old kid Dolan."

The sword that had licked out at Red from the slit in the passageway wall had missed his throat by the breadth of a playing card. Red claimed that he had felt the cold steel of the flat of the blade against his Adam's apple. The edge had cut the skin under his chin to the very jawbone.

Afterwards, the Yid could always get an argument out of Red by saying, "Vell, if you felt it de blade against de Adam's epple, *gondif,* how could it de edge be out to under de chin, I esk you? Dere iss three inches of space between."

To which Red would answer hotly, "I felt it, ye Hester Street flat-faced duck. What do I know about inches—or ye either, ye monkey beneath notice?—This I know, I felt the blade. 'Twas cold and slithery, and it made me Adam's apple go back in me t'roat."

"How could it you feel it mit de cut so far away?—" And so on...

But now Red began, "Well, I was takin' a walk to stretch the legs ave me, thinkin' ave nothin' in particular. All ave a sudden, out ave the wall comes a sword, like out ave the mouth ave a blue and red snake, and I feels the—"

"Wait a minute," Grigsby interrupted. By this time the charge had been driven back and the soldiers of fortune were all there. "Wasn't it dark in the passageway? How could you see—a red and blue snake?"

"I had just lit a cigarette, and the match was still burnin' in me hand. I was just snappin' it out ave me hand, when out come the sword—and I could see it was held by a blue and red snake, I'm tellin' ye!"

"Never mind that part right now, Red, Then what happened?"

"Mary mother! How do I know? I felt the blade, and I knew the damn snake had missed me. Thinks I to meself, quick as lightin', if there's one there may be more. So down I goes, as if me t'roat was cut. Then I felt the blood, and I thought it was. I played dead to throw the scuts off. Wan sword comin' out ave the wall was enough, widout invitin' more—and me in a place I couldn't see to shoot."

"Fast work, oldtimer," Jimmie said, with a grin. "How long had you been there when I came along?"

"I dunno. It seemed like ten million years, Jimmie darlin'. Maybeso a minute or two."

"Did you hear any one leaving?"

"I did not. I heard nothing."

"**WELL, WHOEVER** saw you coming tried for you through the slit. What I don't get is why he didn't swing at you when you passed the open space near the roof."

"Maybeso dere vasn't room enough to make it de swing," the Yid offered, "und a thrust vould have gone over Red's head. A down von might have missed, and den Red vould have got him. De slit vas sure, if de timing vas—"

"That's right, Yid. We'll try to figure it out later. Maybeso the bird that's after Red may tell us, when we catch him. Red, you say it looked like a blue and red snake which held the sword. Sure it wasn't a colored sleeve?"

"It was not! Ye know, Jimmie, the way ye can see a thing in a flash ave the eye? There was no sleeve or anything else on me snake.—It was the skin ave him I saw, all blue and red—wavy like."

"Yeah? Well, maybe the lad that's after your scalp has got him a trained snake. Right now, you're good and dead, Mr. Dolan.—And you are going to keep that way until further orders."

"Who? Me? I am like hell! Wance I get some more blood, I'll go and find the scut who has the trained snake; and I'll make him eat it, sword and all."

"No, you won't. You'll play dead, and we'll all mourn you like the devil and all. Listen, while old man Cordie's son Jimmie tells you all a story."

And while Jimmie Cordie was telling the story, far away from the machine gun section a man was reporting to another man.

"He, the big one called Red, is dead," that man was saying. "I timed it perfect—"

"Do not talk so much! You are sure?"

"Yes. The sword reached his throat. He fell and lay still, face to the ground. I waited and watched for a sign of life. Then Captain Cordie came."

"What did he do?"

"He threw his flash light on the walls. I had barely time to get back from the slit. He is as fast as a—"

"Again you talk. Tell me what happened—quickly!"

"He saw the slit in the wall, and then he threw his light against the roof. He saw the opening and went to it, pulling himself up. He threw his light along the other passage, then he went back to the body."

"That is what any veteran would do, fool. What then?"

"He called out, mourning. Then he lifted the body up and—"

"How do you know this? You were away from the slit?"

"I came back to it from my hiding place as he lifted the body to his shoulders. He carried it down the passageway, and some Manchus came. I did not follow further, because the Manchus—"

"Silence! You have done well, so far. Lieutenant Dolan is the first. Captain Cordie himself shall be number two. He will be on guard, and whatever happens must be— Get to your work, someone comes."

CHAPTER III

A MONGREL OF MANY BLOODS

TZU YU STOOD with his officers at attention as a coffin was lowered in a grave dug near one of the ruined temples. Jimmie Cordie, Carewe, Grigsby, the Yid and the Bean stood on the other side of the grave. They were also at attention, their faces sad and grim, their eyes mournful. A firing squad and a Manchu bugler stood ready to pay the last honors to Lieutenant Dolan.

After the bugle had blown taps, Tzu Yu said to Jimmie Cordie, "Captain Cordie, the name of Lieutenant Dolan shall be engraved in letters of gold on the scroll of the House of Tzu. His spirit now sits with the mighty chieftains of the House of Dolan, on High, where it has been welcomed as a resplendent warrior."

Jimmie Cordie answered, gravely, "I thank you, O Peerless Head of the House of Tzu. Our war brother has gone on High, as you say. I ask that you pardon me if I beg your permission to depart. This I ask for the war brothers of Lieutenant Dolan. We are not Manchus, and therefore cannot hide our emotion."

"You have my permission to depart, Captain Cordie. You and your war brothers. I know that your hearts are—"

At that moment the guns of Chan-king began shelling, and Tzu Yu stopped talking. When shells started to drop, it was not necessary to ask permission to depart. Everyone ran for cover.

Pierre de la Brive, the artillery officer who had lost his guns, ran with Jimmie Cordie.

"I go with you, Jimmie, *mon ami.* Now that my guns have

gone *'pouf,'* what else have I to do? *Sacrebleu!* It is of the seriousness, this affair. Is it not so, *mon enfant?* Name of ten million names! If those species of camels get over the walls—what then?"

Jimmie grinned, as they went underground. "You'd better get yourself a sword, Pierre. If Chan-king's men get over the walls, the first thing they'll have is skinned Frenchman for dinner—plus boiled Yank."

"Name of a name! You are right, Jimmie. Were you at Lukshun?"

"No. I was in the South, with General Wang T'ang."

"Sang' Dieu! What the Chinese did to the Legionnaires who defended the city!—Me, I will save a bullet for myself. You have of the time a little, Jimmie?"

"Why—yes, I guess so. Why?"

"At my quarters I have so grand a bottle of the brandy. Let us go and drink it."

Jimmie laughed. "Well, I guess one little drink won't do me any harm. I can only stay a minute, Pierre. I'm worried about the machine gun ammunition."

"But yes, Jimmie! I understand. See, we take of the drink so little, and then I help you count the ammunition. Ah, what I would give to be once more back in *la belle France.* Back where the ladies are kind and the— Turn here, *mon ami.* My quarters are to the right."

JIMMIE TURNED automatically, as did the Frenchman. Jimmie was thinking of a thousand and one things, and not of where he was walking. He was thinking of the shortage of ammunition, the finding of the rat who gnaws, of the blue and red snake that Red insisted had held the sword that had very nearly really finished Red, of the Yid and the Bean, and of many things. Pierre de la Brive was chattering away about Paris and its joys, but Jimmie wasn't paying any attention to him.

At a fairly narrow place in the dark passageway, Brive suddenly stopped and leaned against the wall.

"My ankle! Name of a name! I turned it. Ten thousand curses on the—"

Jimmie halted, a little ahead of Brive, then he turned. As he did so, a big stone fell from the roof. Jimmie sensed it coming down, rather than saw it. There might have been the slightest warning creak as it fell, and there might not have been. The only thing certain was that Jimmie Cordie's number was not up. His brain and muscles were in perfect coordination, and so acted together. He jumped, much as a big jungle cat jumps from under the shadow of the wings of some great bird of prey. The stone grazed his left shoulder, tearing the sleeve away and drawing blood.

Pierre de la Brive, against the wall, was raked on the left side of his face by a jutting point of the stone.

"Mon Dieu," he gasped. "I—I—à chaque saint sa chandelle! That was à l'improviste!"

"That's right," Jimmie said, with a grin. "In fact, a *double* candle to every saint.—And it sure was 'of a sudden.' Are you hurt, Pierre?"

"Non—non—mon Dieu! What a place! The roof falls, and—"

"Well, it didn't get us. I think we both need that little drink now. Stick around a minute."

Jimmie looked up at the hole which the stone had left. "I can't make it up there. Maybeso there is another room above. I'll see if I can—"

"But no, Jimmie! What is the use? In this so bad place, there is always stones to fall. *Mon Dieu,* I feel of the faintness!"

"Yeah? Take hold of my arm. How far are your quarters?"

"Not far now. Name of a thousand names! I am bleeding like a stuck pig!"

Jimmie practically held Brive up until they got to the Frenchman's quarters, which consisted of several rooms under one of the temples.

Later, he told Grigsby, "Brive was all in—no foolin'. That stone blame near got him. It must have weighed a ton or more.

Whoever pried it loose must have wanted to get him as well as me."

"How do you know it was pried loose, Jimmie?" Grigsby asked.

"Well, on the way here I did a little look-seein'. I found a room above, and in the said room I found the crowbar and the block of wood which he used."

"Yeah? Red's blue and red snake may be after you, also."

"That's right, George. And also after Pierre de la Brive."

"Who is this Brive guy, Jimmie? I mean, outside of being artillery officer for Tzu Yu?"

"Well, one of the Manchus told me that the Frenchman had been here about a year. But we were talking about other things at the time and I didn't ask any questions. Where Tzu Yu got him, I don't know. Probably he was an officer in some colonial regiment for *la belle France.*—Where's the Yid and the Codfish Duke?"

"They said they were going up on top for a little fresh air. Carewe went with them."

"When they get back, warn them to watch their step. Whoever Chan-king has put among us, he evidently intends to mop up on the machine gun contingent. There's no doubt about that."

"That's evident, Jeems. Any line on him?"

"Divil a line up to date, old settler! But he'll slip sooner or later. They all do."

"It better be sooner than later. Twice he's come pretty close. It may be three times and out for one of us—or the whole gang."

"What is written is written!" Jimmie answered, with a grin. "I'll go in and see Mr. Dolan, and then get to G.H.Q. Did you check on the ammunition?"

"Yes. It's all here. Talking of step watching, Jeems, watch yours!"

"I'll do that little thing," Jimmie answered as he started in to where Red was holed up.

IT WAS after eleven o'clock when Jimmie Cordie left Tzu Yu and the officers who had been called to their stations to plan defense in the event that Chan-king's men should get over the walls. As he walked along on top, he passed several Manchu patrols. While the guns of Chan-king were still, the defenders of the city came on top and stayed as long as possible. The patrols would salute as Jimmie passed, and once in a while the officer in command would stop and chat for a moment. The Black-Eyed Smiling One was liked and highly respected by all the Manchus.

Just after one of the patrols had passed him, two Manchus of high rank came from the ruins of a street of shops, near the wall. Jimmie was just going to go down a ladder that reached to the level below when he saw them. They smiled and waved their hands to him, and then walked over to where he was.

"We have been hunting for rat holes, Captain Cordie," one of them said. "And truly, we have found more than we expected. They are all set with traps, now."

"I guess it will be hard to set traps in all of them, Fan Ch'ih," Jimmie answered. "But those that are—"

A Manchu officer ran up and saluted. Jimmie and the two officers with him returned the salute, and Fan Ch'ih asked, "You have something to report, Ch'ao?"

"This, Colonel Fan Ch'ih. My men outside the wall have slain one who came out of a hole. He is a mongrel of many bloods who is not known to any of the men in—"

"Where is the body?" Jimmie asked.

The reply was in Chinese and Jimmie could not get even a tenth of it; but knowing that, the other officer, with the inbred politeness of the Manchu, translated rapidly in English. This he continued to do as long as Jimmie Cordie was present; and whenever Jimmie spoke in English, the officer translated into Chinese.

"It is inside the walls now, Captain Cordie. My men brought it in so that it might be examined. It is back of the—what was once the Temple of the Lower Gods."

"I would like to see it. It may be that you have caught the messenger of the rat who gnaws."

"Come then," Fan Ch'ih answered. "We will all look at it. It may be that I know him, having had command of the gates for many years."

THERE WERE four or five swordsmen standing around the body as Jimmie and the officers came up. It was lying face up, a gaping wound in the head—a sword wound.

The moon was out, and it was almost as light as day as Jimmie looked down at the upturned face.

The swordsmen saluted and stood back as Fan Ch'ih asked, "Has search been made?"

A young Manchu saluted again, then answered, "Yes, Colonel Fan Ch'ih. There was nothing found in his clothes."

"Strip the body and tear the clothes apart, carefully. Everything it has on, especially the shoes. I have never seen this dog before. Truly, you spoke correctly when you said that he was a mongrel of many bloods, Ch'ao. Tartar, Chinese, and also what seems to be European blood. That is faint but— Look, Captain Cordie. Do you see it?"

"I see it," Jimmie answered, absently. He was watching the body as it was stripped of clothes. While the clothes were being ripped apart, he played his flash light on the body, and even as the young officer was saying, "There is nothing, Colonel Fan Ch'ih," Jimmie was kneeling beside the body and looking closer at it.

"Was the ground searched where he fell?" asked Fan Ch'ih.

"Yes, colonel, thoroughly. He dropped nothing. We were on him before he had time to do anything—but die."

Jimmie Cordie looked up. "There are means of hiding things other than in the clothes."

He turned the body over on its face, and then ran his fingers through the thick black hair.

"Here it is!" he announced. "It was held to a shaven place by adhesive tape. The hair above, falling over it, hid it. It feels like rice paper and— Any one got a knife?"

CH'AO PRODUCED one, and a moment afterwards Jimmie stood up with a small square of rice paper, tightly folded.

"Colonel Fan Ch'ih, I ask that this body be taken somewhere and kept—just as it is—until orders are given concerning it by the Lord Tzu Yu."

"The body will be taken to a place and kept there, Captain Cordie."

"All right. Let's go and give this to Lord Tzu Yu."

Jimmie put the square of rice paper in the upper pocket of his tunic. And as he did so, a man hidden in the shadows of a ruined gateway started to ease back, then halted as Fan Ch'ih spoke.

"We cannot—for two hours, Captain Cordie. Lord Tzu Yu worships at the shrine of his ancestors—alone. Until he comes from the shrine, none may go there. To do so would be to receive a well merited death. Pardon me for intruding matters concerning the code of a Manchu House, Captain Cordie, into strictly military matters, but the Lord Tzu worships as the Head of the House of Tzu—not as the War Lord Tzu Yu, in command of this city. Do you understand, Captain Cordie?"

"Why—yes, I think so, colonel. Manchu code stuff is too deep for me, though—and I've always admitted it. Being only a Yank," he added with a grin, "I can't be expected to grasp the whys and wherefores."

The Manchus of the House of Tzu who stood there clicked their heels together, then saluted as Colonel Fan Ch'ih said, "You are the honorable War Brother of the Head of the House of Tzu, resplendent one. We fully understand that your—what you call code—as a Yank, is equal in all respects to a Manchu code."

"And that's some compliment!" Jimmie answered, returning the salute. "Now, how about this message? Will I keep it? I'm going back to the machine gun section, and I will remain there until word comes that the Lord Tzu Yu has left the shrine.—Here's something that puzzles me. Supposing that while the

Lord Tzu Yu is in there an attack comes, or something else, very important, comes up that must be attended to at once. No matter what happens, he must not be disturbed? Is that correct?"

"If attack comes, the Lord Tzu Yu would hear it, Captain Cordie, and perhaps come out. If he heard and did not come, then we, of the House of Tzu, would receive the attack until he came. Nothing is of more importance than his absolute privacy when he worships."

"I see. The Lord Tzu Yu can come out any time he wishes, but no one can go in to him. Is that it?—I've been with Manchus a great deal, but a case like this has never come up before. I am asking now, so that in the future I will know."

"Yes, Captain Cordie, that is it," Fan Ch'ih answered. "The message will be safe with you; but if you wish, I will accompany you to your section."

"All right, come on. I guess you and I can get there, if we put our minds on doing it."

The Manchus permitted their tight lips to relax a little. They knew that Jimmie Cordie was rated as one of the bravest soldiers of fortune in the Orient, and one of the best shots. And Colonel Kan Ch'ih was a master swordsman, a veteran of years of fighting.

ON THE way underground, Jimmie asked, "Did you observe closely the body of the one caught in a trap, colonel?"

Fan Ch'ih understood and replied in English. Once in a while he slipped up on the letter "r," as all Chinese do. Manchus have spoken Chinese for hundreds of years, their own language being discarded after they had reached the Peacock Throne.

"No, Captain Coldie," he answered. "Except that it seemed to be coveled with dilt of valious colors."

"That wasn't dirt, colonel. That was— Here's a good place to get to the next level; I found it yesterday. Be careful on the stairs.—The second stone turns."

Colonel Fan Ch'ih was careful, but not quite careful enough.

He would have fallen if Jimmie Cordie had not reached out and steadied him by taking firm hold of his Sam Browne belt.

"May the culses of the Ten Thousand Devils be on the monglel Chan-king, who has brought Kitai to this," Fan Ch'ih announced with deep feeling, as he recovered his balance. Jimmie, behind him, grinned; and in watching that Fan Ch'ih did not fall again, he forgot for the moment what he had been about to say about the body of the spy. The passageway they were in sloped down at an angle of about fifteen degrees, and in a good many places the roof came to within four or five feet of the floor.

Hence there was not much conversation, Fan Ch'ih leading the way, once they got fairly started. Jimmie's thoughts turned to Tzu Yu, and he wondered idly what would happen if a Manchu Lord's wife or daughter became suddenly, desperately ill, and had only a few minutes to live—if she was crying for her master. He wondered if the Manchu Lord would permit himself to be interrupted at the shrine even for that.

These thoughts, of course, were idle, disconnected. Subconsciously, Jimmie was trying to place the dead man back among the living, trying to place him somewhere in the scheme of things.

After five or six minutes, they came to a place where another passageway crossed the one they were in, and there the roof as well as the walls receded. As they started across, Jimmie came up with Fan Ch'ih.

A faint moonlight seeped through somewhere, but hardly enough to dispel the gloom. Just about enough to make the use of a flash light unnecessary.

"This is a shorter—" Jimmie started to say; but he never finished the sentence.

A man stepped out of a hole in the wall just ahead of them, on Fan Ch'ih's side. As he brought his right foot down beside his left, he executed a swift, turning step, and lunged at Fan Ch'ih, a dagger held rigidly out in his right hand, his right arm stiff. It was a thrust, not a downward stroke. A man—or a woman—expert with a dagger, always holds it as a sword is held, which gives greater length than if the dagger is held in the fist, point down.

The thrust was fast, very fast; so fast that Colonel Fan Ch'ih had no time for defense. The dagger entered his heart and he instantly dropped dead. The man who had attacked disengaged the dagger, and again executed that swift sidestep, so avoiding the falling body of Fan Ch'ih. He then closed in on Jimmie Cordie, the dagger coming from the side—in and up...

CHAPTER IV

A PARTY

NEAR THE WALL, the Fighting Yid, the Boston Bean and Carewe found a pile of stones over which there seemed to be a little breeze blowing. As they sat down, the Yid said:

"My, vot vouldn't I give for about seex fingers of brandy—weet' seex more right after. Of all de dry fights I ever been in, dis is de vorst, no foolink!"

"What's the matter with the rice wine?" the Bean asked, as he settled down with his hands behind his head and looked up at the moon. "Isn't that rich enough for your blood, Mr. Cohen?"

"Dot stuff? *Oi,* Codfisher, how can you esk it? Tell you vot: let's go and raid de Red Cross supplies dot Jimmie thinks he has got hid safely avay from us."

"Why, you di-ert-ty snooper," the Bean answered. "Get away from me!—Where is it?"

Carewe laughed. "I say, you'll be having Jimmie in your hair, old dears. You're on the firing line—what, what, what?"

"Ve are not! Ve are under a vall, und dot make de cheese more binding for needin' some Red Cross brandy. Ve are sick mit de—de vall sickness.—Are you caming, Codfisher?"

"Go and get it, Yid, and we'll drink it right here."

Pierre de la Brive came around the pile of stones and sat down next to the Yid. "Did I hear the word 'drink,' *mes braves?*"

"You did," answered the Bean. "The Yid is organizing a raid on the Red Cross supplies. Want to join up with us?"

"Mon Dieu, non, mes enfants! Jimmie he say, 'Ha, you raid

the so-valuable Red Cross? Name of a name! You shall face me with pistols at ten paces, advance firing.' And that Jimmie he go *bang-bang-bang* while poor Pierre de la Brive go *bang* once—and then miss!"

They all laughed. The Frenchman made it sound more dramatically real than actual life.

"You had me seeing, or rather hearing, that Jimmie go *bang-bang-bang.* It was so vivid that I think I will withdraw from the raid. I don't want him going even one *bang* at me. Help yourself, Yid, I don't care for any," the Bean said.

"Vot? *Oi,* since ven did you get it cold feet? If I do go, I vill sit here und drink it, und you von't get it even—"

"BUT WAIT!" Pierre de la Brive interrupted. "I have had of the thought. See, *mes amis,* in my so grand quarters, I have of the cognac a dozen bottles. When could be a better time to drink them? Look you, where is Jimmie and the so sober Grigsby? Get them and we will go and drink."

"Dot's a bet!" the Yid said, promptly. "Only Jimmie he is at G.H.Q., mit Tzu Yu; und George he is vatchin' dot some bad man don't come in und slap de ammunition on de wrist.—Ve go mit, Pierre."

"But—why not, Monsieur Yid? You three, and then, after we drink, you will take some bottles back with you for the brave Jimmie and the so sober faced Grigsby. It is a good plan, no?"

"It's a darn good plan—yes," the Bean said as he arose. "We're not on watch unless attack comes, and our boy friend seems to be laying off the night frolicking. We'll help you kill a couple of bottles, Pierre. No harm in that. Yid, you can have two drinks and—"

"Who? *Me?*—Listen, Beany. I can drink it de dozen bottle, und den fight a machine gun mit—"

"Your eyes shut! Come on, let's go."

Once in Brive's quarters, he looked around for his batman. "Sacred name of ten million camels! Where is he? I mean my servant, *mes enfants.* Never is he here when I want him, the pig of all pigs! Soon the day will come when I can—"

"Never mind it de day," interrupted the thirsty Yid. "Vare is it de likker? Ve be our own servants, ain't it?"

Pierre de la Brive laughed. "I will get it, Monsieur Yid. I see that if I do not you will die of the so great thirst."

He went into a back room and brought our four bottles of cognac, glasses and a pitcher of water. "These we will drink—one each. Then, there will be to take back with you five more. I will have enough left for me."

"My, dot is good stuff!" the Yid said a little later. "Vere did you get it?"

"It came in a caravan, long before Chan-king attacked, *mon ami.*"

"I vish I had been here and got me some. Mit it I vould stand off all de Chinks in China."

"Take one more, and throw in the Afghans and Tartars," the Bean said. "Let's be starting back."

"I will get the bottles for you to take with you," Brive said. "But first, I have some things to eat. In the caravan there were many good things, *mes braves.*"

IT WAS an hour later when the Yid, the Bean and Carewe started for the machine gun section. As they walked along, the Yid said, with deep conviction:

"Dot is von svell guy, I'll say!"

Carewe was carrying the bottles, and before they arrived the Yid and the Bean got into an argument as to the advisability of holding out a couple of bottles for future reference, the Yid being for it and the Bean against it. The Bean claimed it was a question of ethics; the Yid held that ethics whatever they were, didn't have anything to do with it. He was talking about likker, not ethics.

The argument was still unsettled when they got to the section, and so it settled itself in favor of the Bean-eater.

Grigsby looked up from the machine gun he was cleaning. "You birds look as if you'd been at a party."

"We have," the Bean answered as Carewe put down the bottles. "A bearcat party, George.—Where is Jeems? Pierre de la Brive sent him a bottle of likker. He sent you one also."

"Und von for each of us," added the Yid.

"Yeah?—I feel as if I could take a little drink without doing the world any harm. Jimmie ought to be here any minute. Let's wait for him."

"Vy not open von now, und all take a little von?" suggested the Yid. "Und take it von in for Red. I bet you dot right after, he gets up and vants to lead it a charge."

"Control your appetite for red likker, Mr. Cohen," ordered the Bean, sternly. "Sit down and look at the bottles. Anticipation is far better than realization."

"I never did think dot," answered the Yid with a grin, as he sat down. "Vell, I hope dot Jimmie von't be long!"

CHAPTER V

A TIGER-FOX

THE MAN WHO had passed his dagger through Colonel Fan Ch'ih's heart may have counted on a split-second of time during which Jimmie Cordie would remain motionless. But if he did count on that, it failed him.

In spite of his absolute surprise, Jimmie Cordie met the attack with the quickness of a wolverine suddenly attacked by a hitherto unseen enemy. His body drove against that of the man with the dagger with all the power he had. Jimmie's left arm was rigid, and moving out and away from the side. The man's arm, the hand of which held the dagger, struck against Jimmie's left arm and stayed there long enough for Jimmie's right arm to go around the man's neck. It was so fast that it all seemed to happen at once. The man's right arm dropped from Jimmie's left and drew in to enable him to make a short arm thrust with the dagger.

As the dagger arm was drawing back, Jimmie Cordie's left hand came up, palm in, against the man's face, and Jimmie's knee also came up. It was a hold learned in the Foreign Legion; a deadly one where a twist to the left and a pressure behind snaps the spinal cord. The knee being brought up, starts the body down, which helps.

There is a way to break it before the twist comes, but the man trying for Jimmie Cordie either did not know that trick, or did not have time to use it. The hand holding the dagger had started forward when the snap came, but Jimmie's left hand, dropped as it felt the give, struck hand and dagger away.

He let the body fall, and took the three steps necessary to put his back to the wall, drawing his Colt.

One minute went by without further attack, then two—three. The passageway was as still as the two bodies that lay upon the floor.

At last Jimmie took his flash light from his belt and played it along the walls and roof, as he had done when he found Red. There was no break in either walls or roof that he could see, except a hollowed out place where some statue or image had once stood, and out of which the man had evidently come.

"I guess you tried it by yourself, oldtimer," Jimmie said, looking down at the man's body. "Stick around a minute. I'm going to take you somewhere and look you over."

He knelt by Colonel Fan Ch'ih, and saw that the Manchu was dead. Then he rose, put his hands under the shoulders of the man who had relied upon a dagger, and began dragging the body down the passageway.

As he neared the chamber where the soldiers of fortune were waiting for him, he heard the Yid say, "Vell, Jimmie is late, ain't it?"

"If you're waiting for me," Jimmie called back, "come out here, one of you apes, and give me a hand with a newfound boy friend."

The Yid and the Bean, being nearest, joined Cordie, and as the body was brought into the candlelight, the Yid said:

"*Oi,* such a business!—Dot is Gaston Figeac, de batman of Pierre de la Brive. *Oi,* und ve just had it some—"

"You mean, it *was* Gaston Figeac," Jimmie interrupted, grimly.

In dragging it along the passageway, the soft shirt had been pulled from the pants, which were belted, so that a section of the abdomen showed. Jimmie stooped and ripped the shirt away, all of the front.

"HERE'S RED'S blue and red snake!" he went on.

"Dot guy," the Yid said, looking at the chest of the corpse, "vas mitout question de most—"

"Never mind that for a minute," Grigsby interrupted. "What's it all about, Jimmie?"

"Wait a minute!" Jimmie answered. "I'm hooking something up.—Holy cats! I wonder if— It doesn't seem possible that Brive can be the rat we're after! And yet—"

"Are you crazy, Jeems?" the Bean demanded. "We just came from the Frenchman's quarters. He gave us some cognac, and sent you and George a bottle."

"Und also, von for each of us," added the Yid, who had seen too many dead men to get at all switched from the main line. At present, that, to him, was his bottle of cognac.

"Maybeso, Codfisher. I dunno. You say you just came from Brive?"

"Yes. He invited us to split a couple of bottles with him and—"

"Did you?"

"Does a duck svim?" demanded the Yid. "Dot's foolish question num—"

"Yeah? It was, at that, Yid. Knowing the Bean and— Who went? All of you?"

"No. George stayed here, Jimmie," Carewe answered. "I say, old dear, what is the jolly old mystery—what, what?"

"Let's see that stuff he so kindly sent for George and me—and of course, the Hester Street booze fighter."

"*Oi*, Jimmie! For vy you pick it on me? Did I did you somethings? Pick it on der Codfisher. He started de whole thing, no foolin'."

"Why, you double-damn liar!" protested the Bean. "I wasn't even thinkin' of—"

Carewe had brought the bottles over, and Jimmie took one. "We'll hold the courtmartial later.—Pipe down for a minute, you playboys!"

He looked at the seal, felt of its edges, broke off a little piece with a thumbnail, then asked, "Did he say anything about this likker? When he got it, or anything like that?"

"Yes," answered Carewe. "I remember he said that it came in a caravan that arrived long before Chan-king attacked."

"Yeah? Well, it's been sealed within an hour. What do you know about that, Mr. Cohen? What's the number of that foolish question?"

"Dot ain't a question," answered the Yid, with a smirk. "Dot's a statement. Vy is it dot you are mad mit me, Jimmie?"

JIMMIE'S NERVES were taut, more so than he realized; but when the Yid asked that, Jimmie grinned at him. "I'm not, Abie, old kid. You and I are pudners. Only—don't kid for a few minutes—I esk you."

"Get down to it, Jimmie," Grigsby said. "There may not be much time. You think the stuff is drugged?"

"Yes. Either with enough to put us all to sleep for a long time, or to send us West. Probably the latter."

"Try it on the Yid," suggested the Boston Bean, then hastily added, "I mean it. That's not kidding, Jeems, me good man."

"I'm thinking of using both you and the Yid," Jimmie answered. "If this stuff is drugged, Brive will come and take a look-see after awhile, to see if it has worked. He mustn't see Figeac's body.—I've got to get to Tzu Yu, pronto and in haste. Let's set the stage for him."

"Wait a minute," Grigsby said. "How about the Manchu swordsmen that are supposed to be on guard all around here?"

"There's probably passages that they don't know anything about, but I'll have several ways left open for him."

"Are we to kill him if he comes?" asked the Yid, cheerfully.

"No. Let him come and go. You are all drugged. If he comes up and examines any of you, hold him. You can't fake it and get by if he comes close—assuming he knows anything about drugs, which he probably does. He'll probably take a look-see from around the boxes, or over them, not wanting to get too close on account of the Manchus. So open the bottles, pour the stuff out, and then flop in various positions over the boxes and whatnot. Make it artistic. I'll get back as soon as I can get here."

"All right, Jimmie, we'll attend to it," Grigsby answered.

"Fair enough. The likker may be good and he may be in the clear, in spite of what his man Friday has been a-doin'—but he may not be. Right now, I don't want to take any chances. Here—I haven't time to go into it, but you can all amuse yourselves by figuring this out: Gaston Figeac was a Bat d'Af. A man was killed just outside of the walls not long ago who was also a Bat d'Af. He was carrying a message that, doughnuts to dollars, was to Chan-king. Pierre de la Brive has been a French officer, and he was with me, leading me down a passageway when a stone blame near got me. Just before it fell, he turned his ankle. Red insists that the sword was held by a red and blue snake. Take a look at Figeac's arm.—De la Brive invites you to a party and serves you good likker, and then he sends you home with some stuff for all of us to drink. Think all that over, and then help yourselves to the mustard. Personally, I don't care for any of his likker.'"

"Oi," the Yid announced. "I don't neither care for none. Codfisher, you can have mine, mit my compliments!"

TZU YU had returned from the worship of his ancestors and was in his headquarters when Jimmie Cordie arrived. With him were some of the nobles of the House of Tzu. Jimmie reported the death of Colonel Fan Ch'ih, which was received by Tzu Yu with impassive face and eyes, then he handed Tzu Yu the rice paper message.

Tzu Yu opened it, looked at it for a moment, then looked up and said, "I speak in English, so that Captain Cordie may understand. Chi K'ang, you will translate into Chinese for those of the House of Tzu who do not understand the English that Captain Cordie and I speak...

"The message reads: 'To Chan-king, Ruler of the World. The bombs reached the target. Before two suns have risen, the ghosts—'you will understand, Captain Cordie, that I am translating Chinese characters into English and it may be that the meaning will not be clear to you. This character 'ghosts,'" Tzu Yu touched one of the drawings with a finger, "means 'outsiders' or 'barbarians' or 'devils who come from afar.' I translate it as meaning 'the ones who serve'...

"To continue with the message: 'Before two suns have risen, the devils from afar who serve will be dead. When I send the one word, come, attack with all your force. The guns will then be served by ignorant men.'

"That is the message, Captain Cordie. It is signed by a character poorly drawn. *'Hu'* means 'tiger,' and another *'hu'* means 'fox.' With the drawing of *'li'* after it, it usually means an animal belonging to the small cat tribe. I cannot tell what this pariah cur meant to sign. It is either 'tiger' or 'fox.'"

"Well," Jimmie Cordie said, "we'll try to make a dead rat out of Mr. Tiger-Fox. Too bad the message cannot be delivered to Chan-king."

Tzu Yu and the officers looked at Jimmie Cordie, their grim faces and eyes showing no emotion. They were all fighting men, bred of a race that had fought and conquered all foes for a thousand years, and they were Manchu nobles, raised in the strictest code of honor in the world. All of them liked and respected the American soldiers of fortune who fought at their sides. But they could not understand why he wanted the message delivered. There was no question about Captain Cordie's loyalty to whatever cause he was fighting for, or about the loyalty of the men who used the machine guns with him. But his words puzzled the Manchus, even though they did not show it in the slightest degree.

Finally Tzu Yu said smoothly, "The message can be delivered, Captain Cordie."

"How?"

"The Manchus have many times, shall I say, delivered messages to the Chinese, captain."

"I've heard about Manchu tricks," Jimmie answered, with a smile. "If you can pull one now, it will help a lot, Tzu Yu."

"Deliver the message for Captain Cordie, Lord Hsai." Tzu Yu looked at an old Manchu officer.

THE OFFICER shut his eyes and was silent for a moment, then began to speak. "Chan-king will be asleep in his tent. An officer will come to him and report that a Chinese boy who was stopped at the outposts tells a tale of a message to be delivered to Chan-king only. Chan-king will ask if the boy has been searched, and the officer will answer that the boy has been, and also that no weapon was found on the boy. Chan-king will order that the boy be admitted to his presence. The boy will hand Chan-king the message and tell the following tale. He and some companions were crossing the hills, beyond Chan-king's lines, going toward—Lukshun, where the boy's grandfather lives. They found a wounded man, wounded to the death. This man begged them to take the message to Chan-king, promising that whoever did so would be richly rewarded. The boy's companions were afraid and fled, but the boy was not afraid and he agreed to do it. As he agreed, the wounded man died... Consider the message delivered, Captain Cordie."

The officer spoke in Chinese, Tzu Yu translating rapidly. As he finished, the old Manchu opened his eyes.

"Wait a minute," Jimmie said. "I know that you understand Chinese psychology, all of you. But there's a darn weak link in the chain—at least to an American. If that story came to me, I would go to, or would send men out to bring in, or at least see, the body."

"Explain to Captain Cordie what you did not mention, knowing that we would know the details," Tzu Yu commanded the officer.

This time the officer did not shut his eyes. "The spy's body will be there, Captain Cordie. I did not mention it because I thought that you would understand that without it the messenger tells an idle tale."

"I can understand how one or two Manchus or Chinese can slip through the kind of lines the Chinese maintain anywhere. But to pack a body along is what we call in America 'something else again.'"

"You said, not long ago, Captain Cordie," Tzu Yu said, "that as a general rule there are many rat holes leading out of a Chinese city. That is true—and it is also true regarding Manchu cities. Do you know this also? In most Manchu cities there is buried the treasure of the Manchu house which rules that city. And from the buried treasure there leads a tunnel, known only to members of the house, a tunnel that leads far out from the city.—There is such a tunnel here, captain, and its outlet is beyond the jackal Chan-king's first and second lines. His third line is held so loosely that it may be ignored. The body will be taken through the tunnel, Captain Cordie."

"Well," Jimmie answered, with a grin, "that's that! Can an unidentified Chinese boy come into the presence of a war lord in the field without trouble?"

"Without question, Captain Cordie. To a war lord, or even to the emperor, if there was one in China—if the boy states that he has a tale to tell, and will tell it only to him who commands. For thousands of years such tales have been brought by unknown persons, and have decided the outcome of battles and the fate of provinces. The Chinese, and other Oriental races as well, listen to all tales, Captain Cordie. It was an unknown youth who insisted upon seeing Genghis Khan, and who told the tale that sent Jagatai, Genghis Khan's second son, against the Khorasan to burn and slay."

"**THAT SETTLES** that. The only thing that remains to cause a doubt, as far as my American mind goes, is whether the Chinese youth will be able to carry out the part."

"Tell Captain Cordie, Lord Hsai."

"The youth is able, captain. He is one who was born in my household, and has delivered messages before."

"All right, Tzu Yu. Send the message to Chan-king."

"The message will be sent, Captain Cordie. Have you anything to tell us?"

"Well, I think I have a line on who is the rat that gnaws. I may be wrong, at that. What I want to do is to frame him, so that he will send the message 'Come.' If he does that, we'll make Chan-king think that the message should have read, 'Come and be killed.' We'll collect the rat at the same time that we mop up on Chan-king."

"You say that you think you know who the rat is, Captain Cordie. Have you considered that while you are what you call 'framing' him, he might put into action a 'frame' of his own that might cost us dear?"

Jimmie Cordie was silent for a moment, then he grinned. "That's right, Tzu Yu. In thinking of framing him, I forgot that he might be doing a little framing himself. I'll start by telling you gentlemen a story... The guillotine in France is called The Red Lady, and it is a favorite trick to tattoo a picture of it on a man who is serving in the Bat d'Af."

"I beg your pardon for the interruption, Captain Cordie," Tzu Yu said. "You speak of the Bat d'Af. Will you explain to us what the Bat d'Af is?"

"I beg your pardon, all of you, for thinking that you knew. The Bat d'Af is the French Bataillon d'Afrique, who serve on the edge of the Sahara Desert, which is a hell hole—all of the time. The Foreign Legion is considered a hard-boiled—I mean a tough outfit. But compared to the Bat d'Af, the Foreign Legion is like the gentle patter of rain on a tin roof compared to a typhoon in the China Seas. All the incorrigible cases in the French military forces, who are so tough they cannot be handled, are sent to the punishment battalions, the Bat d'Af. And I'll state in passing that any old time the French army and navy and Legion gents can't handle a tough case, the said case must be some tough! Well, they are sent to the Bat d'Af, and once there, they get tougher if possible. A Bat d'Af is the last word in general no good, hard-boiled cussedness.—You understand, Tzu Yu, and gentlemen all?"

The officer translating had hard work translating Jimmie's talk into Chinese, but he did it. Enough, that is, to allow the officers to understand.

"NOW," JIMMIE went on, "in the Bat d'Af they do not have much time or money for pleasures. So they specialize on tattooing each other. As I said, one of their favorite subjects is The Red Lady. They tattoo the guillotine, the executioner, the crowd watching the execution, and all the details—all over the man's body. His legs, his arms, his breast; and with it they tattoo things like 'Consecrated to the Red Lady' and whatnot. You all get that?"

"Yes, Captain Cordie, we all—get it," Tzu Yu answered, smoothly.

"All right. Now, the man killed to-night outside the walls was a Bat d'Af, who had such tattooing. Later, I killed the man who slew Colonel Fan Ch'ih; and he also was a Bat d'Af, and had on his body the same tattooing. He was Gaston Figeac, the batman or servant of—Pierre de la Brive, colonel of artillery."

The youngest officer present drew a long breath, and his right hand went to his pistol butt. "The dog shall—! I crave your pardon, O Head of the House of Tzu."

Tzu Yu looked at the officer through cold eyes. "Your petition for pardon is not granted, Major Kweiyang. Go to your quarters. Your showing of weakness is not pleasing to the Chieftains of the House of Tzu who sit on High with the conqueror, Nurhachu. I speak as the Head of the House of Tzu. You have my permission to depart."

The officer bowed instead of saluting, and began to back out of the chamber. Jimmie Cordie got one good look at the officer's face. It was getting gray. Jimmie had been with Manchus enough to know what the officer would do on reaching his quarters. He would either blow his brains out, or pass his sword through his heart.

Jimmie liked the officer, and he did what he had never done before. He interceded with the head of a Manchu noble house in the cause of one of its members.

"I ask you to halt Major Kweiyang, Lord Tzu Yu," he said, curtly.

Tzu Yu looked at Jimmie for a moment, then he ordered, "Halt, Major Kweiyang!"

The young officer halted, straightened up and came to attention.

"You have said, O Head of the House of Tzu," Jimmie went on, "that the House of Tzu was in my debt."

"Yes, Captain Cordie. The House of Tzu is in your debt. I, the Head of the House of Tzu have said it, and now I repeat it."

"Very good. I do not have to say that I know that a Manchu house pays its debt—always."

"That is correct, Captain Cordie. A Manchu house pays its debt—always. All the House of Tzu is possessed of is yours—to do with as you will, flesh and blood included."

"I ask only this, in payment of the debt. I ask that all that has been spoken, since the mention of Pierre de la Brive, be wiped from the memory of the House of Tzu."

Tzu Yu did not hesitate the fraction of a second. "It is wiped from the memory of the House of Tzu, Captain Cordie. Major Kweiyang, what are you doing out of line? Return to your place at once!"

The young Manchu officer saluted, his face now like that of a stone image. He went back to where he had been standing. His face and eyes did not show it, neither did the faces and eyes of the other Manchu officers, but inside their hearts were singing with joy. He was a loved relation of all of them. And with the singing a vow was being registered that if the time came, the Black-Eyed Smiling One was to be repaid, full measure.

"NOW," JIMMIE went on, "that which I have told you does

not prove that Pierre de la Brive is the rat that gnaws. But I think he is."

He went on, telling of Red's statement about a blue and red snake holding the sword; and of Pierre de la Brive leading Jimmie Cordie himself down a passageway where a stone fell; and of the party given by Brive, and of the bottles he had offered as gifts. Tzu Yu and the officers knew that Red was alive and getting well.

Jimmie finished with, "Now I want to see if we can catch him as he is sending the message.—Holy cats! not so good. I've put his go-between out of commission, and Manchu swords have slain Chan-king's runner. Tzu Yu, we've got to keep Brive from becoming suspicious because of Figeac's absence."

"The servant of Colonel de la Brive," Tzu Yu answered, slowly, "became involved in a fight with one of— No, this is better! the one named Figeac was found drinking with three of the Chinese bearers, in a forbidden place. He resisted arrest, and struck a Manchu officer. I ordered him placed in solitary confinement. When questioned about this by Colonel de la Brive, I will state that I will release him if the Manchu officer—you, Lun Wie—say that the memory of the blow is wiped from your mind. You will say to Colonel de la Brive that if after forty-eight hours' confinement the one who struck you will make public apology, the memory of the blow will fade away."

"Fine!" Jimmie said with a grin. "Now he will probably take the message himself—unless he's got several Chinese in here as second-string runners, which I doubt. No doubt the Bat d'Af slain outside the wall used to come in, meet Figeac and carry back any messages. I know that you can have Brive watched all the time, Tzu Yu, and you don't need any suggestions from me regarding the clearing his way for him, both outside and in.— Here's something," Jimmie added. "It may be that once out, he'll stay out and watch the assault."

"If he does," Tzu Yu answered, blandly, "we will go and get him after destroying the mongrel Chan-king's troops."

"All right.—I'll get back to my pals. If I get there before he's come to look at them, I'm dead also, when the bodies of the machine gun section are found by your swordsmen. If he's already taken his look-see and has gone, I will find the rest of my pals all dead and then go more or less goofy myself—too goofy to handle a—" Jimmie saw that Tzu Yu and the officers did not understand what he meant by "goofy," and that the translator had stopped. "That word 'goofy' is American slang," he explained. "It means 'crazy.'—Well, I find the rest all dead, and I go crazy. You order me confined, Tzu Yu, and then say that the Manchu helpers at the machine guns will have to fight them. If Brive is present, he'll know that they would jam 'em after a couple of rounds; and that if they didn't jam them, they at least couldn't hold them on a target.—All set?"

Tzu Yu answered, impassively, "All set, Captain Cordie."

CHAPTER VI

THE RAT IS TRAPPED

WHEN JIMMIE GOT back to the chamber, he found the Yid, the Bean, Grigsby and Carewe sitting around on cartridge boxes.

"He came, Jimmie," the Yid said, "und peeked over de top row of cases. My, how dead ve all vas! He only looked a minute, like he vas counting us, und den he pulled his head back. De Manchus are back now in every hole, so dot he can't get it back. Dey know it all de holes coming in here."

"Yeah? Well, that's that. The next thing is, I find you birds all dead and I go goofy. Be dead for a minute. I want to get the mental picture, so I can—Say! Do I smell fuse burning?"

"*Vat?* You smell it a fuse! I don't. Vere de—?"

"Jimmie has just come in from the fresh air," Grigsby said, quietly. "Keep still, Yid. Let Jimmie locate it."

As Grigsby spoke, Red Dolan came out of what the Yid called "de Irisher's room mit bath."

"Wan thing is damn certain!" Red announced, truculently, "I'll stay in that— What the hell are ye sniffin' for, Jimmie?"

"He smells it a fuse," explained the Yid. "Keep still, Irish loafer!"

"I'm man enough yet to—" Red stopped talking as Jimmie pointed over to the left corner.

"Over there behind the boxes!" Jimmie said. "Never mind any playing dead stuff now. We're all blame liable to be real dead any second.—Line up! We'll pass 'em back. I'll start 'em.—Behind me, George. Yid—next. Bean, Carewe, take the boxes from the

Yid and carry 'em behind that wall. Get out of the way, Red, if you can't handle the boxes.—*Allons, mes enfants!* And make it snappy!"

The line was forming as Jimmie talked; and as he finished, the first box of cartridges was being lifted.

Red got behind Carewe and the Boston Bean. "Hand 'em to me," he commanded. "Weak as I am, I'm better than eight Carewes and eighty-wan Codfish Dukes from Bosting!"

Box after box went back, the soldiers of fortune working smoothly and with no flurry. They all knew that whatever was at the end of the fuse was likely to explode any second and blow them all to pieces; and yet there was not the slightest evidence of fear or even excitement.

One minute—two minutes—three minutes; then Jimmie Cordie held up his hand. "I can see it," he said, calmly. "No chance to get to it by moving boxes. It's a fifty-pound box of dynamite, and the fuse is burning within two feet of 'er. I think I can crawl over the rest of the boxes and cut it. Back out, you gents. Get behind the wall. Good-bye, John, if I don't make it."

He was already climbing up on the tier of boxes in front of him. The Chinese bearers who had placed the boxes in rows, close to the wall of the chamber, had not piled them close to the roof; and Chinese-like, owing to some small piles of debris, they had put the boxes down in the easiest places, leaving quite a hole in one place, which had made a fine pocket in which to put the dynamite. Also, as if the Nine Red Gods of War had planned it, there was room enough in that spot for anyone with sufficient nerve to crawl in and cut the fuse—if he had time.

"Come back here!" Red ordered. "I'll go in. Jimmie, ye scut, come back here!"

"Shut up, you big ape!" Jimmie answered, as he started crawling. "There's barely room for me up here. Stick around, and we'll get blown up to— Hold your breath, you birds."

RED DOLAN, Grigsby, the Yid and the Bean stood relaxed, just exactly where they were when Jimmie started. None of them had even taken a step back. It was a place where few men would have cared to be, no matter how much nerve they had. In the Orient, the men who fought beside Jimmie Cordie had the reputation of being there with bells on. And they one and all, right there, proved that the reputation was founded on fact.

To stand relaxed in a dark chamber, underground, knowing that a fuse was burning towards a fifty-pound box of dynamite and that it had less than two feet to go, took Simon-pure nerve. Fuse burns at the rate of two or three feet per minute—depending on what company made it. Some fuse—not all. There have been fuses that delayed, and other fuses that burnt too quickly, as men who use fuse have found out. Men make a fuse, and like everything else made by man, there is likely to be a flaw. But the average fuse burns two or three minutes to the foot.

They all knew that; and they also knew, counting the time it had taken Jimmie to get up and along the boxes, that inside of the next sixty seconds they would either still be living or would be torn apart.

The Boston Bean stood, thumbs hooked in cartridge belt, the same sleepy you-be-damned look in his eyes. He was breathing easily, his eyes on the tier of boxes. The Fighting Yid stood beside the Bean, a little smile on his lips and in his china blue eyes. He came of a race that had charged and destroyed Roman Legions, and he ran true to his blood. There in the semi-darkness, underground, the Fighting Yid showed that he had more than fighting ability, which many men have. He had the courage of his race, undiluted.

George Grigsby, pure American stock, bred in the Kentucky hills, an Anglo-Saxon, stood as his ancestors had stood when awaiting an Indian charge. Cold and calm, no emotion of any kind showing on his clean-cut face or in his eyes. On his lips there was a little frozen smile. His hands hung by his sides, absolutely quiet.

Red Dolan was Irish from the top of his head to the tips of his toes, red-headed and excitable, with the hot temper of the Irish and the vivid imagination. He was bigger than any of them, and he loved Jimmie Cordie better than he did his patron saint. He stood one side of Carewe, his big body balanced easily on his toes. The only thing Red thought about was Jimmie Cordie, in there trying to cut a fuse in time to prevent an explosion. Red never thought about himself in time of stress. To himself, he was saying, "Come on, ye shrimp ave the world! Come on! Get it cut! Get it cut! What the hell's keepin' ye?" No thought for Red Dolan, about to be blown sky high unless Jimmie Cordie cut the fuse.

Carewe, English gentleman, whose ancestors had put out in a fishing smack to fight the Spanish Armada, armed with a one-pound cannon and their swords, stood as they had stood when they watched a Spanish three-tier gun galleon come around so that the broadside would bear. A cold, contemptuous smile was in his blue eyes and on his lips.

They all waited, either for the explosion or for Jimmie Cordie's call: "She's cut, gents!"

TEN SECONDS is a long stretch of time—in some places and under some conditions. Twenty is much longer, and men supposed to be strong have broken when it stretched to thirty. That much time went by, and then Jimmie Cordie called: "She's cut, gents!—And in the well-known nick of time."

The Fighting Yid laughed. "You know vot I vas thinking of, Beaneater? I vas thinking dot you vould be shovelin' coal down below vhile I was up dere playin' on a harp, sittin' on a damp cloud, ain't it?"

"Oh, yeah?" the Bean answered. "Well, listen, Mr. Cohen. I was thinking, 'Poor Abe Cohen! He's got to go to hell yet, and I'm going to walk the golden streets that are guarded by the Marines.' You know, 'If the army and the navy ever reach to Heaven's scenes, they will find the streets are guar-ah-ded by United States Mu-ah-rines.'"

"Ye are a damn liar!" Red said joyfully as he pulled Jimmie Cordie back by the ankles. "Ye was so scared, ye long-legged piece ave Bosting tripe, that ye was shakin' like a leaf. I was watchin' ye, ye scut!"

Jimmie grinned as he got to his feet. "Our boy friend wanted to clean up. We'll give him his explosion, a little delayed. Bean, you're the skinniest. Come on with me." ...

PIERRE DE LA BRIVE, with Tzu Yu and the Manchu officers, heard a dull, rumbling explosion that seemed to come from the walls. Brive had been called, with other officers, to Tzu Yu's headquarters.

"Sang Dieu!" he said to the officer nearest to him. "What was that?—It sounded as if it was the machine gun ammunition."

"I do not know, colonel," the Manchu officer answered politely.

Pierre de la Brive never knew how that officer's hand itched to feel the hilt of his sword.

"See what has happened, Major K'ung Ch'iu," commanded Tzu Yu, curtly.

Five minutes later the officer came back, supporting Jimmie Cordie, whose uniform was torn and dirty. Blood was streaming from a cut on his head.

"You are wounded, Captain Cordie?" asked Tzu Yu.

"I don't care," Jimmie yelled, a broken, raving maniac. "My buddies are all gone!—Blown up, with all the machine gun ammunition! I'm blown up, too.—I can't stay here! I've got to find the pieces and put 'em together again. Where are you, Red? Get the hell out of the way, you ghosts! I've got to—"

Tzu Yu signaled to two officers, who closed in on Jimmie Cordie. Jimmie fought them, raving all the time. It took four of the Manchus to get him down and hold him that way.

"Take Captain Cordie to a place where he will be safe," commanded Tzu Yu. "His clever brain is sick."

"Mon Dieu!" Pierre de la Brive said softly. "The poor Jimmie.—Now he is of the craze. First my guns and now—his."

The Manchu officer looked at him. "The gods order all things,

Colonel de la Brive. Who are we to protest? Now we fight with swords against the pariah cur Chan-king's men. We will show the jackals Manchu swordplay, as their ancestors were shown by the swords of the Chieftain Nurhachu."

"To your battle stations!" commanded Tzu Yu. "If this is the work of Chan-king, there will be an attack shortly. You have my permission to depart. Colonel de la Brive—inspect the walls."

Two hours later, Tzu Yu sat with Jimmie Cordie. "The rat who gnaws but will gnaw no longer has left the city. It may be that he bears the message 'Come.' I have offered up a prayer to the gods that he return. I wish to see his face as the machine guns open."

Jimmie Cordie grinned. "We took the box of dynamite back in a passageway and put it behind some thick walls, then we cut it loose. The fuse didn't give Captain Winthrop and me much time to get away. This cut on my head isn't faked, Tzu Yu. It blame near got both of us... Well, if Chan-king gets the message and comes, he's due for one big surprise. Maybe-so he'll come in person, so as to be in at the finish. If he does, do you want us to save him for you, if we can?"

Tzu Yu looked at Jimmie Cordie, then he permitted himself a smile. "Yes, Captain Cordie, I would like to have him—saved for me, if possible. Truly, war brother, the gods smiled on me when they crossed our paths in England."

THE GUNS of Chan-king rained shells on the city for an hour, just before dawn. The planes went back and forth, dropping bombs; and then, after the fire and the bomb-dropping had ceased, Chan-king's men came from the hills—more than had ever come in any two charges. He was attacking with every man he had. Behind the regiments there came a swarm of swordsmen, and the men of some hill tribes who fought for him.

The charge came on and on, Tzu Yu and his staff officers watching it from the top of a ruined temple. With the officers was Pierre de la Brive, standing between two Manchu officers.

As the charge neared the walls, Brive said, "Sacred name of

a pig! We are lost! They reach the walls and—and—Why does the Lord Tzu Yu man the walls with his rifles?"

"It may be that the Lord Tzu Yu has other plans," answered the Manchu officer, blandly, turning so as to face Brive.

"But if the Lord Tzu Yu does not have other plans, the enemy will come— *Mon Dieu!*"

What made him pause and then call on whatever deity he worshiped, was the snarling voices of six perfectly handled Browning machine guns, and the roar of rapid-fire one- and two-pounders, operated by Manchus trained by Jimmie Cordie. It was a searing, destroying fire, and Chan-king's troops melted away under it. They were approaching in more or less close formation, so as to have as many as possible hit the wall at the same time, for the sake of the added protection against the Manchu swords that Chan-king thought were his only obstacle.

"The guns! And served by—!"

One of the Manchu officers suddenly jerked Brive's pistol from its holster, and as he did so, another did the same to Brive's sword. From behind, his arms were taken in a steel-like grasp.

"You seem excited, rat who gnawed from within!" Tzu Yu said, blandly. "Stand and watch the pariah cur Chan-king's mongrels being destroyed by my war brothers.—Do not be afraid that you will fall.—Your face is gray, rat. Truly, you are excited."

"What does this means?" demanded Brive. "There is some mis—"

Tzu Yu struck him on the mouth, drawing blood. "Silence, rat!"

Then Tzu Yu and the officers turned to watch the charge melting away. Within fifty feet of the wall it ceased to be a charge and became but a writhing, wailing mass of dying men.

Tzu Yu turned to Brive and said, suavely, "You do not mind waiting here a few minutes before going to the House of Punishment, rat who gnawed? Captain Cordie may want to ask you a few questions."

"Torture? You do not dare, Manchu. My country would—"

"No. You are beyond the pale, rat who gnawed. I will explain the matter to the complete satisfaction of France—if she even asks about a disgrace like you. You die by the death of the thousand-and-one cuts. I— Here comes Captain Cordie. Answer very fully, you who are a rat and who also was once an officer and a gentleman. By so doing you will delay the first cut that much longer."

Jimmie Cordie came up. With him there came the Fighting Yid, the Boston Bean, Grigsby, Carewe and Red Dolan.

Jimmie, his eyes cold, looked at Pierre de la Brive. "You die, Brive, for what you have done and what you have tried to do. It may be that I can make the death an easy one. Will you answer some questions?"

"Why not?" answered Pierre de la Brive. He had good blood in him, this renegade to his own land and every other. Now, at the finish, he braced himself. If he was no longer an officer and a gentleman, as Tzu Yu had said, he would at least die like one. "First, command that the grip on my arms be loosened. It is hurting me."

"**ORDER THAT** his arms be freed," Jimmie said to Tzu Yu. As Tzu Yu gave the order he stepped up beside Jimmie. The Yid and the Bean and the rest were behind Jimmie. Back of Brive there stood the Manchu officers. Close to one side stood Major Kweiyang and some of the younger Manchus. Pierre de la Brive could not have broken through them if he had tried.

"First," Jimmie Cordie said, "did you send the map to Chanking? The one that enabled the flyers to reach the ammunition?"

"Yes."

"By whom?"

"By a man who came into the city to get it."

"I will tell you now that your batman, Gaston Figeac, is dead. Also the Bat d'Af that came for the message."

"Name of a name! You know that my—?"

"How did a Bat d'Af come to be with Chan-king?"

"When I took service with Chan-king, the two were with me. I was— A long time ago I was with the Bataillon d'Afrique, as an officer."

"I see. When did you take service with Chan-king?"

"Three months before I—came here."

"So that's it? You were sent by Chan-king to take service with Tzu Yu, so that you could be on the inside?"

"Yes. I had not been in the North, and none of Tzu Yu's men knew me. I had done some work for Chan-king in the South, and—"

"We can figure that out later. You left one Bat d'Af with Chan-king and brought one with you?"

"Yes."

"Where did you get the dynamite?"

"Figeac stole it from the Chinaman who was in charge of it, after the work of hollowing out the wall had been finished. If I had only made the fuse shorter, after—"

"That word 'if' is a hard hurdle to jump, colonel. You ran the fuse back to where you thought there was no chance that the Manchus would see you light it?"

"Yes."

"The black-hearted scut had things figured out, didn't he, ye Yid gibboon?" Red whispered to the Yid.

"Und how!" the Yid answered. "He is von bad hombre, dot frog-eater—no foolink! See how easy he stands, knowing dot de death of—"

"I—I—" Pierre de la Brive said. "You were once an officer in the army of your country, Captain Cordie! I ask you to prevent my torture at the hands of these Manchus. See—I, Pierre de la Brive, a noble of France, go down on my knees to you!"

"He is breaking," the Yid said. "I didn't think he vould did it. My, vot a—!" He stopped talking.

SEVERAL THINGS happened at once. Jimmie Cordie

stepped back, a surprised look on his face. Brive had been so cool and collected and had answered so calmly, in spite of the cut on his lips, that Jimmie was totally unprepared for his sudden cracking. Brive almost wailed out that last sentence.

As Jimmie stepped back Tzu Yu stepped forward, with the idea of interfering with the kneeling. And as Tzu Yu did so, Brive, instead of kneeling, swerved and snatched Tzu Yu's pistol from its holster. He had planned to get Jimmie Cordie's.

"You first!" the traitor yelled as he brought the pistol up in line with Jimmie's heart. "Then me!—I will not live to be—"

As he was bringing up the pistol, Major Kweiyang jumped between it and Jimmie Cordie. Everything happened swiftly. Afterwards, the Yid and the Bean spent hours in argument as to who moved first.

Kweiyang took the bullet meant for Jimmie Cordie's heart, took it in his shoulder, being a shorter man. When that happened, bullets from several guns tore into Pierre da la Brive. Red, the Yid, the Bean, Grigsby and Carewe fired from where they stood, and they were all "dead shots."

Pierre de la Brive went down, dead before his body had even hit the ground. "The rat who gnawed," Tzu Yu said smoothly, "is dead."

As he spoke, the advance guard of Marshal Chang Hsueh-Liang's route army came over the tops of the hills. Chan-king and his staff, caught between two fires, died—to the last man.

"The war brother of my honorable father comes," Tzu Yu went on. "Thanks to you, resplendent one, I have held until the coming."

Jimmie Cordie grinned. "I guess we all better offer up thanks to the Nine Red Gods of War. Without their help, and that of the tattooing on the Bat d'Af, the chances are that the war brother of your honorable father would have found Chan-king inside the walls of Kitai."

The Yid turned to the Bean. "Maybe-so he had it some likker

dot he did not spike mit de poison.—Let's go and take a look, Codfisher!"

"That is the first sensible idea you have advanced for a long time," answered the Bean. "Ease over to the left, Mr. Cohen!"

Which shows about how much the previous doings had affected the Boston Bean and the Fighting Yid.

A MANCHU ROBIN HOOD

Jimmie Cordie and his adventurous comrades were right at home in the warfare between Japanese soldiers and Manchurian swordsmen

CHAPTER I

MANCHU SWORDS

"**NAY, LITTLE FLOWER,** be not afraid. See, your father and brothers are here to protect you, as always. The little men of Nippon cannot reach their greedy hands this far, from where they have put the boy, Henry Pu-Yi, on a tinsel throne and named him Emperor of the new state of Manchukuo. Come and sit in my lap, lotus bud, and I will tell you a tale of the days when the proud Manchus held Manchuria in the hollow of their hands. Then this land was known as their home, Manchuria, and not as it is known today, a land called Manchukuo, ruled by a puppet emperor backed by Nippon guns. In the olden days, peach blossom, the little men of Nippon, had they dared to come even close to the land of the Manchus, would have met Manchu swords and died. Now...

"Truly, it is a bad storm out. Listen to the wind gods howl with anger because they cannot get into our warm house; and see them fling the snow crystals against the window-panes. Put your head against my heart, little flower, and listen to a tale of the Manchu heroes. Once there was..."

The Chinese noble, sitting in the big living room of his house near Fu-Yu, one hundred miles northwest of Harbin, Manchuria (or to give the state its new name, Manchukuo) told a tale while his wife, his two sons and his little daughter listened.

Also present in the room, sitting as close to the fire as they could get, and just outside of the family half circle, were several

The Japanese raiders had not expected resistance

old servants. Outside the house a storm was raging, and as the Chinese noble had said it was "truly a bad one."

"... And so the Manchu war lord drew his sword there in his audience chamber, saying, 'You hill jackals do not know Manchus. Who comes first to die? I will—'"

There came a sound of the crashing in of a door, the ring of steel, and the snarled commands of an officer speaking Japanese. Then there was a strangled cry, and into the room ran an old Chinese.

"The men of Nippon, lord!" he gasped, holding his right side, blood from a bayonet thrust running out between his fingers. "They have—*aie! aie!* I—" he pitched forward to the floor.

The two sons rose and drew swords. The father put the little girl down from his lap and rose also.

"Put up your swords, my sons," he commanded. "For the little men of Nippon want me. Put up your swords and do not resist. I command it."

The little girl, hardly more than ten years old, stood rubbing her eyes with her little fists. The wife of Prince Chiang had also risen, and as her husband spoke, she went over to him.

A Japanese officer came into the room, followed by a file of soldiers, their rifles bayoneted. As the infantrymen came in, they lined the walls of the room. Others followed, forming behind the officer.

"You are Prince Chiang?" demanded the officer, a middle-aged man with thick, sensual lips and cold eyes.

"Yes, I am Prince Chiang," answered the Chinese noble, evenly. "For myself I ask nothing, but—I beg your honorable consideration for my family."

The Japanese officer laughed. "You Chinese dog! I have been sent to teach you not to intrigue against Nippon. Take him out and shoot him!"

The last to a non-commissioned officer who stood a pace in front of the soldiers.

The little girl had stopped rubbing her eyes. She was looking at the Japanese officer and the soldiers as if she were fully convinced that she was dreaming a bad dream. As the officer said "take him out and shoot him," she walked directly up to him, her bright silks making her look like some lovely little butterfly.

"No," she commanded royally. "You must not. You are a bad

man, and you are not to touch my honorable father. If you do I will—"

The Japanese officer struck her across the face with his open hand. It was a hard, cruel blow; and the little girl, her face already bloody, was lifted by it and hurled against the legs of the soldiers who lined the wall on the right.

As the officer struck, the two sons drew their swords again and charged in upon him. Prince Chiang, driven almost crazy by the sight of his little daughter being struck in the face in this brutal manner, drew also.

The officer laughed again and pulled out his service revolver, shooting twice. The two sons of the Chinese Prince Chiang went down, dead before they hit the floor.

"Disarm him!" the officer shouted. "He dies with his face to a wall."

THE NON-COMMISSIONED officer stepped forward, as did several of the soldiers, their bayoneted rifles advanced. And as they did so, a machine gun opened outside the house. There was an instant's pause, as if all in the room were frozen. The Japanese knew that if their machine gun had opened up, it meant an attack. Prince Chiang knew it also, even as he knew that he stood no chance against the bayonets of six or seven soldiers.

The machine gun reports came clearly, *tat-tatatat-tat-tat* and then there came the sound of other machine guns, firing much more rapidly. *Ratatatatat—atatatat—r-r-r-r-r-atat.*

"Brownings!" snarled the officer. "Who is—? Out! Out! We will—"

The clash of steel against steel, the cries of mortally wounded men, and into the room, through the windows and doors, there came Manchu swordsmen led by a Manchu noble whose grim, scarred old face was as impassive as that of an idol.

The Japanese met the rush with their bayonets, and those who could used their rifles. The officer killed the first two swordsmen that came in his line of fire, and then Prince Chiang reached him. He fired pointblank at the Chinese, and missed him. A

Manchu swordsman, charging in upon the men at the wall, had brushed against the officer's shoulder, so that the bullet meant for Prince Chiang's heart went high over the head of the man who sought to avenge his little daughter and his sons.

The sword licked out twice, like the tongue of a snake. The hand of the Japanese officer, the one with which he had struck the girl, fell from the wrist to the floor; and a split second later the officer's body joined it.

The Japanese machine gun maintained its fire for a little more than a minute, then it stopped. The men who operated it were dead, and there were none to take their places.

There was a final ring of swords on bayonets and rifle barrels, and then—silence.

The big room was a shambles of dead and dying Japanese and Manchus. The Manchu leader, his sword red, went up to the Prince Chiang, who was kneeling by the bodies of his sons.

"I am Chang-Lung Liang of the House of Chi. The spirits of the mongrels of Nippon have gone howling into the outer coldness, Chinese swordsman. I saw you kill the Nippon dog. Rise and come with us."

Prince Chiang looked up. "My sons are— May their spirits ascend on High as lightly and smoothly as the flight of a swan, on—"

A dying Japanese soldier raised himself up on an elbow. "To me, Akita!" he called loudly. "Where are you?—The Big Swords are—" he fell back, dead. His brother at arms could not answer or come. His spirit was already in "the outer coldness."

"The bodies of your sons shall receive honorable burial. Gather your family and your servants.—You are under my protection. Make haste, Chinese."

PRINCE CHIANG rose. "My little daughter and my wife were here in the room when—"

"There is a woman there by the wall, lord," a Manchu swordsman said to Chang-Lung Liang.

The wife of Prince Chiang had reached the little girl as the Manchu swords entered the room and had shielded the little form with her own delicate body. In the mad swirl and press of the fight, either a bayonet or a sword had reached her heart; but even as she died she covered the little girl's body with her own.

"My wife has—also gone on High," Prince Chiang said, evenly, as he lifted her in his arms. "And it may be also my little flower, who only a few min—"

The little girl stirred, then opened her eyes. "I want my honorable father," she whimpered. "He will—"

Then the proud old Manchu, head of the House of Chi, whose chieftains had ridden stirrup to stirrup with Nurhachu to the Peacock Throne of China, did something that caused the eyes of his swordsmen to widen a little, in spite of the Manchu code of utter impassivity. He held out his arms and said to Prince Chiang:

"I will carry your broken blossom. Take the little golden one in your arms and comfort her."

A man entered the room, plainly an Anglo-Saxon. The swordsmen near the door bowed as he passed them. Around the man's waist, strapped outside a sheepskin coat, was a cartridge belt from which hung a holstered forty-five Colt's revolver.

"Make it snappy, Chang," he said curtly, speaking in English. "The Jap regiment is closing in. We cannot hold them with the men we have here with us."

"You have destroyed the bridge and the tracks, Captain Cordie?" asked Chang-Lung Liang. His English was as perfect as that of the man who had entered, for in his youth Chang had been sent to England for his education, and afterwards he had been one of the secretaries of the Chinese Embassy at Washington. Most Manchus and Chinese cannot pronounce the "r" when speaking English, there being no such letter in the Chinese language, which is now spoken by Manchus. But Chang had mastered it in England and America.

"Yes. The bridge is down and the track torn up, both in front of and behind their troop train. They are marooned, Chang. But that does not stop them from coming in on foot. We'd better pull our freight."

"Very well, Captain Cordie. We will, as you say—pull our freight. You, K'ung, and you, Yang Huo. Carry the bodies of the sons of this Chinese, whose excellent swordplay entitles him to honor."

CHAPTER II

A PRAYER OF THANKS

THE CAFÉ OF Meng Yi, in Tsitsihar, had been a good place to keep away from, even in the days before the Japanese occupation of Manchuria. Unless the person who went there for wine, women and song was fully able to protect himself in every way. And now, when the army of the Chinese General Ma was camped close to the city, and when the Japanese troops were occupying the city, it was more than ever not a place for any one not utterly reckless.

At the moment, General Ma was friendly with the Japanese, and was accepting their gold. He firmly believed that the more "foreign devils" he could get to command his troops, the better off he would be. The Japs didn't like this, but Ma's friendship was vital just at that time, and so they tolerated as choice a collection of adventurers in Tsitsihar as had ever been brought together. American, English, German, French, Russian, Italian, Turkish and cross-breeds of all kinds. Soldiers of fortune all, and hardbitted; held only in leash by the knowledge that old General Ma would just as soon line them up with their backs to the wall, facing a firing squad, as he would to take a drink of strong French brandy—and he liked to do the latter very much.

One night about two weeks after the Big Swords had destroyed the Japanese unit, the big main drinking room at Meng Yi's was crowded. There was no space cleared in the room for dancing, and the tables were placed as close together as possible. At them sat the soldiers of fortune who fought for General

Ma. Chinese and Japanese officers, civilians of twenty different races, they were—the kind who always follow an army or come looking for favors from the victorious side. And with them sat the painted ladies of Meng Yi—who also were of many races and breeds. All of the men wore their side-arms, and most all of them, since the time was one o'clock in the morning, were more than half drunk.

A RUSSIAN who had once been a colonel in the army of the Czar and who now was an artillery officer for Ma, got up from his table and started over to speak to a friend at another table. As he passed a table about halfway over to his friend, a man who looked to be about as broad as he was long, got up. His back was turned to the approaching man, and so he did not see him. As the fat man got up, he brushed the Russian's arm.

As soon as he had regained his balance, the Russian turned and glared at the other. He saw an unmistakably Semitic face, and he began to curse hotly. Then in Pushtu, the universal language of the border, he shouted:

"You Jew dog! You dare touch me with your foul—"

He struck at the man with right hand clenched.

The Jew, whose china blue eyes seemed to be popping out of his head with surprise at such bad doings in a naughty old world, appeared to be absolutely unprepared to receive the attack. Yet, as the Russian struck, in a way that seemed clumsy and slow, the Jew closed in on the Russian. His right hand, the heel of it, struck the Russian under the chin, and as it did so his left knee came up. It looked as though he was only trying to avoid the blow, but a big red-headed man, sitting not far away with some ex-Légionnaires, grinned.

The Russian yelled in pain, and staggered back as the Jew, who was in civilian clothes, began yelling, "*Oi! Oi!* Mine persecuted race! Vot did I did to him? Don't let it him get at me! I am no fighter! Let me out! Make vay—please! I am no fighter!"

The big red-headed man muttered into his glass of cognac,

"Ye're as good a fighter as ye are a liar, ye Yid monkey-faced gibbon."

"You said?" asked the Légionnaire sitting beside him.

"Nawthin'. I was offerin' up a prayer to the good saints that all Yids be driven into the deep sea. Did ye see that—?"

The Russian had staggered against a German, who had been brooding over the fact that when *"der tag"* had come, Germany had found that others had also been ready for the day. He, the German, had drunk himself into the idea that in spite of everything the Germans were the best people on earth and entitled to the respectful acknowledgment of the same from the rest of the world. When the Russian bumped against him, therefore, the German was fully primed. He rose and said, *"Schweinhund! Ich bin ganz kriegs-schiff!"*—Which, roughly translated, is, "You pigdog! I am all man-of-war." After which the German planted himself squarely and knocked the Russian into the lap of a Jap officer, who had pushed back from the table.

He knew, this Jap officer, what was coming. A blow struck in Meng Yi's meant a general rough-house, which was one of the reasons why Meng Yi's was no place for a cripple. Why it meant that, no one had ever been able to say. In other places the crowds would sit and watch the fight, but in Meng Yi's—never.

The fastidious little Jap pushed the Russian off, and as he did so, another Russian hit the German over the head with a bottle. An ex-Légionnaire did not like the way the second Russian had sneaked up on the German, and expressed his dislike by hitting the Russian over the head with a chair.

In a split-second the room became a madhouse. Germans went to the rescue of Germans; Russians tried to fight their way toward the first two Russians; Japs started for the officer who had pushed the Russian off, who in turn had been knocked down by an Englishman who didn't like Japs anyway.

AT FIRST it was fists, bottles and chairs. The painted ladies got under tables or ran for the nearest exits. Some of them made it and others did not. Some were caught in the maelstrom and tossed about like corks as the fighting men milled around.

The ex-Légionnaires formed a wedge and started for the main door, the big red-headed man at the point. They had had plenty of experience in that kind of fighting, as well as in other kinds; and they went about the business of getting out as coolly and calmly as if forming on parade. Fighters who came close to the wedge went down, and if the man nearest to him didn't put him down, the next man in the wedge attended to it. The big redheaded man steered the wedge toward the spot where the Jew stood behind an overturned table, meeting all comers with a table leg for a weapon. He was yelling at the top of his voice, "*Oi! Oi!* I am no fighter! I am no fighter!"

The fight began to get messy. At first no side-arms were drawn. But, as the wedge went across the room, an ex-Légionnaire got a hard rap on the knuckles from a bottle and immediately afterward he shouted, "*La Rosalie!*" which is the Legion's name for the beloved bayonet. What is more, he used *La Rosalie* to make payment for his skinned knuckles. As the bayonet flashed, other bayonets appeared, and guns as well.

The big red-headed man at the point of the wedge drew neither bayonet nor gun. Whoever came within range of his fists passed out of the picture for the time being.

The wedge reached the place where the Jap officer who had pushed the Russian was fighting gallantly against three drunken Russians who were pressing him hard. As yet, the Jap had not drawn his gun, using his knowledge of jujutsu to keep the Russians off. Just as the point of the wedge reached him, a bottle hit him on the side of the head. The fighting little Jap staggered back, and the nearest Russian closed in with a yell of drunken glee.

The Jap's game stand appealed to the red-headed ex-Légionnaire, and he reached out a hand as big as a ham and drew the Russian close to him by the scruff of the neck. Turning him around he said, "Take somewan the size ave ye, ye scut!" And as he said it, he slapped the Russian across the face with an open left hand.

The Russian went down as if he had been hit with an ax.

"And ye the same, ye big squarehead," said the red-head to one of the two left.

This one was blond—and to the big red-head, all foreign blonds were squareheads. When he got to the word "squarehead," his right fist reached the Russian's jaw. That ex-trooper of the Czar left his feet as if shot from a cannon, and he landed across a table, six or seven feet away.

The Jap officer grinned as the second Russian was picked off, and he closed with the one remaining. There was an instant when the Jap's small body seemed part of the big Russian's, and then the Jap sprang away as the Russian fell. The little man of Nippon had put all his remaining strength into the effort, and as the big red-headed man went past, he swayed forward.

"Come in here, banty," the red-headed man said. " 'Tis a good little man ye are!" And he lifted the Jap officer as easily as he would have a baby, tossing him into the open space of the wedge. "Take care of him, ye half-baked black-and-white kitties," he shouted.

One of the ex-Légionnaires, back in the right wing of the wedge, an American, laughed. "I'll keep him for you, Red," he called, tucking the little Jap under a long, steel-like arm. *"Allons, enfants perdus!"*

THE WEDGE kept on, and when it reached the place where the Jew was still yelling that he was no fighter, and at the same time cracking any and all heads that came within his reach, the red-head halted his marchers.

"Wait till I collect me a Yid to go wid me little banty," he shouted. "Hold the scuts off, ye duck faced apes, till I get him."

The ex-Légionnaires laughed, and the wedge became a line in front of the red-headed man and the Jew. The Jap officer was still under the arm of the American.

"Get avay! Get avay from me!" yelled the Jew. "Irisher bum!

Did it you come von step fudder und I smack it you on de sconce. Loafer vot you are! Get avay! *Oi,* I am no fighter! I am no fighter!"

"Put that club down, ye Yid monkey! 'Tis rescuin' ye I am, ye hook-nosed gibbon. Put it down or I'll—"

A machine gun sent a burst of steel-jacketed bullets over the heads of the fighting men, and then there was a snarled command, first in Chinese, then in Pushtu. Every man in the room looked up at the balcony that ran across the south end of the room. There the muzzles of two machine guns showed, and standing between them was one of General Ma's staff officers.

The command was, "Stop fighting and return to your commands—or die.—Clear the room! Make haste, little brothers, before the guns begin to talk."

No man there but knew that if he did not get out as fast as he could, more than likely he would feel machine gun bullets crashing into him. When old General Ma sent one of his staff to deliver an order, it was best to obey that command very promptly. Ma had the reputation of meeting with bullets any reluctance in the obeying of his orders. In this case, he had sent a machine gun company in, knowing that if a fight started anywhere in Tsitsihar, it must be stopped as quickly as possible lest it spread; and the best way he knew to stop it was with machine guns.

In less than three minutes, the big room was empty, save for several dead and badly wounded men.

The big red-headed man, the Jew, and the Jap officer, were all swept along in the rush for the exits. The Légionnaire line was broken as it became *sauve qui peut* for all. The Jap was dropped by the American, but luckily he landed on his feet. His head had cleared a lot, and as he found himself alongside the red-head, who in turn was alongside the Jew, he said:

"In here! In here! I know this place. In here!"

He spoke in English, and he was already at a door in the hall. Feeling along a panel, he pushed it in. The door swung open, and he entered, followed by the red-headed man and the Jew.

The men behind also tried to squeeze in, but the Jap turned and shut the door in their faces.

THEN, IN the dim light of a lamp that stood on a table in the middle of the small room, he clicked his heels together and saluted the red-headed man.

"I am Major Mito," he announced. "You saved my life—or at least, you saved me from serious injury. I thank you."

"I saved ye, banty, because av the good scrap ye was puttin' up," the redhead answered. "I'm Captain Dolan av the Chink's—I do be meanin', av General Ma's army. And who the hell this Yid is, I dunno—and care less."

"I have got it a right to be here, Mister Captain. I have got it papers signed by de Japanese High Command to be here und trade mit all peoples. Did I vant to get it into a fight, I esk you? I am no fighter. I am in bitzness."

"I'll soon find out who he is, Captain Dolan," Major Mito said. And to the Jew, "Let me see your papers."

The Jew produced a long, official looking envelope and handed it to the Japanese officer; and as he did so he smirked at the big red-headed captain of General Ma's army. "I got it dem, Mister Captain."

"Abraham Cohen, born New York City, United States of America," Major Mito read. "Occupation—trader. Description—" He stopped reading aloud. Finally he looked at the Jew, then said, "His papers are in order. You may go, Cohen." He handed back the papers.

"I vill did it. But first, I vish also to thank de brave captain of de Chinks for rescuin' me. An Irisher mit Chinks! Vat could it be sveeter? Thank you, Mister Captain."

Mr. Abraham Cohen went to the door, and after peeking cautiously out to see if the way was clear, he departed.

Major Mito smiled and said, "And now, Captain Dolan, if you will come with me while I get someone to attend to my ringing head, I will take you to a place where there will be no fights, and where the liquor is of the best."

"I would like to go wid ye, banty, but I must be gittin' back to camp. The old divil's commands are not to be sneezed at, if ye want to keep widout holes in ye."

"No doubt you are right, Captain Dolan. Are you with the guns? Many of you soldiers of fortune are."

"I am not. I am on the old boy's staff. And what the hell good I am there, I dunno!"

"Well, if you cannot come with me now, some day I will look you up and then we will go to the place I know, and over a bottle I will thank you properly for what you have just done."

"Come any time ye get the chance," Captain Dolan answered, as he started for the door. " 'Tis a good little man ye are, for all your lack o' inches."

Dolan himself was six foot three, and broad in proportion. He weighed some two hundred and thirty pounds, all of it bone and muscle. Ex-Foreign Legion and once lieutenant of military police, A.E.F., "Red" Dolan was simon pure fighting Irish, from the top of his red head to the tips of his toes. Hence there was some excuse for his having called the trim, dapper little Japanese officer by the name of "banty," since he had no wish to insult.

Major Mito, Military Intelligence, stood still for a moment after Captain Dolan left. Then he said aloud, though very softly, "To the great Buddha I offer a prayer of thanks."

CHAPTER III

INTELLIGENCE

THREE MEN SAT in a darkened room, over the shop of Hsai Chu. One was Captain Dolan, another Abraham Cohen, and the third was Captain James Cordie, the man who had told Chang-Lung Liang to "make it snappy."

"All right, let's have it, Yid," Captain Cordie said.

Wherever soldiers of fortune gathered in the Orient and the talk swung around to shooting ability, someone would say, after Jimmie Cordie's name had been mentioned, "Yeah, that's so. Those guys are there like a duck, but did you ever see Jimmie Cordie really strut his stuff with a Browning, or with a forty-five Colt?—Listen. One time Jimmie and I were up in the North and—" Generally the story told would bring a delighted grin to the lips of the men who listened, and nine times out of ten, the story contained somewhere in its length the expression, "So Jimmie framed 'em."

He was slim, black-eyed and usually smiling, was Jimmie Cordie. Ex-Foreign Legion sergeant, and once captain of a machine gun company, A.E.F., since the war he had been a fighter in the far places. Among the Chinese he was known as "The Black-Eyed Smiling One, whom it is best to obey quickly."

Mr. Abraham Cohen grinned when Jimmie demanded to hear his story. "De intelligence ain't got it much to report, Jimmie. Last night, de Japs started three or four regiments, mit cavalry, artillery and tanks, towards Lao-Tzu. De vay I got it is dat dey is goin' to mop up, using Lao-Tzu for a base."

"Holy cats! And you don't call that much of anything? Lao-Tzu is full of Manchu refugees and Chinese who're wanted. They've got their families there.—I can't fool around here with you birds! You got anything, Red?"

"I have not. General Ma is gettin' good and sore at the Japs. If he could be given a push, I think he'd fight."

Jimmie Cordie laughed. "I wish we could give it to him, Red; but at the minute, we've got other fish to fry. I'll be getting back.—Stay with it, you gents! You're doing nobly."

"Hey! Vait it a minute," protested Mr. Cohen. "You said it dot if Red und me took it dis end for a little v'ile, dot vould be enough, und ve could join de gang again. I don't like it dis intelligence stuff."

Mr. Abraham Cohen, besides being that and a trader, was the Fighting Yid. He had received the name while he was first sergeant of Jimmie Cordie's machine gun company in France. And later he had lived up to it fully in the Orient. The Yid would fight anything, at any time and at any place. That was why Red had muttered something or other when he heard the Yid yell, "I am no fighter!" during the café scrap.

The Yid fought for war lord or general, whoever needed a man afraid of no odds, and one who could handle men and make a machine gun sing the death song. Jimmie Cordie had once said, "The Yid is a soldier of fortune—neither pure nor simple," and that about summed up the Yid. Ever since the A.E.F. days, the Yid had been with Jimmie Cordie as much as possible. If by chance he fought on the other side, once he found out that Jimmie and "de gang" were his enemies, the Yid would promptly desert, and with great cheerfulness turn a machine gun on his former employer.

"WELL, YE Hester Street ape," Red Dolan said, "are ye kickin' about the soft job av ye? Nawthin' to do but bum around and guzzle wine and play wid de ladies.—Look at me! I've got to put up wid an old scut that—"

"I'll tell you what you can do," Jimmie broke in. "Weep on

each other's shoulders, for both of you will stay right here and keep right on doing what you are doing now. I've got to have an intelligence department, and you're it. No telling how soon our information is going to dry up; and while we're getting it, the place for you two birds is right here. Have you been recognized, Yid? I mean, as the Fighting Yid, by any of the bunch that are with Ma?"

"Sure have I. Plenty of dem. Dey say, 'Vot de hell are you didin' up here, Yid?' Und I say 'I have quit de fightin' end und am now a trader. Vot you got it to trade?'"

"Yeah? Well, maybe the Japs won't hook it up. You've fooled around with a lot of outfits besides mine; but if they find out I'm with Chang, and some one tells them you are the Fighting Yid who is with me a lot, there'll be a new Yid face in the angel chorus immediately afterward."

"And it will be good riddance to bad rubbish!" Red stated, firmly. "Too long this monkey-faced gibbon has been breathin' the good air into his lungs and spoilin' it for a better man, Jimmie darlin'. I hope the little men catch him."

"Quiet, you Irish bummer!" the Yid answered, loftily. "Or me und Jimmie vill kick de slats in. Put it de jaw tackle, v'ile us intelligencers vork."

"Oh, ye will? Ten Yids and twenty-nine Cordies couldn't do that to wan sick Dolan—let alone a well wan. 'Tis—"

"For Pete's sake, Red, pipe down! We all know what one Dolan can do. I'm going to leave the Boston Bean in T'ai. He will be a missionary; and, Yid, you contact him. I can't make it in here so often. He'll pass the word to Carewe.—I don't think the Japs will get wise to us—if they ever do—before we can get all the Manchus out of the dangerous territory. Let's have a drink, and then I'll beat it. I've got a gang of Big Swords holed up in the outskirts of this man's town, and I'm afraid they'll start something."

"How did you get it dem in, Jimmie?" asked the Yid.

"Last night. We came in as peasants bringing beans to the

Japs. One by one, a Chinese outfit that's with Chang joined the parade, and the Big Swords faded, leaving the Chinese to unload the stuff at the Jap depot."

"And wan av them Chinks will sell the news to a Jap, and hell will pop for ye and the Big Swords. I'll go wid ye, Jimmie, alanna."

Red Dolan had one other love, besides the love of battle, and that was his love for the slim, smiling Jimmie Cordie. Red, ever since the day when he met Jimmie in the Legion, had adopted a simple rule of life. He would ask, "What now, ye shrimp?" or "How about that, Jimmie?" The answer always satisfied Mr. Dolan; and in addition, he had only one thing to say, when confronted with the enemy. "Aw, slap 'em to hell outta the way." That was always his suggestion.

Jimmie laughed. "These Chinks won't tell, Red. Thanks, just the same, old kid Dolan! Up to date, we've outplayed our new boy friends from Nippon, and I think we can keep on doin' 'er.—Let's get that drink."

CHAPTER IV

TRAP-SHY

AS JIMMIE CORDIE said, "Let's have it, Yid," two Japanese military intelligence officers, in G.H.Q., not half a mile from the shop of Hsai Chu, were doing the very thing that Jimmie did not think they could do. They were "hooking it up."

"I am sure of it, colonel. So sure that I will stake my commission on it. At Fu-yu, before he died, one of our soldiers told of a Manchu who said, 'I am Chang-Lung Liang of the House of Chi,' and a little later a man came in whom the Manchu addressed as Captain Cordie."

"Admitting that," Colonel Nagoya answered, "how are the two men you mention connected with the Big Swords? All it tells us is that the new leader of the Big Swords is the Manchu, Chang-Lung Liang, and that he has with him a soldier of fortune named Cordie. But that is all, as far as I can see."

"Have you not read the report from our intelligence in Hongkong that I placed on your desk, soon after the affair at Fu-yu?"

"No. I have been too busy with other matters. What bearing has the report on this matter?"

"I have heard much of Captain Cordie. He is the man who killed Captain Samie, in the Northwest, and he is also the man who persuaded Sahet Khan to hold the Thian Shan Passes against us if we moved towards Siberia. After I heard the soldier's story, I wired Hongkong and got the report—a very full one—on Captain Cordie. With him there are generally five men, named Grigsby, Carewe, the—"

"I do not care what their names are! Get to the point, major. I am very busy."

"This, then: the two men of the café are Cordie's men. He is with the Manchu leader of the Big Swords. One of the men is called Red Dolan, and the other the Fighting Yid. In some way, they are getting the information that permits the Big Swords to strike at us. I had the descriptions of all of Captain Cordie's men sent up in the report. Tonight, by the grace of the Lord Buddha, two of them I met. I believe that they are the ones who send the information to the Big Swords."

"**WHAT ARE** they doing here?"

"One, Dolan, is a captain in General Ma's army. The other—the one called the Fighting Yid, poses as a trader."

"We can get this man Dolan any time from General Ma. Send a detachment for the other one. That is the quickest way to find out if there is anything in your theory. If there is, you have earned your step up. If there isn't—in the future, be more certain of your knowledge before you bother me again. Have the man brought to the questioning room at military police headquarters. He will very soon tell us whether or not he is a spy for the Big Swords. I will be there in an hour. See that he is there, also."

Major Mito saluted and left the room. As he did so, he decided to go with the detachment to take the Fighting Yid. He had not been in the café for the purpose of looking for any of the men who generally fought with Captain Cordie; as a matter of fact he had dropped in to get a couple of drinks before going to see a lady whom he knew very well. He had had other things to think of at the moment when Red picked him up, and he had not then noticed that Red fully corresponded with the description of Red Dolan which had been sent up from Hongkong. When the Yid was reached, Major Mito did not even see him. It was not until they were in the inner room, when he looked at the Yid's papers, that it dawned on him that he was in the presence of two of the men described.

Up to that moment he had thought that in all probability

Captain Cordie's men were fighting at his side, under the old Manchu war lord. He was clever, this Japanese intelligence officer, otherwise he would not have been a major in the intelligence, and it did not take him long to guess that there was a connection between the leak, the two men in the Tsitsihar café, and Captain Cordie of the Big Swords.

Where the leak was, and who was responsible for it, he did not have the slightest idea; nor how it connected with Red Dolan or the Fighting Yid. But the colonel had cut the Gordian knot with "He will very soon tell us whether or not he is a spy for the Big Swords." Major Mito was very sure the Fighting Yid would tell, once he had entered what was called the questioning room at military police headquarters.

When he reached the military police headquarters, Major Mito asked for a detachment. When asked how many men he wanted, he answered that four men would be enough. Then, as he thought of the possibility of the shop having secret exits, and since he did not want the Fighting Yid to slip through his fingers, he asked for two squads, intending to surround the shop.

The men, under a young lieutenant, were promptly furnished him, and he started for the shop of Hsai Chu. The place where the Yid lived he had learned from the Yid's papers.

JIMMIE CORDIE put down his glass and rose, "Well, that's that! I'll get back to my gentle playmates and—"

The door of the room opened and the old shopkeeper ran in. "Soldiers come," he shrilled, in Chinese. "On street—in shop—every—!"

A shot came from the hall, and the old man pitched forward on his face. Major Mito stepped into the room, revolver in hand, followed by two Japanese soldiers; their rifles were bayoneted.

The room was dimly lighted, by only one small oil lamp, and Major Mito expected to find only the Yid there. But instead of meeting one man, who would put his hands up at a command, it was as if Major Mito had stepped into a cage of black leopards. He and the two soldiers met three men whose muscles were perfectly coordinated with their brains, and who reacted instantly to danger. Before the major had time to speak, Jimmie Cordie and Red Dolan had drawn their forty-five Colts and had them full on the two soldiers. The Yid hurled the chair he had been sitting in at the gun hand of Major Mito, and even before it had struck, followed it up by a crouching spring, straight at the Japanese major's throat.

The Yid, of course, was about as broad as he was long. His hands reached below his knees when he stood erect, and his powerful body was as strong as that of a grizzly bear. Few men, no matter how big, could stand up to a hurtling charge by the Yid, and the little Japanese major was far from being one of those few. He went down as if hit by a shell. But since he was a fighter himself, as he fell he pulled trigger and shouted, "Forward!"

The bullet went into the ceiling as the two soldiers, in spite of the guns that were being held upon them, dropped their rifles to a charge-bayonets, and started to obey the command.

They did not live to take the first step. Both Jimmie Cordie and Red Dolan knew that unless they could fight their way out, it would mean death right there, or a little later, with their backs to a wall. And so they killed.

The Yid rose from the body of Major Mito. "He is out und down und all in," he announced, cheerfully, drawing his Colt. "Come mit. I know a vay out. De shopkeeper told me it ven—"

"Listen to what's coming up the stairs.—Get going, Yid! The intelligence department is busted up."

The Yid went to a door on one side of the room and opened it.

"Down de steps und out de vindow und over de roof. Vot could be sveeter—?"

"You first, Yid. Follow him, Red."

AS RED went through, bayonets and rifle barrels showed at the door where Major Mito had entered, and behind the rifles, faces. Jimmie Cordie fired, and the *bang-bang-bang-bang* of his forty-five sounded like a drumroll. Then he ran, closing the door behind him.

He took the short flight of stairs in one jump, and kept on down a narrow, dark hall that made a sharp right-hand turn about twenty feet away from the stairs. Immediately after he had made the turn, bullets crashed into the wall where a split-second ago his body had been.

The hall ended at a window some fifteen feet from the turn. There was no one in sight, and Jimmie naturally thought that Red and the Yid had gone out that window. How far the drop was he did not know, but he did know that it was up to him to take it. The window was open, and large enough to permit Jimmie to throw first one leg and then the other across the sash. As his head came out, he saw that the drop was about twelve feet, to a shed roof.

As he jumped, he heard the Fighting Yid say behind him, "Dot's de boy, James!—Hurry mit de rescue, if dey don't kill me right here."

Jimmie was in the air, and so he could not turn—although he tried it, and also tried for the window ledge. As he hit the roof, he said bitterly, "You Yid ape!" Then he bounded to his feet, and jumped to reach the ledge.

Jimmie's height was between five feet seven or eight, and he was dressed in heavy furs. He missed the ledge by a foot and a half. As he crouched to try again, he heard what sounded like a hundred cats fighting, with a scuffling of human feet and a dropping of rifles mixed in; and he knew that the Japanese had arrived and that they were trying to take the Yid alive.

The Yid's yells broke upon the air. "I am no fighter! *Oi! Oi!* Take dot—und dot! Get goin'!—Und here is von for you. Come mit de gang, later! Und here is von for—" The rest of the Fighting Yid's swan song was drowned out by the snarled commands and the shrill yelps of the soldiers as they closed in, swarming over him.

Jimmie Cordie knew that nothing he could do at the moment would help the Yid, and so he ran across the roof, jumping down a few feet into some kind of a yard that gave upon an alley.

Red was standing there, looking up; but from where he stood he could not see the window.

"Where is that Hester Street scut?" he demanded.

"Fighting the Jap army. We'll take the alley to—"

"He's *what?*—Well, the di-ert-ty bum. He fooled me, the—"

"He fooled me, too. Come on."

As they ran toward the alley, Red was sounding off. "All the time that Yid wants all the fun—bad luck to the monkey-faced gibbon! He tells me that it's a cinch there will be some av the little men waitin' below, and for me to go and mop up on them while he was waitin' for you.—And, begorra, I took bait, hook, line and sinker.—Wait till I get the two hands av me on the coco av him. I'll—!"

They reached the alley, Jimmie a little ahead of Red. Jimmie looked first to the left, where all was clear. Then, as he looked to the right, he laughed.

"The Yid was telling the truth, Red," he said. "Here come the Japs for you to mop up on."

Entering the alley on the right, about a city block away, was a platoon of Japanese infantry, on the double, their rifles down to charge-bayonets.

"Come on, Jimmie! We'll slap 'em to hell outta the way."

"No slapee, Mr. Dolan! See that fence? Jump it and run, Red. I'll hesitate these—"

"Like hell I will. Wance is enough to be sucked in. I'll stay right—!"

"Come on, then. We'll both jump it. *Le bon Dieu* knows what's on the other side, but—"

They jumped the fence.

"Are you all right, Red?"

"I am. Only I lit in a garbage box, by the smell av it. Are ye, Jimmie darlin'?"

"Yeah, boy. Let's go."

"Where?"

"Through that house, dumb bell.—Bust the door in."

RED'S WEIGHT would have smashed in a heavier door than the one against which he put his shoulder and pushed.

They ran across a dark space—some sort of a storeroom—and then through a door that was about half shut, and on into a kitchen. Four or five Chinese were sitting around, drinking tea. When the two foreign devils suddenly appeared, the Chinese squeaked and dropped their cups, falling off their chairs to the floor. Cries went up. The two demons were begged not to hurt them, the mouths of the frenzied Chinese held close to the floor.

"We beg your pardon, mighty war lords," Jimmie said with a grin, as he and Red went through. "Some day we will return and buy you all the—" Another door had been reached, and Red was through it. So Jimmie stopped talking and followed. This door led into another hall, and the hall led to a larger room which fronted a street.

"What now, Jimmie?"

"Wait till I take a look."

Jimmie went to the window and looked out.

"Everything seems quiet along the Potomac, General Dolan," he said. "We'll walk out as if we owned the place, and saunter along. You're Captain Dolan of Ma's Army, and I've just arrived to jine up. We don't know a darn thing about any fight or anything else. We're hunting for a wine shop which you thought was down here."

"Come on. Where are we goin', Jimmie?"

"To the Big Sword hole-up. The Intelligence Department is hereby abolished. You can send your resignation to General Ma later.—Be Captain Dolan for a few minutes more. Think of the joy of being a Big Sword, and of having a sword to play with."

They walked out of the house, down the street to the corner, and down the next street, absolutely unchallenged all the way. Then they proceeded to the Big Swords, in the same way. The course along which they had come, turning and twisting during their run, jumping fences and going through the house, had somehow put them outside the ring of Japanese soldiers closing in on the shop.

CHAPTER V

TO DIE AT DAWN

THE FIGHTING YID stood in front of a long table in military police headquarters. Behind the table sat several Japanese officers. Sitting in a chair at one end of the table was Major Mito, his head heavily bandaged.

The Yid had not yet been placed in the "questioning room" for the simple reason that immediately after he was downed an officer of the Japanese staff, attracted by the shots, arrived on the scene. A moment or so later, Major Mito got to his feet.

The staff officer had once been in military intelligence, and he still thought that, irrespective of the fact that he was now a lieutenant general, he was the best intelligence officer in the world, bar none. And so, after hearing Major Mito's story, he promptly took charge—which helped to save the Yid's hide.

The other officers, of the military police and the intelligence, who were present, would have varied the questioning by a little high class third degree stuff, with the Yid on the receiving end. Now, not knowing exactly how Lieutenant General Yiabu stood in regard to such things, they sat still, their eyes on the Yid. And every eye had a look like the look in the eye of a hungry tiger whose meat is being kept from him.

The Yid was not bound in any way, and his papers were on the table in front of Yiabu. The prisoner's head was cut in two or three places, but none of them serious. His shoulder and arms were sore, where jujutsu holds had been put on him, but otherwise the Yid was intact.

"You are Abraham Cohen?" asked Yiabu smoothly, in English, which was spoken by all officers present.

"Dot's right," answered the Yid, cheerfully.

"Known also as the Fighting Yid?"

"Vell, dot vos a long time ago, ven I vos young und didn't care about noddings. I made it a reform, und now I am a trader. If you got it anything to trade, Mister general, I give you a bar—"

"Silence—dog! Answer my questions promptly, unless you wish to feel a bayonet point in the fat of your body!"

The eyes of the officers lighted up a great deal at that. Perhaps the lieutenant general was all right, after all.

"I am diding it," the Yid protested, his china blue eyes full of injured innocence—or what he tried hard to make innocence.

"You fought for the War Lord Tseng Wang, a year ago. Before that you fought the machine guns for General Shan. Still earlier, you fought as commander of a machine gun section for the War Lord of Hunan, and previous to that you fought for many war lords and generals. Originally, you were the first sergeant of a machine gun company in the American army in France.—Is that correct?"

"My!" answered the Yid, admiringly. "Vot an intelligencer department you must got it.—Dot vos all before I reformed!"

"Who was the captain of your machine gun company in France? His name?"

"Captain James Cordie," answered the Yid, promptly. "Und von hell of a captain he vos! Dot guy ain't got no—"

"Silence! For the last time I warn you to only answer my questions.—For years since the world war, you have fought under Captain Cordie. Tell us about it."

"Vell, I vill admit dot I have fought in de same push dot he was fighting in. But dot don't make him und me friends. *Oi,* how I hate it dot stuffed shirt!"

YIABU SMILED, and suddenly his tone became warm and personal. "You cannot, as you Americans say, 'make it stick,' Yid.

I know that you are not at all afraid, and that you will do your best to protect your friends. And because you try to do that, you die. How much better it would be for you if you told us all about it. We could find work for a man like you to do—work that will pay you far better than being a spy for the Big Swords.

"We know that Captain Cordie is with them. We know that Captain Dolan, of the staff of General Ma's army, is the Red Dolan of Captain Cordie's organization—just as you are the Fighting Yid. We know also that of the two men who were with you tonight in that room, one was Red Dolan. Tell us who the other was, and tell us from whom you or Red were getting the information of our troop movements. When it has been proved that you are telling the truth, you will be given employment, as I have said. Refuse, and you face a firing squad at dawn."

"*Oi!* Such a bitzness! I vould tell it to you right avay, did I know it. Dot's right about Red Dolan. He was dere mit. Me und Red is old buddies, und he come to see—"

Major Mito rose and saluted.

"What is it?" rasped Yiabu.

"May I ask this man a question, general?"

"I am asking the questions, major. Yet since it was through you that this matter was brought to light, yes. You may ask your question."

Major Mito looked at the Yid, who smirked at him.

"You say that you and Red Dolan are old buddies. If that is the case, why did you not recognize him as such, after the fight at the café?"

"Vell," answered the Yid, "me und Red had a falling out, und ve vasn't speakink. He vas a captain in de army of General Ma, und I vas only a trader. I vaited for him to speak, und ven he said, 'Who de hell iss dis Yid?' I thought dot he vos still mad mit me, so I didn't know him, either."

The Japanese officers laughed, and Yiabu said, "Very poor, Yid. Too bad you didn't have time to think up something better. Now, who was the other man in the room?"

"Mister general, I don't know—honest! Red come in mit him, und said dot his name vos Sharlie, und dot he had been it in de Legion mit him. I never saw him before."

"From whom have you been getting information regarding troop movements?"

"*Oi,* such a question! Did I did it, I vould tell it to you. Honest Injun, Mister general. I am a trader. Vot do I care vich vay de troops move mit movement, I esk you?"

Yiabu looked at the Yid steadily for a moment, and several of the other officers stirred a little in their chairs. It was plain to them that the Jew was flouting them.

Finally Yiabu asked silkily, "Is that the attitude you are going to take—all the way through, Mr. Cohen?"

"Vot other could it I take? I am reformed, und a trader. Dot is all I know."

"Take him away," Yiabu ordered. "He is to be executed at dawn."

As the Yid, protesting loudly, was taken from the room by the file of soldiers who had brought him in, one of the officers said something to Yiabu, who answered:

"We will give him a few hours to think it over in the cold darkness of a cell. Then I will have him brought to a place I know of. I had much rather get what he knows without using—er—force, if possible. This way, if he decides to tell us, it will be the sane truth. The other way, he will say anything to stop the pain. Either way, however, he will die at dawn. We will wait here a few minutes to see if General Ma honored our requisition for Captain Dolan."

CHAPTER VI

MR. HOOD OF ENGLAND

THE PLACE WHERE the Big Swords were holed up was, at least, on top of the ground, an old warehouse. Under ground there had been dug out a series of big rooms, large enough to hold a regiment, if necessary.

In one of these underground rooms Jimmie Cordie stood talking with two young Manchus. In front of them stood a Chinese. One of the Manchus was translating into English as the Chinese spoke.

"The one you ordered us to find, honorable elder brother, is in the cells of the building where the men of Nippon maintain their police. This we found out by showing one of the pariah curs who act as servants for the police that it were better for him and all his relations that he talk promptly."

"Ask him if he means a Jap?" Jimmie said.

"He means a Chinese. The servants are all Chinese. Those who clean up and remove the refuse, honorable one."

"I didn't think a Jap would open up.—Ask him about the building. How many men are on guard there at night, and how close is it to any large body of troops."

"He answers that he does not know, but that he can have the information here within an hour."

"Tell him to get it—and as fully as possible."

As the Chinese went out, one of the Manchus smiled and asked, "Is it your intention to take the military police headquarters of the Nippon dogs, honorable captain?"

"And how!" Jimmie answered, with a grin. "We've got a couple of hundred men here, Wang-Lu. With that many, we ought to be able to take a gang of mere military police for a buggy ride."

"That is true, resplendent one," answered the Manchu noble, gravely, although he did not have the slightest idea what "take a gang of mere military police for a buggy ride" meant. "We can do it, as you say."

The fact that there were at least two divisions of Japanese troops in and around Tsitsihar did not make any difference either to the Manchu or to Jimmie Cordie. Now that Jimmie knew that the Yid was alive, and also where he was, he would try for him. It would not have mattered if the Yid had been behind the south gates of hell. And the Manchu's idea of a perfect day was to get close enough to a rifleman to use a sword on him.

Red Dolan, on arrival, had seen a lean, lanky, broad-shouldered man sitting with his back to the wall, his legs straight out. Red stared for a minute, as if not believing his eyes, then he shouted:

" 'Tis ye, ye long-legged scut from Bosting! Ye swapped legs wid a crane and got beat in the trade. Come up from that wall, ye codfisher, till I see what makes ye tick!"

The Boston Bean, whose name in the Massachusetts Social Register was John Cabot Winthrop, rose to his feet.

"Well, well, if it isn't Terrence Aloysius Dolan. How does it happen you are once more in our midst, Terrence, me good man?" he demanded.

It would be impossible to print Red's answer to that "me good man" thing. He was so glad to see the Boston Bean once more that he had to spend a few minutes blackguarding him.

The Boston Bean had served in the Legion with Jimmie Cordie and Red and in the A.E.F. as a captain in the artillery. After the war, whenever he could make it, he went with Jimmie Cordie and the other adventurers, no matter why or what their objective was. Whenever he was unable to do that, he would hunt up the Yid, provided the Yid wasn't with the outfit; then he and the Yid would go, as the Bean put it, "wildcattin' hither and yon."

The Boston Bean was a millionaire two or three times over, thanks to his mother and father and the two old maiden aunts. The maiden aunts had said in their wills, "So that dear John may not come to want."

Yet all the Codfish Duke of Massachusetts wanted was to be in a tight place behind a machine gun, and to have a cigarette to smoke. He had town and country houses, apartments in several world capitals, yachts and all that goes with unlimited money, and he was always leaving them in charge of hired men in order that he might go "wildcattin'." His face was sorrowful in appearance, which was misleading. The Bean was really happy-go-lucky to the last degree; and with him anything went. He fought with a bored "you be damned" look in his eye, and if he had any nerves, no one had ever seen them displayed.

FINALLY RED calmed down enough to tell about what had happened, ending with, "An' where the Yid is, I dunno. Wait till I get the two hands av me on that scut av the world! 'Tis worried about him I am, Beany."

"Cease worrying, old timer. The well known luck of Hester Street will pull him through. You say that Jimmie thinks the Yid was captured? If that's right, my money is on the Yid, not on the Japs. The Yid is too flip for them, Mr. Dolan."

"I hope the dirty lying flat-faced duck av a Yid polecat is, Codfish," Red said, as he stretched out on the dirt floor. "I always liked him."

The Bean laughed. "I'll tell him you admitted that, as soon as I see him."

"Ye do," Red answered, grimly, "ye do, and see what happens to ye, right after. Beany, what's it all about? All Jimmie would tell me was to go and get a commission in the old Chink's army, and to keep my ears open and tell the Yid what I heard—which wasn't much. Jimmie said that what I didn't know wouldn't hurt me, the half-sized shrimp."

"Well, I don't know anything about the end you and the Yid were on, but I can tell you some anyway about our end. Have you heard, by any chance, Mr. Dolan, of a gent named Robin Hood?"

"I dunno. There was a lad in my company in France named Hood, but I don't think his first name was Robin. That's a hell av a name to hang on a man, ain't it, Bean?"

In the Orient, if any one asked a soldier of fortune "Do you know where John Cabot Winthrop is at the moment?" the answer, nine times out of ten, would be, "Don't know him." But if the question were worded, "Where is the Codfish Duke of Massachusetts?" or if he were referred to as Beaneater, or the Boston Bean, or any other name that even remotely suggested Boston, the answer would be, "He's up in the North, with the Fighting Yid," or "He's in the south with Jimmie Cordie," as the case might be. The Bean didn't care. He answered to any and all of those names.

"No doubt Robin Hood's father and mother liked it," the Bean answered gravely. "But I don't think it's the same man you knew, Red. In fact, I'm sure it isn't. The Mr. Hood I'm talking about lived in England quite a long while ago."

"He did? Then what the hell are ye wah-wahin' about him for, ye long-legged piece av Bosting tripe? Tell me about—"

"I was trying to paint in the picture for you, Terrence, me good man.—This Robin Hood I'm talking about was an Englishman who had been grievously injured by—"

"Been *what?*—Talk United States, not Bosting!"

"This Englishman had been done wrong by some high-up gents," said the Bean, slipping into talk that Red could understand, "and he spent the rest of his life smackin' 'em down. He collected a merry band of archers and swordsmen, and between times, when he couldn't find any of the higher-ups to smack, he went around helping the poor and needy. He'd rob the rich and give the coin to the poor, and woe betide the higher-up who hurt any of said poor, if Robin Hood or any of his lusty men were around.—You sabe 'lusty,' Terrence?"

"I do not, and I don't give a damn! What has this got to do wid us? At that, this lad was all right, wasn't he, Codfish?"

"He was. Now, up here in the North, there is a Manchu noble whose name is Chang-Lung Liang, and he is head of the House of Chi—which, for your benefit, Mr. Dolan, is a house that furnished some of the chieftains who led the hordes to the Peacock Throne of China. Are you fully and duly im—?"

"GET ON wid it!—Get on wid it! The tongue av ye is tied in the middle and wags at both ends. In wan more minute I'll come aboard ye!"

"Go and get all the rest of the Dolans to help you, then. I see there's no use in trying to paint word pictures to you, you moron! Here it is in words of one syllable, then. Chang-Lung Liang lived in the Nonni River area, in a walled city named Lueh. The Jap Eighth division took it, and in the taking, their planes destroyed the palace of Chang—and with it, all of Chang's family. He was in the South when the Japs attacked without warning. When he got back up North, he became the Robin Hood of the North. Now you see why I told you about the Englishman."

"I do! And so he is the lad that Jimmie and us are wid?"

"You guessed it! Chang swore by the chieftains who sit On High with Nurhachu that he would kill as many Japs as he could, and that he would also prevent them from doing any more dirty work at the cross roads until he, too, went On High. It seems that he is an old friend of Jimmie's, and he called on Jimmie to come up and help him work his hate out on the Japs. Jimmie didn't like the way the Japs acted towards women and children in Shanghai, so—here we are, Mr. Dolan. Now you know all about it."

"I don't either!—I mean, I don't like the way they shot 'em down. I'm wid the old coot.—How about the Big Swords, Beany darlin'?"

"Well, at first the Big Swords were bands of Chinese bandits, and what not, with a lot of other breeds mixed in. They spent their time looting and slaying. They'd take a village or a city, and when they left, the jackals couldn't live there.

"They fought the Japs on general principle, the same as they fought any one else, I guess. And they were called Big Swords because their weapons were swords, daggers and lances. Blame few of them had guns.—You now know the meaning of Big Swords, Mr. Dolan."

"I know more about swords than you ever will, Codfish. Get on wid it. Is it them divils that—?"

"Not exactly. That is what they were, and not what they are to-day, Red. Chang got together all the swordsmen of the House of Chi, and all the relations who could hold a sword, and he started out to the place where the biggest band of Big Swords were camped."

"To mop up on 'em?"

"He was like the old boys up in New England, Red—the preachers and the deacons and the elders. They'd go out to convert the Indians with a Bible in one hand and a blunderbuss in the other. The Indians either got converted or blown apart. Well, Chang pulled the same stunt with the different leaders of the Big Swords. He got to 'em one by one, and he said, 'Either fight under my banner, obeying orders always—or die by Manchu swords.'"

"Holy mackinaw! He must be a bearcat! Did they do it, Codfisher?"

"THE FIRST Big Sword leader answered 'Pooh-pooh for you and your Manchu swords!'—or words to that effect; and Chang mopped up on the entire band, not leaving a man alive. That Chink didn't have good sense at all. He should have known that his men wouldn't stand up to Manchu swords. The Chinese never have and never will. Pie was probably full of hop. Well, the next one saw the light, pronto and in haste, and he joined up with his gang. Most of them did, for that matter, and those who didn't went On High to tell their troubles to their ancestors. A big reform movement took place. Finally, Chang had an army and—"

"How much av an army?"

"Jimmie tells me that all in all, counting everything, there are around a hundred thousand men. Of course, that means the three or four men back of each front line man. I think there's about twenty thousand shock troops, Red."

" 'Tis more than I thought there'd be, at that! Haven't they got anything to fight wid but swords?"

"Oh, yeah, Mr. Dolan.—Heap plenty rifles, machine guns, one- and two-pounders and what-nots. Also, heap plenty ammunition. Jimmie's friends in Hongkong sent up everything except the mortgage on the old home. And now the Big Swords are an organized, disciplined army, with divisions of artillery and everything."

"Yeah? What are those lads out there in the front room doin' wid swords, then?"

"They are some of Chang's personal bodyguard—men he sent with Jimmie. They're Manchus of the House of Chi. All that bunch still fight with swords. I mean his own gang. They'd charge the whole Jap army with 'em, and sing while they were doing it."

"Yeah? I misdoubt if they could keep on singin' long. A sword is fine if the scuts are close to ye, but—"

"Depends on the swords, Terrence. Remember how the fuzzy-wuzzies broke a British square? And all they had was swords."

"The who?—Why don't ye talk—?"

Jimmie Cordie came up to them at that moment. "We're going in after the Yid," he announced. "You birds will be safe here. Don't worry about any bad old Japs getting you while we're gone."

"What?" yelled Red Dolan, getting to his feet faster than one would have expected a man of his size to do. "Stay here and—?"

He paused, seeing Jimmie's tantalizing grin.

"We'll go along—just for the ride," said the Bean who was also on his feet, "I'll take Terrence Aloysius by the hand."

CHAPTER VII

THE HORNETS' NEST

THE BUILDING OCCUPIED by the military police was an old one, built of wood. It was almost in the center of the city, surrounded on all sides by the smaller houses and shops of the natives. At one time the building had been the palace of a local magistrate—also his courtroom. The Japanese had built a row of steel cells at the rear of the first floor, not many of which were needed because it was very seldom that anyone was held long. These natives which the military police brought in generally faced a firing squad soon after; and Jap soldiers who became too obstreperous (which rarely happened) were turned over to their respective commanders for punishment.

About five o'clock in the morning it was still dark, and a snowstorm was gaining in intensity. A captain of military police was sitting at a desk; two lieutenants were writing letters at a table; and a sergeant was dozing in a corner, out of sight of the captain. An orderly stood at the door, and in a squadroom to the left of the entrance, half a company of military police loafed. A couple of Chinese servants were sweeping and dusting in the squadroom, being careful not to get too close to any of the soldiers.

That any attack would be made upon the military police headquarters of the Japanese army in Tsitsihar was, to the Japanese, beyond the bounds of possibility. It was not even thought of.

One of the lieutenants looked up, then rose and went to a

window. "There is a bad fire. I thought it was getting light very suddenly."

"Let the fire department attend to it," the captain answered, yawning. "Where is it?"

"I think it is in the Street of the Wise Men. It seems to be getting worse. Those native houses are like tinder and— Shots! Something is happening. It may be that— Another fire breaks out!"

The captain got up and came to the window. "The fires are in Captain Nobioka's district. He will soon put them out. The natives have probably gotten out of hand once more. They always—"

The phone rang, and the captain answered it.

"Send all available men you have to assist Captain Nobioka in preserving order," said the voice over the wire. "This is Colonel—"

The connection was broken. The voice, speaking Japanese, had come over the wire in the familiar rasping snarl of command.

The captain tried for a moment to regain connection, then hung the receiver up. "It is evident that Captain Nobioka needs help. Lieutenant Yoyama, take two platoons and report to Captain Nobioka."

The young lieutenant, glad of a chance for action, ran to the squadroom. In less than two minutes, half the soldiers at military police headquarters were on their way to the fire.

The captain yawned again, stretched, then reached for a cigarette. As he was lighting it, he heard a noise at the rear of the building.

"Sergeant!"

The sergeant rose and came to attention. "Yes, sir."

"See what is loose at the back of the building. It sounded like a door or shutter. Secure it."

The sergeant saluted and left the room. The captain put his feet up on the desk and began thinking of gay nights in Tokyo.

Then his pleasant dreams were rudely interrupted. From the rear there came the sound of a shot, then the fall of a body, and the quick thud of running feet.

The captain's feet came down from the desk abruptly, and he stood up, drawing his revolver. The soldiers in the squadroom rushed to the wall where their rifles were racked, as surprised as the captain was at the sound of a shot in headquarters. Five or six of them got to their rifles before the others, and once they had them, ran into the room where the captain stood beside his desk.

"Come with me," he ordered.

THROUGH THE door leading to the cell block there came, first three Americans, forty-five Colts in their right hands, and right behind them an orderly file of Manchu swordsmen, led by two young Manchus.

"Steady!" the first American said, in Pushtu, as he entered. "Stand perfectly still. No one will get hurt if my orders are obeyed. I am Captain Cordie—of the Big Swords. We have come for a man whom you hold, captain. Give him to us and—"

The spell binding the Japanese captain was broken. Whatever else they are, good or bad, there is no question about the courage of the Japanese. The officer laughed, "You Americans! You come to the—" He snapped his revolver up and fired at Jimmie Cordie.

His bullet went wild, for a bullet from the Boston Bean's gun reached his brain even as his finger tightened on the trigger. As the soldiers raised their rifles, more Manchus came into the room from behind the soldiers, and the sound of fighting came from the squadroom. The Japanese did the best they could, but that was hardly good enough—not against three of the most deadly guns in the Orient and against Manchu swords.

In less than two minutes the headquarters of the Japanese military police in Tsitsihar was in the hands of the Big Swords.

"Go along that row of cells, Red," commanded Jimmie. "That bird you smacked down probably has the keys. Don't waste any time telling the Yid how much you love him. Get him out—and make it snappy!"

The "bird" Jimmie had referred to was an old Japanese non-commissioned officer who had been asleep at the end of the cell block, his chair tilted against the wall. The sergeant had died as he drew his revolver upon seeing what had made the noise that had awakened him.

"We're after the Fighting Yid!" yelled Jimmie Cordie

"Get to the front door, Codfish," Jimmie went on. "You go with him, Wang-Lu. If those fires are put out pronto, this buggy ride will end about the same time."

It was an old, old trick that Jimmie Cordie had played; so old that it had whiskers on it in the days of Rameses. He had started trouble in one place in order to draw his opponents temporarily from another place. The fires had been started by the same Chinese who had helped the Big Swords reach the warehouse, and the panic among the natives drew further reinforcements.

The Japanese "Colonel's" voice, on the telephone, was that of a half-breed whose father had been a Japanese and who had been born and reared in Japan.

It was no discredit to the Japanese that the trick worked. It generally works—unless suspicion has somehow been aroused before. The military police were there to quell disorder. There was disorder, and they had gone to quell it, on what was thought to be the order of a superior officer.

RED CAME back into the room, dragging after him the old Japanese whom he had slapped down in passing. The old man had risen and was fumbling at a holstered revolver when Red reached him.

"Jimmie! He's not there!—The Yid! He's not in the cells!"

"*What?* For Pete's sake! You sure, Red?"

"I am! 'Tis all over the damn place I've been. He's not here, Jimmie! This scut I got by the scruff av the neck won't tell me nawthin'. He knows, I have a hunch."

"Stand him on his feet.—Chau, you speak Japanese. See what you can do with him."

The other young Manchu stepped up to the old man whom Red was holding up. The Manchu's grim face came to within an inch of the old man's face, and then his sword flashed between the faces. The old man shrank back against Red.

"Speak, old one of Nippon—and quickly! I am Chau of the Big Swords. Speak, or I will cut your lips and nose off. Where is the Jew that was brought here?"

If he had been asked anything about the Japanese forces, the old man would have died before he told anything, knowing that he was not a traitor to Nippon. But to tell of a Jew prisoner—what harm?

"He was here," the old man quavered. "But an hour ago he was taken away."

"Where?"

"I do not know. I am only in charge of the cells."

"He is telling the truth," Jimmie said. "Put him on a chair, Red. Get your men together, Chau.—Get the Bean and Wang-Lu, Red. We will go out the same way we—"

"Jimmie, how about the Yid? Are ye going to leave him in the hands av the—"

"Like hell! But he isn't here, Red, and there will be heap plenty Japs here, in another five minutes.—Get the Bean and Wang-Lu."

The Manchus collected their wounded, and the party that had taken a Japanese military police headquarters—at least for a few minutes—went out the rear and melted into the storm and the darkness.

On Jimmie Cordie's command, the Manchus, once they had left the Japanese headquarters, scattered out to make it back to the warehouse.

"Go with them, Codfish. You also, Red. I'll see if I can find out where the Yid has been taken to. If I do, I'll come and—"

"Me?" demanded Red Dolan. "Go wid them?—I will not! Not wan step! I stay here wid ye, Jimmie."

"This is one hell of a time for you to get pig-headed, you big ape! I can do better alone. You do as I—"

"Hold 'er, Jeems!" the Boston Bean interrupted, calmly. "It's also no time to quell mutinies. You've got one, right smack on your hands. Red and I are going to stay alongside. Any time we leave you in this hornets' nest—we don't. And that is that!"

"Oh, for Pete's sake!" exclaimed Cordie in disgust. "What's the use? What's the use?—Come on then, both of you. I hope to hell and high water you both get killed nine times. I'm going to see if I can grab off some high military police officer and make him come through.—Or a military intelligence high-up gent. And where to start I—"

"Jimmie! Wait! Let's get Casey. That scut knows all about everything. He was chief av intelligence for the old divil Ma, before he got his division to command. That scut can—"

"Wait a minute! Never mind what he is for Ma. Who is—?"

"Don't ye remember him, Jimmie?—Mike Casey?—Him that was in the Ninth Company? They was wid us at Milsidi?—Sure ye do. He was the lad I fought twenty-wan rounds wid at—"

"I remember him now. Where is he?"

"Commandin' the left wing av the Chink army, wid headquarters on the river bank. We can get to him widout any trouble. Wance there, we'll say, 'Ye big flat-footed black-muzzled pup, find out where the Yid is for us—and be quick about it!'"

Jimmie laughed. "Here's hoping he'll be at home. Lead off, Mr. Dolan!"

CHAPTER VIII

THROUGH THE JAP LINE

THE EX-FOREIGN LEGION adjutant greeted them with a yell of joy. Often, of course, he had seen Red, since Red had joined General Ma's forces. But Jimmie and the Boston Bean he had not seen for years.

"Do ye know that there is an order out to bring ye in, dead or alive, ye great red-headed spridhogue from the pe-dif-e-rus north av Ireland?" Casey demanded, before they could tell him what they wanted.

"Is there? Try and do it, ye gibbon! Ye couldn't take the big toe av me, let alone—"

"Did I say I was goin' to? For that I'll knock the head off ye—after we've had nine million and wan drinks.—Wait till I chase me little yaller brothers out for some more nose paint. There's only a dozen bottles here, and—"

"Hold it a minute, Mike. Business before pleasure. I won't ask you if you're with us, because I know you are. The—"

"Am I wid ye, Jimmie? I am—all the time. And well ye divils know it. Did ye not pack me on the backs av ye, the time the Riffs were creepin' up wid the big knives? And did not this red-headed wild man from Antrim stand them off the while ye was do in' it? And me in the Ninth Company? I am wid ye to the bitter end, Jimmie Cordie, and well ye know it."

"Fair enough! Listen. The Fighting Yid was taken by the military police. We came in to rescue him, and after mussing up their headquarters, we find that he's been taken somewhere else. Now—to come clean with you. The Bean and Grigsby and I are with the Big Swords. Red and the Yid were our intelligence department. But the military police jumped us last night. Red and I got away, but the Yid was caught. That's what the order out for Red means. If you throw in with us, and in any way it is found out that you have done so, it'll be good-by Mister Casey. If the Japs don't get you, old General Ma will, and—"

"To hell wid the Japs and to hell wid the old scut! Am I Casey av the Ninth Company, or am I some delicate young lady? I'll answer me own question. 'Tis Casey, the old buddy av ye I am. To hell wid all else but us av the old Legion. Drink up what likker there is here while I do be thinkin'. This Yid ye speak av has either had his back to the wall, facin' the firing squad before now, or—"

"Hivin forbid!" Red whispered. "If they've done that to Abie, 'tis I that will—"

"Quiet, Red!" Jimmie said, softly. "Give Mike a chance."

FINALLY CASEY, after taking a drink, said, "I can find out easy enough if this Yid av yours has gone west wid his back to the wall. Wan av the Jap intelligence officers and me are thicker than two thieves. 'Tis many a trick we've pulled together.—Lemme see, now. I'll tell him that I want to know about— No—what the hell should I care about a Yid and the doin's av the Big Sword intelligence, now that I'm a commander av a—av a—

"I have it! The order to take the big red-headed scut named Dolan came to me; and always on me toes to help me dear Jap friends, I watched and I waited and I waited and I watched until me bowld Dolan walked into me trap. I have him fast, and he opened up a lot to me. I want to know what this Yid—"

"Me? Opened up to the likes av ye?" Red demanded, hotly. "No Dolan ever opened up to any one, let alone wan av the black Caseys, who are all—"

"Put a jaw tackle on, Red! Go on, Casey."

"What wid? 'Tis a fine story, and me little Jap will swaller it whole. If I find out that the Yid is still alive, and where he is, what then?"

"Why, then," Jimmie Cordie said with a grin, "we'll go in and get him, Mister Casey of the Ninth Company."

Casey laughed—a great uproarious, happy laugh. "A divil ye was in the Legion, Jimmie Cordie; and a divil ye are yet. 'Tis us that will do that little thing, in spite av the Jap army. Wait now! 'Tis to be approached wid the strategy av a Casey, which is the best in Ireland. I go in wid wan av me Chink regiments as a bodyguard. They'll go to the bottom av hell for me. In the middle av it, dressed as Chinks wid the toothache, march the three av ye.

"Me little yellow brothers will ask no questions av Giniril Casey. They know better, the duck-faced hellions! Wance I find out what is what, if this Yid be dead, back we will march, and I'll help ye to the hills. If he isn't dead, then in some way we will take him.—Wait! I change me plans. Whether this Yid is dead or not, I am goin' wid ye to the hills. What the hell do I be wantin' wid a lot of Chinks, when you lads are jazzin' around? I go wid ye!"

"And wance we are wid the Big Swords av Jimmie Cordie, I'll play the 'Wearin' av the Green' on yer coco, to knock some av that Casey conceit outta it," Red announced, firmly.

"If ye do be man enough!" Casey answered over his shoulder as he started for the door of the shack which he dignified with the name of headquarters. "Stay here till I make the arrangements."

"Jimmie," Red asked, "do you think that—that Abie has—that the Japs have sent him west?"

"I don't know, Red, but it doesn't look very good to me.—That taking him out of his cell and out of the building makes it—What's the use of trying to dope anything out? We'll know, soon enough."

THE JAPANESE made no objections to Lieutenant General Casey's coming through their lines with one of General Ma's regiments at his back. There was no reason why they should. Most commanders traveled with a full regiment wherever they went, because attack might come any minute, and from any quarter. Those Jap officers in command of the troops which Casey and his regiment passed through, knew him, and so he was greeted with smiles, and was waved on.

Once in the city, he led the regiment to a park near the military intelligence headquarters, and left it there while he went in to the headquarters.

It was very cold, and the storm had now become almost a blizzard. Those Chinese and Japs who were out in it were bundled up to the ears with everything they had in the way of coats and wraps, and they were too cold to pay any attention to who was beside them, also wrapped up to the ears. Jimmie, Red and the Bean had slipped into the ranks, and now marched with the rest. Nobody even looked at them. The discipline of a Chinese regiment does not amount to much, and the ranks were not at all orderly.

It seemed like a thousand years to Red Dolan before Casey eased beside them.

"Well, first, the Yid ye are so worried about is alive. He was brought to intelligence headquarters and he wouldn't talk. I misdoubt but what the Japs didn't roughhouse him some. But accordin' to me friend, the Yid stayed right wid it. Divil a thing could they get outta him, but that he was a trader. Just as they was gettin' ready to go to work in earnest on the Yid, the main lad there was called to report to G.H.Q., right away. So he orders the Yid to be taken to the prison av Hiang Wu-tze and have him held there. And he told the Yid that he wasn't goin' to fool around any longer. Either the Yid would tell him, or he'd face the rifles. There would be no more tryin' to make him tell. He could tell or die, whichever he saw fit."

"How long ago was that?" Jimmie asked.

"Two hours, Jimmie."

"Where is the prison of Hiang Wu-tze?"

"About a mile from here, down on the canal.—Ye know where the railroad yards are?"

"Yes."

"Down there. 'Tis that big old stone building."

"How is it guarded?"

"Damn if I know, Jimmie. 'Tis well guarded now, I bet. What ye did at the military police headquarters has got the Japs all het up."

"Well, there's one way to find out, and that is to go down there. How about this regiment, Casey? Will they go through for you?"

"They will, as I said. 'Tis me pet regiment. I'll pass the word that I have sold out to a war lord in the hills, and that every man will get double pay and a bonus av gold, wance we get there.—Before we start there is a man we got to get outta prison. On the way to the double pay and the bonus, we fight any and all that steps in our way. That's the kind av thing they will understand, and 'tis up to you to make me word good."

"It will be made good, Mike. Can you get near the prison without being stopped?"

"Sure. 'Tis very drunk I am, and I'm marchin' me men around to teach 'em how to take a joke. 'Tis on the way outta town, and me good friends the Japs will pass me along. Me and me regiment—wid a laugh."

"Come on," Red Dolan said. "What the hell is all the wah-wah about? A Casey does nothin' but talk—all the time."

Jimmie grinned. "Mr. Dolan is in a hurry. Let's go."

CHAPTER IX

AN ABDUCTED TRAIN

CASEY WAS RIGHT about the Japs passing him along. The storm was still very bad and it was constantly getting colder. All Japanese officers whose rank was high enough to enable them to do so were holed up in places near their commands, leaving their subordinates in command out in the storm. Casey acted the part of a truculent, drunken Irishman to perfection, and the Japanese out in the storm gladly cleared the way for "me and me regiment."

The canal bank was reached, and Casey led the way down the railroad tracks that skirted it. A young Japanese officer, who had suddenly appeared out of the storm with a platoon of soldiers at his back was in Casey's path; but he laughed as he watched the dimly outlined files of men pass him.

"Truly, the Irish are a great people," he said to another young officer. "That is Casey of General Ma's army. He thinks he is a king leading his army to battle. General Ma will soon teach him otherwise, once he is back to camp. See how the Chinese dogs straggle along behind him."

The other officer also laughed. "They'll soon be out of our lines. I wish that I also was—very drunk. The cold eats into my bones!"

As they got deeper into the yards, Jimmie Cordie, Red and the Boston Bean came up and marched just behind Casey, as if they were his staff officers.

"There it is—right ahead of ye," Casey announced, a minute

or so later. "And how the hell we are to take it, I— Scatter out!" That much was in English. Then he yelled a command in Chinese.

Bearing down on them was the rear of a train. Both the English and the Chinese command were obeyed promptly. Jimmie, Red, the Bean and Casey ran to the right of the track. Three, four, and then five cars went past! It was an armored train, as could be seen by the steel sides and the gun muzzles sticking out of slits. It wasn't going very fast, and as the engine reached the front of the prison, it stopped.

A few Japanese soldiers began to get off. Jimmie Cordie looked at the train, at the prison, and then back at the train. Then he grinned as the Boston Bean said, gravely:

"Me lud, the carriage awaits!"

"The Nine Red Gods draw cards," Jimmie said, softly. Then, "Take it, Casey!"

Casey laughed. " 'Tis me that will do that little thing for ye, Jimmie."

He snarled an order in Chinese that was repeated down the line of his Chinese soldiers, and was then relayed up the other side. The Chinese whipped out their bayonets, and with a shout swarmed over the train. To them, this foreign devil who took such good care of them and gave them much food and warm clothes and gold, was to be obeyed in all things.

The engineer and fireman did not last a split second. The train was backing in practically empty; the Japs who were on it had been hooking a ride into town from their various divisions; and they did not last much longer than the train crew. They were hopelessly outnumbered and they died before they could begin any defense.

A single shot was fired, by an officer who attempted to head a group of men; and there was one other shot; inside the train, and therefore muffled. Bayonets took the train so fast that the few scattered Japs did not even have a chance to use their rifles or revolvers.

Casey, who already had led the nearest of his men on board, swung off. "She's took, Giniril," he announced, with a very snappy Legion salute. "What now?"

"We take the hoosegow," Jimmie answered, with a grin. "Drag some of your men out of his ludship's carriage, and leave the rest to hold it."

OUTSIDE, THE prison was guarded by a company of Japanese infantry, and inside there was another company in the guardroom. The company outside had been standing around half frozen when the train was attacked. Some of them, not on actual post, were sitting down, huddled together in corners where they were sheltered from the wind. As the Chinese climbed on the train, the officers of the company, after one incredulous look, shouted orders.

The company was falling in, a good many of the men rubbing their eyes when they met a charge led by four big men who had forty-five Colt revolvers in their hands. The Japanese fought bravely, and retreated not an inch; but the men charging knew what it was all about, and the Japs did not. To them, a Chinese regiment had suddenly materialized out of the storm to attack them.

The officers, out in front, went down under the deadly Colts, and then the bayonets were at work among the men. The Japs were again outnumbered, and three minutes later Jimmie Cordie, Red Dolan, the Boston Bean and Mike Casey reached the big double doors of the prison. Right behind them was what was left of the Chinese who had charged with them. The Japanese company had been destroyed.

The doors opened. The company inside had heard the fight, and was coming out to mix into it. They knew as little as the others what the scrap was all about.

There was a bad jam for a few minutes. Japanese were trying to get out and the Légionnaires and the Chinese were trying to get in. It was what Kipling called a "messy" fight, in which men fought breast to breast—until the forty-five Colts cleared the way.

In surged Jimmie and the others, and behind them came the Chinese. Once again, a Japanese company of infantry was wiped out, fighting grimly to the last man.

Red, as soon as he was clear, ran through the rooms on the ground floor, shouting, "Yid! Yid!—Abie, ye Hester Street scut! Where the hell are ye? Yid! Answer me! 'Tis Red, ye monkey-faced gibbon!"

There were no cells on that floor, and Red charged up a flight of stairs. At the top of it he halted for a minute, and his Colt went *Bamb!—Bamb!—Bamb-bamb!* Then he began to call to the Yid again.

There were cells on that floor, and from one of them came an exultant yell. "Here I am, Red! De fifth von down on de left! Oi, Irish bummer, how glad I am to hear old mister Colt. Come und get it, Poppa!"

Red yelled back, a wild Irish yell, then he shouted, "Stay put, ye Yid scut. Jimmie will be here in a minute. There may be some more av the little men up here for me to slap outta the way. Is yer cell locked?"

"Mit bars on de outside. Come und loosen dem und I vill help it—"

Jimmie Cordie and the Boston Bean came up. A half minute later, the Fighting Yid walked out of the cell. "My, I am glad to see it you all! Oi, vot a time I had mit de—"

"Get going," Jimmie interrupted. "We're behind time now."

"Vot de hell does Jimmie mean, about it vay behind time?" the Yid asked as he and Red ran down the stairs.

"I dunno—and care less. The next time ye get pinched, stay in the first place, ye Yid beneath notice! Do ye think we are goin' to jazz all around town after ye?—The next time, stay put."

"Oi! Could I help it, I esk you?"

"And that reminds me. Ye fooled me, didn't ye? For that, when we get back to the Big Swords, I'll—"

"We're not there yet," Jimmie said, from behind. "Step on it."

OUT, AND to the train. The Chinese were firing at Japanese who were advancing up the track, in the rear. As yet, no heavy Japanese force had arrived to see what the shooting was about. Those coming were the nearest detachments on guard duty.

"Get on, Yid! You and Casey also," Jimmie commanded to the Bean.

"Who de hell is goin' to run it?" demanded Red. " 'Tis no engineer we have, Jimmie, and no fireman either."

"I'm going to be engineer, and you are going to be fireman, Mr. Dolan. Hop up there and get up some steam—and make it snappy. This is old Ninety-Seven, and we got to put 'er in Danville on time!"

"Oi! Now I know it vot Jimmie meant. Vate! How do you know it, vare de switches are, und vare de track goes to?"

"I don't know, and I don't give a durn. All I know is that old Ninety-Seven is going away from here—pronto and in haste. Get on board or you'll be left at the depot."

Casey laughed as he and the Bean and the Yid got on board. "Take her across country, Jimmie," he yelled. "Wadda we care?"

"She has some steam up, Jimmie," Red announced as Jimmie climbed up in the engine cab. "I never fired wan av these ding-batted things before."

"Yeah? Shovel in coal, Mr. Dolan—and trust in the Lord. If I blow 'er up more than six or seven times, don't get peeved."

"Holy Moses! Did ye never run one before, Jimmie?"

"Well, I bunked with an engineer once. That makes me a militia hog-head. Lay on that shovel, and don't bother the engineer."

"The likes av ye!" Red muttered as he obeyed. "I never seen it before or since, ye shrimp."

As a matter of fact, Jimmie Cordie had taken mining engineering at Massachusetts Tech, and while with a big hard rock outfit, he had often run the engine that pulled supplies to the mine and ore away from it.

The train gathered speed, and the Japanese dispatcher at the yards, seeing an armored train coming, threw the switch that put it on the main track to the north. He had received no orders about this train, but he figured that, in some way, the storm had interfered with his getting them. Anyway, he threw the switch.

Jimmie did not know whether he had the right of way over other trains or not, nor how long the track was; but he sat there with a grin on his face. Now that the Yid had been found, everything was quite all right in the world. Afterwards, Red said, "Jimmie Cordie took that damn train—engine and all—up in the air. We flew to the north. I can lick the scut that says different."

BACK IN Tsitsihar the Japanese, to put it mildly, were good and fussy.

To have their military police headquarters invaded by Big Swords under command of a group of American adventurers was an insult to their military pride and prestige. On top of that, to have an armored train stolen and their prison broken into and a prisoner removed was like rubbing salt in a wound. There had been two Japanese divisions in Tsitsihar and the surrounding country, and the Big Swords had…

Five minutes later another armored train roared out of Tsitsihar in pursuit, this one crowded to the guardrails with Japanese troops.

Along the line of the Chinese Eastern railroad, which the Japanese had taken over, for as far as their guns would reach out of Tsitsihar, they had at first tried to maintain a regular system of telegraph and telephone wires. But they had soon found out that it would take a regiment or two, plus rapid fire and machine guns, to hold any of the stations or towers.

The moment they withdrew in force, leaving a small detachment as guard, in came the bandits or the Chinese generals who were fighting Japanese occupation, and it was good-by detachment, as well as good-by any and all wires that could be cut and taken away. Finally the Japanese had contented themselves with keeping one track for north-bound traffic and the other for south-bound, the latter consisting only of troop trains anyway. The train crew pulled switches as they went along, and took chances on a rear-end collision, which condition of affairs helped Jimmie Cordie take the train north.

Red fired, urged on by Jimmie's derisive comments on the way in which he moved and at his speed. "What do you think this is, number Thirty-Eight?—This is old Ninety-Seven, feller. Show some speed with that shovel. Us eagle-eyes have got to have service! Snap into and show me something with that shovel!"

Red said something about "To hell wid all shovels! Me back is broke already!" But he kept right on shoveling.

The Yid and Bean crawled over the coal in the tender and stood hanging to a handrail.

"Get out of here!" Jimmie shouted. "No passengers allowed on—"

"Ve ain't passengers," shouted the Yid, above the noise. "I am de front shack, und Beany is de rear shack. Ve come it to tell you dot dere is a train coming up behind us."

The Boston Bean, who loved any kind of machinery, made it to Jimmie's side. The engine he had noticed was bucking like a locoed bronc.

"Let me run her, Jeems," he shouted.

"Help yourself to the mustard," Jimmie answered, grinning as he let go the throttle and got off the engineer's seat. "What's Casey doing?"

"Getting every loose gun he can find in the train to bear on the limited that's behind us. Casey says he'll blow it off the track, 'does she come within range.'"

"Take this shovel, ye Yid troublemaker," commanded Red. "Come on, show me something! What do ye think this is, the slow freight? This is old Ninety-Seven. The front shack does the shovelin' on Ninety-Seven, me bucko. Snap into it and make me some steam."

Jimmie laughed as Red pressed the Fighting Yid into service.

CHAPTER X

DUEL BETWEEN TRAINS

THE TRAIN WENT past several villages, across two bridges, and then the track stretched out in a straight line, north and west, as far as they could see. The blizzard had died down now, and the wind and snow had ceased. Presently the sun came out, revealing that some freak of the storm had caused the snow to blow from the track in most places. Wherever it had not, the engine plowed through the drifts.

"Where are we going, Jeems?" yelled the Boston Bean, the throttle back in the last notch.

"Depends on the life you've led," Jimmie answered. "If we jump the track, we—"

The sound of gunfire came from the rear of the train—*Bang-bang-bang!* Then the snarling staccato of rapid fire and machine guns.

The Yid stopped shoveling coal and announced, "Casey is sayin' hullo to dem fellows from de observation platform."

"We've got to shake them," Jimmie shouted. "Give us more steam, you big apes."

"Look at the water gauge, Jeems," the Boston Bean answered. "She's down below the safety level and liable to—"

"That's the way I keep 'em on old Ninety-Seven. Get off that seat and let a good man take 'er! Is this a slow freight in Arkansas? You're not getting half the speed out of her that you ought to. You got to coax old Ninety-Seven along."

“The hell I ain’t!” the Bean protested. “Make those greasy firemen keep the steam up.”

The Japanese train dropped back a little way. In doing so, they showed good sense, for by keeping the stolen train ahead of them they could come up soon enough whenever it slowed down or stopped. They knew that no engine would continue to function, once two or three one- and two-pound shells had connected with her. And they also knew that their shells were not duds.

AN HOUR went by, and another; then, as Jimmie Cordie’s train went around a hill, the engine crew saw a bridge. And on either side of the bridge were the rifle regiments of the Big Swords, the bridgehead bristling with machine guns.

“Slow down, Bean!” yelled Jimmie. “Give her the sand! They don’t know it’s us. Bring her to a—”

“There ain’t no sand, Jeems, me good man!” the Bean announced calmly, after he had pulled a lever. “Hang on, I’m goin’ to set the brakes, and trust to the luck of the British army.”

As the train pulled to a stop, machine gun bullets shattered the headlight and peppered the front of the engine.

Red, who had been peeking out his side, yelled and leaned far out, “George!—Carewe!—Quit that, ye scuts! ’Tis us, ye gibbons!”

Two white men standing just back of the machine guns raised their right hands high in the air and shouted commands. The firing ceased. The two were George Grigsby and John Carewe, the balance of what was called, in the Orient, “Jimmie Cordie’s outfit.” Grigsby, as big a man as Red, and fully as strong, and an ex-Foreign Legion and a major of infantry, A.E.F., looked at the coal-dust-begrimed men who got off the engine.

“Glad you decided to bring a train with you, Jimmie,” he said with a smile. “We need one badly. We heard you coming and—”

Again Casey’s guns opened up, and this time kept right on firing. The Jap train had pulled up behind Jimmie’s, and Japanese infantry were piling out.

"Holy cats!" said Jimmie. "I forgot all about our boy friends. The Japs have been on our tails with another—"

"Write me a letter about it," Grigsby answered. "Two trains are a blame sight better than one train. You gents take a rest, and watch us take Train Number Two."

He ran back to the Big Swords.

"By the nine blind virgins av Constantinople," Red said, "I'm goin' to do that little thing, also. The back av me is broke, and me hands are blistered beyand all fixin'."

"Dot's right, Irish old lady mit soft hands und back," the Yid answered. "Sit it down and rest, und vatch Poppa help it take de train."

Red thereupon described the Yid as seen from an Irish gentleman's standpoint. Also the Yid's ancestors for several generations back.

He revealed the sultry hereafter where the Yid would go, without question, when he died, as well as the extreme pleasure which it would give Mr. Dolan to help him on his way there.

As Red was orating, the Big Sword regiments swept past to the attack, bayonets fixed. With them went the machine gun section and some hundred Manchu swordsmen.

As Jimmie and the Bean and the Yid ran to join Grigsby and Carewe, Red stopped talking. He forgot all about his back and hands suddenly, and actually beat them all to the machine guns.

The Japanese were caught in a trap, and had to fight the issue out right there.

Casey had disabled the engine, and the train was stalled. To give the Japs due credit, they would not have retreated anyway. They were out to get the men who had put a stain on their military honor, and they were going to do it or die trying.

WHEN JIMMIE Cordie and the others reached the rear of the train, Casey yelled the battle yell of all the dead and gone Caseys, and jumped off. "*Vive la Légion!*" he yelled. "*Allons, mes enfants!*" Then he yelled in Chinese to his men, "Come on, you pie-faced, misbegotten sons of seacooks! Will you let a lot of pink-toed little Japs be played with—and you not there?"

To the last man, his Chinese soldiers boiled off the train after him.

Casey came up with George Grigsby. "Who the hell are—? E-e-e-e-yah! 'Tis ye, Grigsby! Be Judas, the gang's all here, exceptin'—"

"Take your men over to the left, Mike," Jimmie Cordie ordered as he ran up. "Get around their flank."

"Yes, sir, giniril. 'Tis around there we are right now."

The Japanese fought on the ground, and from the train. They fought as they always fight, grimly and well; but they met fighters equally good, and as unafraid as themselves.

At last the train was taken by the Big Swords. The engine, smashed beyond repair, was derailed, and the cars were coupled behind the first train.

"How come you so far east, George?" Jimmie asked.

"We are on our way to persuade a bandit leader that the climate farther south is more conducive to his good health. We heard you coming, and thought that we might as well bag a train *en route.*"

"Where is Chang-Lung Liang?"

"At Dadchin, waiting for you. Better load up those Chinese you've collected, along with Casey, and get up there, Jimmie. This train is just what is needed to get the women and children back from any—"

"The Japs have started for Lao Tzu."

"Yeah? Get going, Jimmie. We'll be back in a week. They can't get up there before that."

"I think I'll go wid ye, George," announced Red.

"Take another think, you big ape!" Jimmie Cordie answered grimly. "You're going to fire that engine to Dadchin."

"Me back is—"

"I know all about your back! I saw you climb on top of the

Jap train, beating Casey to it. Get on that engine with the well known snap, Mr. Dolan, or I won't detail the Yid as your assistant."

"I'm on me way, Jimmie darlin'! Send me assistant promptly."

THE JAPANESE way to Lao Tzu, once they got to within twenty miles, was barred. The Big Swords barred it with machine and rapid fire guns in all the passes and at the river. They barred it with entrenched infantry commanded by Casey, who put "me pet regiment" in the front lines—"because of the honor you covered yourselves with at the train-takin', you little fightin' monkeys!"

At night, on the Japanese front, the Big Swords barred the way with whirlwind charges of cavalry. Manchu swords were on flanks and rear. Chang threw his men at the Japanese with a reckless disregard for life that cost them dear—but it also cost the Japanese dear. And instead of taking Lao Tzu and "teaching" the civilians not to interfere with military operations, the Japs had hard work to prevent being taken themselves. The train had pulled all the women and children, and all but fighting men, out of Lao Tzu and to a place far in the hills.

Finally, heavy Japanese reinforcements arrived; not on the tracks of the Chinese Eastern Railway, because tracks and bridges had been destroyed for fifty miles, but overland. The Big Swords, their work done, withdrew into the hills, their guns snarling defiance from the passes, a defiance which the Japs did not try to overcome. There was nothing of value left in Lao Tzu. For the moment anyway, the Japanese had seen all they wished of the Big Swords, intelligence division and all.

Back in the hills, Red sat down beside the Yid. "Abie, what did the little men do to ye? Casey said that they had roughhoused ye?"

"Dey didn't do it much," the Yid answered, with a grin. "Every time dey touched it me, I yelled my head off and began to tell it dem things dot didn't make sense at de finish. Den dey vould start to tvist de arm some more, und I vould yell und promise to tell it de truth. Just as dey vos gettin' good und mad mit me, de main squeeze vas called it to de telephone. Ven he got back, he said dot—"

"I know that part.—Ye fooled me at the window, didn't ye? You know what I think av the likes av ye? I think that ye're a—"

"Have you got it any more of dot likker vot you had dis noon?" asked the Yid, politely.

"I have not—and well ye know it, ye Yid scut. Ye drained the bottle when I told ye to take a small wan."

"Vell den, vot do it I care vot a low-life Irish bummer thinks?"

At which all the reckless soldiers of fortune around the campfire laughed uproariously, Red included.

THE FACE IN THE ROCK

Never before had Jimmie Cordie and his soldiers of fortune drawn guns to fight a tribe of "spirits" who inhabited a mountain

CHAPTER I

TIMUR THE LAME

"**HERE IS WHERE** we reproduce Custer's last stand," said Jimmie Cordie, ex-sergeant of the Foreign Legion and captain of a machine gun company. He had flung himself to the ground on a narrow ledge in the Thian Shan range of mountains, in northwest China.

"Oi! Could it ve hold it de path mit von little popity-pop, I esk you?" the Fighting Yid demanded as he stretched himself out next to Jimmie Cordie.

"Why the hell don't ye wish for the Thirty-First Division, ye Hester Street Ape?" demanded a big red-headed man as he tenderly felt a bruised knee.

"Did I speak it to you, Irisher? Put it de mind on de shootin' vot you vill be diddin' soon, and let it two gentlemen have it de conversa—"

"Get up to the edge, you kidders," ordered another man, who was wounded. "We can't hold 'em very long, Jimmie." This was George Grigsby, ex-Foreign Legion man and major of infantry, A.E.F.

"Well," Jimmie answered, with a grin, "we will sure hesitate 'em as long as our ammunition holds out. They can't get at us except by coming up the path, and only two at a time can do that. Maybe so they'll get tired and go home."

"Think up something, Jimmie," the red-headed man ordered. He was Red Dolan, also ex-Foreign Legion man and lieutenant of military police, A.E.F. Red, since the day when he had met

Jimmie Cordie in the Legion, had found life much simplified. He would ask, "How about that, Jimmie?" or "What now, ye small-sized scut ave the world?" And the answer always satisfied Red, who was two hundred and thirty-odd pounds of fighting Irish.

"Start growing some wings, Mr. Dolan. That's the best thing I can think of at the moment. Or pick out the best thing to say to Saint— Heads up!"

The Japanese were trying to take the ledge, coming up two at a time; but the .45 Colts in the hands of these soldiers of fortune made the pass one that led to death. In less than five minutes the Japs had abandoned the attempt, and a machine gun had opened fire. The bullets could not reach the men on the ledge, owing to the angle of fire. The Japs, though they knew this, spattered the rock of the hill above the ledge in order to tell the men defending it that any attempt to climb higher, would be just too bad.

A fairly large party of Big Swords had been neatly trapped by the Japanese, in the valley below. The Big Swords, composed of Manchu and Chinese fighters, fought bravely, as they always do; but there were not enough of them to whip the Japs. Finally,

They came on despite the gunfire

some of the Manchu swords of the House of Chi, together with Jimmie Cordie and his soldiers of fortune, saw that it had become a stricken field, and literally cut and shot their way to the hills. When they reached the ledge, there were eight men left: five Americans, two wounded; one Englishman, wounded; two Manchus, unwounded. The Manchus had their swords, and the soldiers of fortune had their .45 Colts—but not much ammunition left in their cartridge belts. Furthermore, there was no food and no water.

When the sudden attack came, the Big Swords had been nearing a little mountain stream, and canteens had been emptied to be refilled with fresh water.

"Our little playmates have thought of something," Jimmie Cordie said, reloading his Colt. "They wouldn't quit that easy."

He was quite right. The Japs—or, rather, the commanding officer—had thought of something, which was that there was a bombing plane at a Japanese base some fifty-odd miles away. He saw no reason for wasting men when a plane could blow what was left of the Big Swords off the ledge with one well-placed bomb. And so he withdrew his men and sent for the plane. Eight or ten Big Swords would not have been worth fussing about, but these soldiers of fortune had been recognized, and the Japanese would give their eye teeth either to bring them in alive or to be sure that they were dead. Hence the sending for the plane.

"**WHAT NOW**, Jimmie, darlin'?" Red asked. "Are we to wait here and let the scuts think up something to get us off this damn—"

"Quit cussin', Red. You are too near the pearly gates, old kid. How do you feel, George?"

Grigsby, readjusting a makeshift bandage around his head, smiled as he answered, "Well, my head feels as if there was a boiler factory inside it, with all hammers going. Outside of that, I'm all right."

Jimmie turned toward another man. "I noticed that you were still able to make old Mr. Colt's masterpiece talk turkey, Codfish. How are you now?"

A lean, lanky, sorrowful-faced man answered, "Outside a piece of red hot bayonet in my leg—anyway that's the way the said leg feels—I'm the same as George, me good man!"

In the Massachusetts Social Register the one called Codfish was listed as John Cabot Winthrop; but in the Orient he was the Boston Bean, or Codfish, or any other name that even remotely suggested Boston. His sorrowful face was very misleading, for the Bean was happy-go-lucky and reckless to the *n*th degree, and he was never sorrowful under any circumstances.

"How about you, Carewe?" Jimmie asked. A slim, boyish looking man, who was wounded in the shoulder, answered, "Well, old dear, I can't say that I'm feelin' very fit, what-what-what? But I can manage to carry on as long as the giddy old show lasts."

He was John Cecil Carewe, former flight commander of a British air squadron, and a fighter from the top of his head to the tips of his toes.

"What difference does it make, Jimmie?" asked Grigsby. "We couldn't get ten feet up the side of the hill if we were all unwounded. The machine gun explained that to us."

Carewe, who was wounded in the left shoulder, said, "You know, old chap, I don't think we should wait here for the rotters to— My sainted aunt! Now I know why they drew back. They've sent for a plane. It's what I would do, if—"

"Why can't they come up like men, and wid Colts in the hands ave them? Sendin' for planes to do the work for 'em, the little shrimps!"

"Nine reasons, Mr. Dolan," Jimmie answered with a grin. "The first one being they don't use Colts.— Never mind the other eight. Calm down, old kid. We've got three wounded with us, and— At that, if Carewe's guess is a good one, I vote we go calling. I'd hate to sit and wait for a gent a few hundred feet up to lay an egg on me. I'd rather go to my Heavenly Home handing out calling cards."

"Come over here, Red," the Bean said, "and fix this bandage for me. I can't reach it.—Tighten it up so that I can go calling also."

"I'll twist it off ye, ye long-legged piece av Bosting tripe!" Red answered, rising to his feet. He was all of six feet two inches, and as he stood upright his head was revealed to a Jap sharpshooter who had remained near the machine gun. The sharpshooter promptly took the tip of Red's left ear off with a steel-jacketed bullet.

Red threw himself down and to one side, so as to avoid falling on the Boston Bean. In doing so, he twisted his body, instead of twisting the Bean's leg as he had promised. His right shoulder came against the edge of a flat rock that seemed to be almost buried in the ground, about a foot up from the ledge. Red thereupon sat up and again began telling what he thought of the Japs in general, and in particular the one who had nicked him.

"Ain't it too bad de bullet didn't go two inches to de right?" asked the Yid, blandly. "Den ve vould have had no more de Irish bum to bodder us."

The Fighting Yid was about as broad as he was tall, with china blue eyes that always seemed to be popping out of his head with surprise at such naughty doings in a bad old world. That look was as misleading as the Bean's sorrowful one. The Yid was never surprised at anything. Furthermore, he would fight anything—at any time and at any place. He had been Jimmie Cordie's first sergeant in France, where he had been renamed the Fighting Yid; and later, in the Orient, he had fully lived up to it. His real name was Abraham Cohen, and he had been born on Hester Street, New York City.

Red's answer, while Jimmie Cordie was binding up the ear with a piece torn from a shirt, concerned the Yid's immediate ancestors, his earlier ancestors and the place to which the Yid was going without question, and how anxious Mr. Dolan was that the Yid go there soon.

"FOR PETE'S sake, shut up a minute!" Jimmie said. "How the heck can I make a tie? Quit moving your head, or I'll bite a piece out of your other ear, you big red-headed chimpanzee!—Getting up—"

"Jimmie! When I hit the rock wid me shoulder it moved. Yer talk has just reminded me."

"What moved?—What are you talking about?"

"Listen. The rock me shoulder hit moved—like a door, I tell ye!"

"Yeah? Well, maybeso it is a little loose, Red. Hold still now."

"Ven Jimmie gets it through, go hit it de door mit de head, Mistaire Dolan. Den de head it breaks, und—"

"Put a jaw tackle on, Yid!" Grigsby commanded, looking at the rock which Red insisted had moved. "And after you do that, go over and do a little hitting of that rock yourself—around the edges. It looks like a slab of some kind to me."

The Yid crawled over to the rock, taking great and exaggerated care to keep his head below the Jap angle of fire, and smirking at Red as he did. Though the Yid was about as broad as he was long, in his massive shoulders there was enormous power. At first he pushed with the flat of his hands against the edges of rock; then he put his shoulder to it, and the rock swung half way around, so that the other side of it was facing the men on the ledge.

On the side now turned outward there was a painted face. It was the face of an Oriental—a Tartar—with a fierce countenance, narrow black whiskers fringing the cheek and meeting the tip of the chin in a scanty, pointed beard. A thin mustache swept in a semicircle from the upper lip. The eyebrows above the almond-shaped eyes were well marked, but they were not bushy. The eyes were black, and whoever had painted the face had known how to put a cruel look into eyes.

Beneath the face there was a line of printed characters.

As the men on the ledge stared at the face painted on the rock, one of the Manchus, jarred out of his usual impassiveness, said to the other, "*Timur i Leng!*" pointing at the face. Then he began to talk in excited Chinese, a language which is now spoken by all Manchus.

Jimmie Cordie looked at the face through narrowed eyes, standing there as if frozen. Jimmie was only some five feet seven, so that he was able to stand upright without danger of being seen by the Japs below. The rock door, too, was well out of sight of the Japs.

"The face of Timur," Jimmie said finally. "Timur the Lame, or Tamerlane. It may be his—"

"What the hell are you talkin' about, Jimmie?" demanded Red. "Is it about the flat-faced duck painted on the rock?"

Jimmie Cordie looked at Red and laughed. "That's right, Red, I'm talking about the flat-faced duck on the rock, and if he were alive and heard you call him that, old kid Dolan, you would be sitting on a sharp stake immediately afterward, if he were feeling in a good humor. If not, you would probably be dipped in—"

"Says ye! That's all. Says ye.—Who was he?"

"I vill tell it you, Irisher," the Yid said, patronizingly. "He vas a lame guy dot kept it a pawnshop on de corner of Samarkand Avenue und—"

"How much water have you in your canteen, Yid?" Grigsby asked quietly.

"Vat? Me? I ain't got it no vater, George. You know dot. Vot are you askin' it for?"

"I thought that it might bring you damn fools down to a realization of what we're up against. Three wounded men and no—"

"*Four* wounded men," Red interrupted, firmly. "The ear ave me is hanging by a thread."

Grigsby laughed. To the rest of these utterly reckless adventurers, George Grigsby was more or less of a sheet anchor to windward. Born in the Kentucky hills, he was usually a silent man who fought with a little frozen smile on his lips and in his eyes. In all the East, there was no more famous soldier of fortune than the Kentuckian.

"I see you're all running true to form. Get at it, Jimmie," he said.

"**RED, EASE** over and see if the Japs are staying put.—Yid, push the rock back half way, and take a look at what's behind it."

The Yid announced a moment later: "Dare is it a flight of stone steps—a vide flight mit—"

"All right, Yid. We'll all take a look at the 'mit' later. Well, here it is waiting for us on a silver platter. A flight of stone steps to walk down, and a rock to push back into place again afterward. The Japs can't see either us or the rock, from where they are. Just what's at the bottom of the stone steps the good Lord only knows; but—I vote we take a little trip down and—"

The Manchu who had pointed at the face interrupted with, "do not do so, Captain Cordie, for it would be better to stay here and die quickly at the hands of the little Nippon mongrels than to brave the wrath of Timur i Leng. See"—he pointed to the line of characters—"it reads: 'He who enters here dies a lingering death. I, Timur i Leng, promise it.' And it is written in Mongolian, which Manchus know." He was speaking Pushtu, the universal language of the border.

"And yet, little brother," Jimmie answered, gravely, "Timur

the Lame has been dead for five hundred years. It may be that time has made this promise of his a little hard to keep, so that—"

Red crawled back from the edge of the ledge. "No wan in sight," he announced. "Who is the flat-faced duck, Jimmie?"

"Mr. Dolan has a one-track mind," the Boston Bean explained patiently. "Clear it for him, Jeems, me good man, or we'll have no peace in the family."

"Wan track or twenty-wan," began Red. "Wan ave us Dolans can—"

"You want to hear about who the flat-face is?" Jimmie asked.

"I do."

"Tell the Bean all about the Dolans later, then. Here it is for you, short and sweet: Timur i Leng—or Timur the Lame, or Tamerlane, whichever you like—was the great-grandson of Karachar Nevian, who was, in turn, the minister of Jagatai, and the son of Jenghiz Khan, also commander-in-chief of Jagatai's forces. In the year 1398, Timur took India and looted it. He had already mopped up on Persia, and Russia, too, as far as the Volga. As he mopped up, Mr. Dolan, he collected treasure. It is said that after the taking of Delhi it took three hundred elephants to carry the loot back to Timur i Leng's capital, beyond the Oxus.—And Delhi was only one of the cities he took."

"Holy cow, Jimmie! Do ye think the old scut's treasure might be buried here? Let's go in and—"

"Wait a minute!—If it was buried here, I'd gladly swap a couple of handfuls of it for a drink of water.—I don't know, Red. I've only heard the stories that have been handed down for hundreds of years. One of them is that a part of the treasure taken in India was buried somewhere in the mountains of Manchuria. Another is that the old boy himself was buried there. These stone steps may lead to the treasure, or they may lead to his tomb. And, then again, they may not."

"Come on. I'll carry ye, Beany."

"I'll carry myself, Mr. Dolan. Thanks just the same. That is, I will if the steps aren't too steep."

Again the Manchu protested, and this time he was backed by the other. Better die by bullet or sword than by the hands of the spirits who, without question, guarded the resting place of the mighty Timur i Leng or his treasure.

Jimmie and the others listened, then George Grigsby said, "We do not believe that spirits guard anything here on earth, little brothers. See—we are here on this ledge, and some of us are wounded. We have but few cartridges, and no water or food. Our enemy waits below, and we cannot go higher. Soon there will come a plane to drop bombs on us. We cannot defend ourselves against it, that plane.—Before us we see a stone with a painted face on it, and behind the stone there is a flight of steps leading down—to what we do not know. Shall we stay here and await death like cornered jackals, or shall we go down the steps—as men unafraid?"

The two young Manchus bowed respectfully, and one of them—the eldest—said, "We will go with you, honorable elder brothers."

CHAPTER 11

IN THIS MOUNTAIN'S HEART

IT WAS DARK when the stone had been turned so that the painted face was once more turned toward the steps. Jimmie Cordie and the Boston Bean had flash lights. Jimmie's was a powerful one, the Bean's a smaller and less powerful. The steps, as revealed in the light, were about fifteen feet long and two feet wide, made of stones evenly fitted together. In the light of a flash the walls and the roof, which was some twenty feet overhead, seemed also to be made of stone.

"I'll go first," Jimmie said. "Red, give the Codfish Duke a hand. Yid, you follow Red and the Bean with Carewe. Not so good. Bean, give Red your flash and come up here with me. George, you and Meng-kau and Kwan-chi come next. Red, you're rear guard—and see that you're a real one, you big ape. If you let any bad spirits sneak up on us from behind, I'll reduce you to the ranks.—Ready? *Allons, mes enfants! Vive la Légion!*"

With their .45 Colts ready for action, held in steady right hands, the soldiers of fortune and the two Manchus started down the steps, Jimmie Cordie's flash light playing ahead on the steps, the walls and the roof. Red, bringing up the rear would take a step, then whirl around and play his light, or rather, the Boston Bean's light. One step—two—three—then slowly down to the last step and onto a level floor, also made of stone. The roof curved now, and there were pillars of stone every ten or twelve feet.

They advanced about fifty feet in the same formation, and for as far as the flash light would carry, the corridor seemed to be the same, without turns.

"Vell," the Yid said, cheerfully, "here ve are, und no ghosts have come it to take tea mit, yet. I hope dot de old gent left it some vater mit de treasure. Anyvay, ve didn't have it nothing on de ledge, und here ve got it a svell place to play hide und seek mit de Japs if dey find it de rock und—"

While the Yid was talking, the party had progressed by twenty-odd feet. When he said rock, the roof to within ten feet back of them caved in. Not a slow bulging out, not a smashing cave-in, but a complete sudden dropping of the roof, and the tons of rock over it, to the level of the floor. It was as if a great stone door had been let down from above.

"I think, Mr. Cohen," the Boston Bean said, as the flash lights played on the rock, which now completely shut off the corridor, "that the ghosts you mentioned a moment ago are getting ready to serve the tea. That's a handmade slide."

Jimmie Cordie laughed. "At least, we needn't worry about the Japs finding the rock and coming in after us. All we've got to do now is to find another way out so we can go home."

"That's all, Jimmie," Grigsby answered, quietly. "Let's be getting after it, old kid. My head feels like—like—steady, you birds!—Egan! Bate! Hold your men in line! Here they come! Come on, Yanks! We'll show the—"

George Grigsby lifted his Colt and fired point-blank at Red, who had come up to Jimmie Cordie. It was fast, very fast. But fast as it was, Jimmie Cordie was faster. The flash light was in his left hand, and as Grigsby's gun came up, Jimmie struck at it with the flash light. The blow did not knock the gun out of Grigsby's iron hand, but it did knock it out of line a little. The bullet meant for Red's heart went between one arm and a side, burning the skin.

Every man there knew that George Grigsby's head wound had driven him crazy. The soldiers of fortune knew that he thought he was back on the Western Front. The two Manchus knew nothing about the Western Front, but they knew a crazy man when they saw one. Both stepped back, their swords held point down, ready to deliver the deadly up and inward cut of the Manchu swordsman.

JIMMIE CORDIE dropped the flash light and his .45 Colt. His right hand closed on Grigsby's right wrist, and as he closed in, he lifted Grigsby's arm up for a moment. Grigsby was normally almost twice as strong as Jimmie. Now, he was three or four times as strong. He laughed and struck at Jimmie's face with his clenched left hand.

The blow landed on Jimmie's cheek, cutting it open. As that happened, Red Dolan twisted the gun out of Grigsby's hand. Whether Grigsby had the strength of a maniac or not, he could not resist the power that Red Dolan put into that twist.

Jimmie, though jarred by the blow, hung on, bringing his body close to Grigsby's, and trying for a Legion wrestling hold with his left arm and leg. Grigsby only laughed again, and threw Jimmie Cordie off with force enough to send him back against the wall. It was absolutely dark; Jimmie's flash light had been smashed by the blow at the gun barrel, and Red had dropped the Boston Bean's as he went after Grigsby's gun.

But before Jimmie Cordie's body hit the wall, Red Dolan had closed with Grigsby. Both were big men, without an ounce of fat on them.

Grigsby, when sane, was fully as strong as Red Dolan; and now, in spite of the blood he had lost, he was stronger. Red tried to bring him down without hurting him, by putting an arm around the neck and a knee in the small of the back. But Grigsby, who thought he was fighting a German at close quarters, twisted and got Red around the throat with his right hand. Then his left hammered at Red's kidneys.

The Yid picked up the flash which Red had dropped and turned it on. The Bean and Carewe stood back a little, ready to help if the chance came.

Red, his breath getting short, lifted Grigsby and tried to put him on the ground. He might just as well have tried to throw a wounded grizzly that had closed with him. Grigsby's feet left the ground; and as they did so, he brought a knee up into Red's stomach. Red went down, Grigsby on top of him.

"Hold it de light, Beany," the Yid said, calmly. "I give Red a hand mit—"

Jimmie Cordie shot past the Yid, in a flying tackle. His brain had cleared and he had crouched and sprung, using the wall as leverage.

No one man, sane or insane, could withstand the combined assault of Red Dolan and Jimmie Cordie for very long. At last Grigsby lay still, his face to the ground.

Red knelt beside him, one big hand on Grigsby's head.

Jimmie Cordie staggered to his feet. "Let me have your belt, Yid. Yours, too, Codfish. Holy cats! I always knew that George was strong! Come on with those belts, you apes. Or are you hoping to see this act all over again?"

"From your last remark, Jeems," said the Boston Bean, as he handed Jimmie the belt, "I gather that our dear George is still with us."

"Gather what you damn please!" Jimmie answered. "Do you think Red and I would try to kill George Grigsby?—Come on, Yid, make it snappy!"

The Yid handed over his belt. "Vell, from vot I saw, dare vos quite a lot of that try it to kill stuff bein' handed out by all three. Some of de holds dot—"

"Tell the Codfish Duke of Massachusetts about it! If you saw any holds like that, George was trying to make them stick. Red and I had to break them, didn't we?"

THREE MINUTES later, Grigsby, still unconscious, his wrists and ankles tied, was placed gently against the wall by Red Dolan, whose throat now looked like a piece of raw beefsteak.

One of the Manchus said to the other, softly, "The spirits have begun to obey the orders of Timur i Leng, war brother."

Jimmie Cordie heard it and answered:

"No, little brother. The falling of the roof could have been arranged by men, years ago. A step on a certain stone in the floor sets in motion certain cleverly placed timbers that hold the roof up.—The wound in Major Grigsby's head merely made him think that he was once more fighting the Germans. There are no spirits here, little brother."

"It is no doubt as you say, honorable elder brother," answered the Manchu, politely. "Give orders that we may obey."

"I don't know any orders to give except forward. It's a cinch we can't retreat.—Red, are you hurt?"

"I am not," answered Red, hoarsely. "The ear ave me is gone intirely I do be thinkin'. George tore the bandage off, and wid it the rest ave me ear, by the way it feels. Me throat is red hot, and the belly and sides ave me is sore. But I'm all right, Jimmie darlin'. What now?"

"Vait till ve get it to a drug store," the Yid said, "und I buy it for you a stick of horehound candy for de throat, Irish bummer!"

Red opened his mouth to answer, then he laughed. The laugh sounded more like the croak of a frog than a laugh; nevertheless it was a laugh. "Ye do that little thing, Abie darlin'," he answered. "Did he hurt ye?" to Jimmie Cordie.

"No, nothing to speak of. He jarred me up a lot."

"That cut on your cheek don't look so good, Jeems," the Boston Bean announced. "Better bandage it, old-timer."

"It's all right. Bean, see if you can locate George's gun. Yid, can you pack George for a little way?"

"Sure can I. Two of him, all at vonce. I am de guy dot dey wrote it de song about. Remember? 'Up de stairs de fireman ran, but de child vos bigger dan de fireman.' I vos de fireman. I vill put it George on de back, mit von arm over my—"

"Ye will not!" interrupted Red. "Since when has a Hester Street scut carried anything when a Dolan was around to do it? I'll carry George meself."

"That's right, start an argument. You've got all you can do to carry yourself, Red. Pick George up, Mr. Fireman. We'll find you some stairs to carry him down."

"Here's George's gun," the Bean said.

"Give it to me. I'll be a two-gun man.—Got him, Yid? Get ahead with that flash, Bean. Our rear will have to take care of itself."

THEY WENT along down the corridor, the Yid carrying Grigsby. It seemed as though they would never end. Half an hour went by, and then another. Rests were frequent. They had to be. Grigsby was a dead weight of two hundred-odd pounds, and in spite of the strength in the Yid's powerful squat body, he was tiring fast.

The Boston Bean was walking with his wounded leg held stiff, and one hand on the wall to help him along. There were beads of cold sweat on his forehead, and his lips were gray; but the bored "You be damned!" look in his eyes was still there. The Boston Bean, as a soldier of fortune had once said, was "a very regardless hombre." Being an old Texas Ranger, the speaker felt that he was qualified to pass on very regardless hombres.

Carewe was walking fairly straight, but once in a while he would weave from side to side of the corridor. His shoulder was inflamed, and the fever was rising. His face was flushed, and every time he took a breath he felt as if a redhot poker had seared his lungs. The young Englishman was of the "bulldog breed"—and showed it. Both he and the Bean were badly in need of water.

Jimmie Cordie's perfectly healthy body had readjusted itself from the jar of Grigsby's blow and the strain of the fight. The blood had stopped flowing from the cut on his cheek.

Red swaggered along as ever. He had exaggerated in telling about his ear. It was still there, minus the top that the Jap sharpshooter had removed. Like Jimmie, Red was always in the pink of condition, and after a few minutes his stomach and sides had stopped aching, for which Red audibly voiced his thanks.

The two Manchus were as fit as when they reached the

ledge—in body at least. Mentally, they were fully convinced that they were surrounded by evil spirits that would strike at any time. So they kept their swords ready, not stopping to think that a sword would have no effect on a spirit.

The rests began to get more and more frequent. At one of them, as the Yid knelt and put Grigsby down, Jimmie said, "Sit down, Codfish. If you raise your leg up the blood will—"

"If I sat down, Jeems, me good man, I doubt whether or not I could get up. I'll stay on my feet."

"Are ye that bad, Beany?" asked Red. "Why didn't ye say something, ye long-legged piece ave Bosting tripe? I'll carry ye, Beany darlin'. What is the weight ave ye to me? Nawthin' at all."

"I'll carry myself."

"Ye will not! I'll carry ye, as I said. Wan word outta ye, and I'll—"

"Dot's right, Irish gonif. Jump it on a cripple. Vonce a guy told it me dot de Dolans vent around huntin' for cripples to jump on. I told him dot I didn't believe it. An' I didn't until I see a big Dolan mit hair of red dot—"

The Yid wouldn't have got that far if Red had not been drawing a long breath. "First," Red began, "let me tell the likes ave ye what ye are. 'Way back in the days when gibbons climbed trees, there was wan tribe that wasn't allowed beyand the first branch. That was the tribe ave Yid gibbons. The great-great-grandfather ave ye was—"

"If you're going that far back, Red," Jimmie interrupted, "tell it as a serial, a little at every rest. How about it, Yid? Can you pack George, or will I have Red spell you? From the way he talks, he's all right again."

One of the Manchus spoke. He understood a little English, enough to know that Jimmie was talking about Grigsby. "I, Meng-kau of the House of Chi," he said, "will consider it an honor to be allowed to carry my honorable elder brother."

"And I, Kwang-chi, of the House of Chi, will also consider it an honor," the other Manchu added, promptly.

They spoke in Pushtu.

Jimmie Cordie shook his head. "You are both more valuable to your elder brothers with your swords ready to meet attack. When Major Grigsby comes back from the sleep, I will tell him of your honorable offer, and it will make his heart glad." Then in English, he added, "All right, let's go. Say when, Yid.—Red, after the next stop, you carry George. Carewe, can you stay with it?"

"Carry on, old bean. What wouldn't I give for a cool drink of water!"

Red looked at him and started to say something about even talking about water; then he stopped and went over beside Carewe, putting his hand under Carewe's uninjured shoulder. " 'Tis a game little devil ye are, Carewe. Lean on the hand ave me. Do ye want me to carry ye?"

"No, thanks, Red. I can stick it."

The flash gave only a little light, but the floor was as smooth as a sidewalk, and they went forward.

THE BOSTON Bean suddenly sat down. "That will be all," he said. "My other leg has given out. Go ahead, you birds."

Jimmie Cordie laughed. "Oh, no! It isn't all, Codfish. It hasn't even started yet, old kid.—Pick him up, Red."

"Really, Jimmie, I wish you wouldn't," the Bean protested. "You're handicapped now with George; and Carewe can't hold out much longer. You have a chance, if you— Get goin', you birds, and leave me in peace. I'll be—"

"We ought to leave you in *pieces,* after that remark. Pick him up, Red. The only thing that will be all, Captain Winthrop, is that kind of talk!" Jimmie interrupted coldly.

The Bean had served in the same company of the Foreign Legion as Jimmie, and in the A.E.F. as a captain of artillery. It was very seldom that Jimmie Cordie ever called him Captain Winthrop.

The Bean looked up, and in spite of the pain that was shooting through him, he smiled. "Sorry, Jimmie!" he said, simply.

"Fair enough.—Come on, Red. And lift the Codfish Duke of Massachusetts gently, you big chimpanzee!"

They went on in the semi-darkness, Jimmie carrying the flash.

"Truly, our mighty elder brothers come of a fighting breed," one of the Manchus said to the other. "They walk slowly and in pain to an unknown death, yet they smile."

The rests became longer. Jimmie tried carrying Grigsby, but could only stagger under the load.

"Give it him back to me," the Yid said. "You be de police, und de Irish bummer und I vill be de firemens. Put it George up on de back, Jimmie. My, I vish de fire was over! Dot's de boy. I got him."

Jimmie walked on ahead to give Carewe a hand, leaving the Yid to bring up the tail of the procession. Red was carrying the Boston Bean easily, and telling him how soon he and Jimmie would "fix the leg ave ye, Beany darlin', wance water was reached."

Jimmie saw that it was only a question of a few minutes before Carewe would go down, so he called another halt. After this rest, either he or the Manchus would have to carry Carewe.

As Red put the Bean down, he looked around to say something to the Yid. But there was no Yid, as far as Red could see. "Jimmie! Throw the flash back.—I misdoubt that the Yid is down."

Jimmie played the light back, and then, with Red and the Manchus, he ran back to the last resting place. There was no sign of a struggle. The walls, the roof and the floor looked exactly the same as ever; but both the Fighting Yid and George Grigsby had disappeared.

"Holy cow!" whispered Red. "What happened to 'em, Jimmie?"

"I wish I knew, Red. You go back and stay with Carewe and the Bean. Go with him, Meng. And you, Kwang, come with me."

"Where are ye going?" demanded Red.

"Back as far as the slide. Get goin', Red."

"What's the use ave doin' that? 'Tis disappearin' ye will also be—"

"I don't think so, Red. Get back, old kid. I just want to see if anything by chance has been left open."

Red went back, much against his will.

On the way, the Manchu asked, "Now do you believe in spirits, Lord of the flaming hair?"

Red didn't care to hear any talk about ghosts, whether he believed in them or not. "Keep that sword ave ye ready!" he answered, loosening his .45 in its holster.

Jimmie Cordie came back with Kwang. "No sign of anything!" he said, curtly.

"Jimmie, do ye believe in ghosts? No foolin', do ye or don't ye?" demanded Red.

"No, Red, I don't. If you've got an idea that ghosts took the Yid and George Grigsby out of this snake hole, then forget it!"

"Who did, then?" demanded Red. "They was here, and now they ain't here. What's happened to 'em?"

THE BOSTON Bean, in spite of the pain, laughed. "Answer that one, Jeems! They was here and now they ain't. What happened to 'em? Answer it, old kid Cordie!"

"I wish I knew, Red," Jimmie answered, gravely. "Right now, you know as much about it as I do. If you want me to guess, however, I'll guess that some outfit is watching us and has started to pick us off one by one."

"Ye nicked it, ye shrimp ave the world!" Red answered, much relieved at Jimmie Cordie's common sense guess. Red didn't really believe in ghosts, but at the same time he was glad to have Jimmie figure it out. "Now all we got to do is find out where the scuts are, and take George and that Hester Street ape away from 'em."

"That's all, Red," Jimmie answered, smiling at the big Irishman.

"You and me will go and hunt for them, leavin'—leavin'—Jimmie, what the hell are we to do? We can't leave Carewe and the Codfish here, and we can't leave George and the Yid in the hands ave them dirty hellions that sneak up from behind in the dark. Think up something, Jimmie!"

"And make it snappy," added the Boston Bean. "I'll take a little nap while you're doin' 'er."

"No you won't, Bean. You stay awake. Red, there's only one thing to do—"

"Shoot your horse, then crouch behind his carcass. And if the herd, in their wild stampede, do—" began the Bean.

"Jimmie, now the Bean is gone bugs!—Lie still, Beany darlin', and don't try to fight while we tie ye up. Sure, ye are the Emperor of China and all that. And I'll lick the man that says different."

"He's all right, Red. As long as he can recite poetry, the Codfish Duke is there.—Here it is for you, Red, the way I see it. George and the Yid have disappeared. We don't know whether they are alive or not, and there doesn't seem to be any place where they could have gone. Here we have two wounded men. Let's get them to some place where we can hole them up with the Manchu swords in front of them, and then see if we can find George and the Yid."

"Jimmie, ye think that they are dead! I can tell it in the voice ave—"

"All I know is that they are not here with us, Red. If they were, they would say exactly the same thing if we were missing. Get the wounded men to as safe a place as possible, and then hunt. There must be some sort of opening in the corridor that we did not see. We'll fix the Bean and Carewe comfortably and then—"

Jimmie had not finished speaking when the wall opposite opened like a door. Through the hole came several big, robed figures.

Kwang-Chi said, "The spirits come, brother!" He and his kinsmen raised their swords bravely and charged into the very thick of the crowd in the doorway.

Jimmie Cordie and Red Dolan opened fire at the strange robed figures. The Boston Bean and Carewe drew also. The confined space rocked with the detonations of the heavy Colts, and the air became supercharged with powder smoke. The Bean was sitting down, with his back to the wall and his legs straight out. Carewe was beside him, standing up but leaning against the wall. As Red and Jimmie opened fire, they stepped in front of the two wounded men.

The two Manchus were fairly through the door and safe from the bullets of Jimmie and his men. Both were firmly convinced that the spirits had arrived, yet they were fighting courageously.

The Bean threw the upper part of his body to the left, so that he might get a line of fire.

Carewe, as Red's body came in front of him, took a step to the right.

The first of the figures went down, but there were many more behind, filling the opening. These jumped over those that were down, and came on, ignoring the gunfire and the Manchu swords, It was as if a cloudburst had begun to rush down a dry stream bed in the mountains. Two of the figures reached Jimmie Cordie at the same time. One wound steel-like arms around him, and the other threw a cloth over his head.

Jimmie Cordie went down as if hit by two All-American tackles.

Then Red went down under three or four of the strangers. Whoever they were, they were big, well-nourished men, and not afraid of anything. The Bean and Carewe did not last even as long as the others. Both were as weak as sick kittens. The guns were torn from their hands, and cloths put over their heads, too.

The two Manchus had been able to cut their way into the mob for a moment, then they were stopped by sheer force of numbers.

A voice shouted two words in some unfamiliar language. It was evidently an order to kill the two Manchu swordsmen. There was a flurry, with the two Manchus in the center, then four cracks were plainly heard, like the snapping of brittle twigs. The milling stopped, and the robed figures drew away. On the floor, just beyond the doorway, lay the two Manchu nobles of the House of Chi, dead. Their necks and backs were broken.

CHAPTER III

NIGHTGOWN JOHNNIES

JIMMIE CORDIE CAME back to the light through what he thought had been a million years of rising through cold darkness. He opened his eyes in a room that was dimly lighted by what looked like a natural gas flame passing an opening about a foot square, high up on one wall. The walls, roof and floor of the room were of stone, the same kind that had made the floor of the outer passageway.

Jimmie's ears heard a disconnected babbling from one corner. As his eyes became adjusted to the light, he saw the Boston Bean lying flat on his back in the corner, stark naked. The wound in his leg had bled again, and the Bean was half lying in a pool of blood. He was babbling of cool things to drink, and of bathing in northern waters.

Near the Bean lay Carewe, also naked, face down upon the stone floor. Then Jimmie's eyes picked up Red Dolan. Red was half sitting up against the wall, opposite Jimmie. He was as naked as the Bean and Carewe. Jimmie did not need to look at himself to know that he also was in his birthday suit.

Red was swaying back and forth like a drunken man, muttering, "Stay wid 'em, Jimmie! Stay wid 'em. Soon as I—get this—damn cloth off the head ave me—I'll—"

Jimmie got up on his feet and went over to Red. Stooping down, he began to shake him.

"Red! Red! Wake up! Wake up, Red! *Allons! Vive la Légion! La Rosalie!* Come on, you big red-headed ape! It's Jimmie Cordie talkin'. *Aux armes!*—Oh, for Pete's sake! Snap out of it, you big mick! The Fighting Yid is giving you the horse laugh. Red! Wake—"

Red opened his eyes, and at the same time struck Jimmie's hands away. He staggered to his feet, looked around, and then he saw Jimmie.

"Is it ye, Jimmie? What the— Look at ye!"

"Look at yourself, Mr. Dolan. I thought you'd never—"

"Jimmie! I thought I was still fightin' the ghosts that— Holy cow, 'tis the Bean and Carewe! Is he dead, Jimmie? Sorry the day we ever saw the face ave the flat-faced duck on the—"

"For cat's sake, Red, don't start that keening stuff! The Bean is—"

A portion of the wall swung back, and an old man, dressed in the robes of a priest, walked calmly into the room. He was followed by four other priests, all of them quite as big as the old man, who was even taller and broader than Red.

"Here they are!" yelled Red. "Come on, Jimmie! We'll get—"

Red crouched to spring at the old priest, but he was unable to do more than crouch. As swiftly as a pair of big jungle leopards, two of the priests had him. They lifted him up and pinned him against the wall. No words, no excitement of any kind. It was as if they had picked up a log and placed it against a pile. For once in his life, Red Dolan was in the grip of men to whom his strength was as nothing. To give Red due credit, he was weak from lack of water and food, and the fights with Grigsby and the other priests.

Jimmie Cordie tried to close with the old man. He sought to get a Foreign Legion hold on the priest. Evidently the old man was of importance, judging from the golden work on the robe he wore. Jimmie hoped to force him to terms. He might have, if he had secured the hold, and if he had been able to speak the language but he didn't even get the hold. The old priest held out one hand, a stiff arm behind it, and Jimmie fell away. One of the other priests picked Jimmie up and held him against the wall.

Red began to curse the priests, starting with the Black Curse of Crum'el. But the robed men paid absolutely no attention to him.

The old man walked over to where Carewe lay, examined him, put him back on the floor, and went over to the Boston Bean. The Bean had kept right on babbling. As the old priest bent over him, the Bean said to him, "Come on in, the water's fine. Come on out from behind that false face. I know you, old kid."

THE PRIEST looked at the Bean's wounded leg, then said something in that strange language which neither Jimmie nor Red had ever heard before. One of the men holding Red let go and picked Carewe up. The other priest picked up the Boston Bean. The old man turned and went out, followed by the two carrying the wounded. Then the two who had Jimmie and Red let go their holds and stepped back. One of them snarled something.

At that instant Red Dolan and Jimmie Cordie, naked as the day they were born, jumped at the priests.

This time, Jimmie came in low and reached the priest's body, only to be torn off much as a clawing cat is torn off and tossed up into the air. Red's man sidestepped, and his right hand and arm, used like a club, drove Red's guard against his own head, and sent him spinning into a corner. It takes real power to do that to a two hundred and thirty pound fight-mad Irishman, even if the said Irishman has been in a couple of hard fights recently, and has been without food or water for some little time.

Then the two priests walked calmly out, and the opening slid back into place.

Jimmie Cordie picked himself up. "Outside of that, our new boy friends like us."

Red's answer, as he got to his feet, was lurid. Jimmie was trying to see how badly one elbow was skinned, and Red had plenty of time to put several assorted curses on "the black-hearted scuts." Finally he calmed down and demanded, "What now, Jimmie?"

"Well, if I were you, Mr. Dolan, I'd step into the nearest clothing store and get some clothes. You're a sight for—"

"And what the hell do ye think ye are, Jimmie Cordie? Ye look like a plucked— First George and the Yid, and now Beany and Carewe. Gone from us! Many's the year we've been together, and now—deep under the ground and in the darkness—they leave us.—Not in a good fight wid the guns roarin' and the swords singin' the death song. Not side by side wid—"

"Red, listen! So help me Saint Peter, if you start that damn keening, I'll climb your big frame! You hear me? Turn that tap off—once and for all!"

"Ye jump my frame? Ten Cordies couldn't do that and get away wid it. Listen ye to me. Wan Dolan—wan Dolan can— No, be Judas, wan Dolan cannot do anything, for I let two ave the—"

Jimmie Cordie, naked and bruised in this semi-dark, cold room, deep underground, and in the power of the priests of an unknown religion, nevertheless had the pluck to laugh.

"Careful, Mr. Dolan! After we get out of here, it would be very sad if I had to remind you that you once admitted that one Dolan couldn't do anything. Now listen to old man Cordie's son, Jimmie. First, we do not know that the Yid and George are dead. Second, it looks to me as if the Bean and Carewe were being taken to the hospital. Third, you and I are still all in two pieces. I'll admit I'd like to have at least a suit of—"

"Jimmie! Do ye think they are still alive?—Ye do! I can feel it in the heart ave me. What now, ye scut ave the world?"

"Right at the minute, I'm going to see how many square inches of skin I'm minus. Go and sit down, Mr. Dolan, and take things easy. When they want us, the door will open. Better than sitting down, see if you can find a loose rock that will turn."

"I'll do that.—Holy Moses! This floor is cold and wet to bare feet."

RED COULDN'T find a loose stone that turned, nor one that did anything else. Neither could Jimmie Cordie. And the door did not open for a long time. How long it was, Jimmie and Red could not tell. The light remained much the same, and no food or water was brought them.

They walked round and round the room, and when they got so tired they could walk no longer, they sat down and tried to sleep—without much success. Red's wounded ear became inflamed, and he was like a grizzly bear with the toothache. The damp coldness ate into their bodies, to the very marrow of their bones.

At Red's worse moments, Jimmie Cordie would say, "Tighten your belt, you big ape!"

To which Red would answer, "I have no belt to tighten, bad luck to them!" And for the next few minutes he would forget about his ear and take to inventing new names to call the priests.

To Jimmie and Red it seemed as if they had both died and gone to a cold hell where they had already been a thousand years. In reality, it was thirty-odd hours before the wall opened and the priests—four of them—came in.

"Steady, Red," Jimmie said. "No use in getting broken up down here. Let's see what the play is."

One of the priests held out a long white robe that seemed to be made of linen. Jimmie took it, and the priest handed another robe to Red.

"Night gowns," Red said bitterly. "Maybeso they are goin' to put us to bed."

"Put it on, Red. We'll obey orders until we make the last try."

The priests stood there, their hairy faces like stone idols, while Jimmie and Red slipped the "nightgowns" over their heads. Then one of the priests motioned toward the opening. Jimmie and Red went through it into a corridor, the priests following close behind, within arm's length.

"Say when, Jimmie," Red muttered. "I don't like walkin' wid this thing on. 'Tis more like a shroud than anything else. Let's try for 'em right now."

"Keep your shirt on, Mr. Dolan. Or rather, keep your little

white nightie on. We wouldn't last a minute. I want to see if we can't get something in our hands before we try. These birds are too big for us to take on barehanded—or even bare-footed. Tighten the belt you haven't got on, and keep on walking."

The corridor began to take a sharp pitch upward, and for the last hundred yards or so it was on a forty-five degree slant. It leveled out after that, and as they walked along they could see doors on either side. One of the priests went ahead for a few feet, and opened a door, motioning Jimmie and Red to go in.

"Will we, Jimmie darlin'?"

Jimmie Cordie laughed. "I've always wanted to see what was behind a door. Let's go in. Wait for a real chance, like I told you."

They entered, and the priests shut the door behind them.

The room was a large one, with a window that looked out on a square roofed court. There were several flames issuing from the ground on each side of the square. Jimmie was right when he guessed that these flames were of natural gas. The room was fairly light, and as Red stepped inside it, Jimmie right behind him, he let out a wild yell of joy. For there, standing facing the door, also dressed in what Red called a nightgown, stood the Boston Bean and Carewe and George Grigsby.

" **'TIS** ye, ye scuts ave the world! George! Are ye no longer goofy? I thought ye was dead, Carewe! Glory be to all the saints!"

"Less noise, me good man!" the Boston Bean said, loftily. "Or we'll turn you out of the lodge. I'm keeper of the sacred nightshirt, and—"

"Yeah?" Jimmie interrupted. "The last time Mr. Dolan and I had the pleasure of seeing you, Codfish, you were asking some one to come out from behind a false face. We may not have much time, old kids. Let's get up to date. First, where is the Yid?"

"I don't know, Jimmie. The last thing I can remember, I was telling you that my head felt bad. The Bean tells me that I went off the track, and that you and Red finally knocked me out. Then the Yid packed me along on his back. All I know about it is that I woke up lying on some kind of a couch, feeling all right. There were two priests in the room, and I tried to get them to talk, but couldn't. Not long ago, another came in with this robe. They put it on me and walked me here. That's all I know."

"Short and sweet! How does your head feel?"

"Perfectly well. My hair is shaved off on that side, and I can feel where a cut has been sewed up."

"For Pete's sake! They must be going to make a Roman holiday out of us all. Bean, what—?"

"Wait," Red interrupted firmly. "To hell wid the Bosting Bean. He's here wid us. Where is Abie? George, when ye came to, did ye see no trace ave Abie?"

"No, Red."

"Maybe they're saving him for something extra special, Red. We'll ask 'em later. What happened, Bean?"

"Well, Jeems, I woke up about the same way George did. Last I remember, I was sitting down on the floor of the corridor, and the wall was opening. I remember drawing my gun and trying to get a line of fire. That's all. Then I woke up on a cot, and my leg felt a million times better. Speaking of operations, let me show you my scar. George's is nothing compared to mine!"

"I say, Jimmie, I can tell a little more. I woke up when one of the jolly old priests was working on my shoulder. He was cleaning out the giddy wound with water, and—"

"Holy cats! Didn't it hurt ye bad, Carewe?"

"My word, yes! It took two of them to hold me still, Red."

"It must have hurt ye," Red answered, with deep conviction, "if it took two ave the black-hearted gibbons to hold ye. Wan of them held—wan damn near held me, I mean."

"Then he filled the wound up with some kind of salve, Jimmie," continued Carewe, "after which he sewed it up. I say, in two hours I was feelin' fit."

"Did ye get any water?" asked Red.

"No, Red, nor any food."

"Ye know what I'd give for a long drink ave cold—!"

"We know what you'll get if you don't shut up!" Jimmie said. "Then, summing up after all returns are in, you three are ready for battle again. Is that it?"

"Cut your wolf loose, Jimmie," Grigsby answered, with a smile. "I will try to stay sane as long as possible, this time."

"Lead on, Jeems," the Boston Bean said.

"Right," Carewe answered. "Carry on, old dear."

"**WELL, ALL** we can do is to keep as close together as possible. I think we are all going to be taken some place and put over the jumps. Up to date, all I've seen in the way of weapons are the mitts on the ends of the priests' arms. Wherever they take us, there will probably be some things to torture us with or whatnot. When I yell 'let's go!' we'll try for 'em. If there isn't anything, I'll holler anyway. We may be able to go through their line, and we may not. Anyway, we'll go to glory making the try. Any one got anything better to offer?"

"Here's a piece of poetry I just made up," the reckless Bean said. "I offer that.—

"Here we stand in our nightgowns,
"With Mr. Dolan as all our clowns,
  "We are going on High
  "Making the try,
"Bucking the line for the last of our downs."

"I'm afraid the last line does not scan, but—"

"Here ye stand," Red said bitterly, "makin' up poetry, and all ave us not knowin' whether Abie is—"

"For Pete's sake, Red! Will you quit that sob-sister stuff? Listen, the Yid has got nine lives, allee samee cat. The last time, we thought he was facing a firing squad of Japs, didn't we? The time before that, we thought he'd gone down with the Bean's yacht, and we found him sitting on the captain's cabin, floating around and eating a piece of pie.—Let's wait until we're sure, this time. If he's gone west, all the yowling in the world won't bring him back, and right at this minute he may be sitting pretty somewhere. You've always got a certain amount of—"

"Who's yowling?" demanded Red. "If ye was full ave mate and water, Jimmie Cordie, I'd knock the coco off ye."

"Perhaps Mr. Dolan does not like my referring to him as more than one clown," the Bean explained patiently.

In spite of the desperate position they were in, and the fact that they had had no water or food for three days, every one of them laughed. In the Orient, it had often been said:

"If you want to get a gang to waltz through hell singing 'There'll be a Hot Time in the Old Town To-night,' go get Jimmie Cordie and the apes that stick around with him.— They'll do it and shoot up the works at the same time."

That was probably an exaggeration, but as they now stood, naked except for a thin robe apiece, and in a stone chamber far underground, waiting for a chance to fight for their lives, they certainly seemed to pay no heed to the seriousness of their situation.

"If I have the time," Red said, "ye will eat that clown thing, ye long-legged—"

The door opened at that moment, and a file of priests marched in. Ten of them, and as far as could be seen, without weapons of any kind.

"Jimmie," Red whispered, "while I jump them, you close the door. We will take the robes and—"

"Easy does it, Red. We're going to go places and see things. Don't start anything until I give the word."

One of the priests motioned for them to get into line. They did so, and afterwards the priest motioned them to the door.

"Fair enough," Jimmie said, as the priests ranged themselves five on a side. "We are going to be brought into the arena all together."

"Whatever that is," Red answered morosely. This walking bare-footed, with only a nightgown for clothing, and between any two men, did not set at all well with Mr. Dolan's idea of what was what for the Irish in general and Terrence Aloysius Dolan in particular.

CHAPTER IV

THE IDOL SPEAKS

THE PROCESSION WENT out into the corridor and on across the square. They entered a big stone building that was set on top of a steep incline. It looked like a blockhouse fort, something that had been built in the pioneer days.

"What is it, Jimmie?" Red asked.

"Darned if I know, Red. Maybeso either the treasure house of Timur i Leng, or else his tomb."

"Bad luck to the rock that—!"

"Heads up, Red! We may have to make a break any second."

The doors that had been open as they neared, swung shut behind them. On the ground floor, there was nothing but a flight of stone stairs leading up.

"Last time, we went down," the Bean said. "This time we go up.—Jeems, if you don't give the word very soon, my bare feet will be so frozen that—"

Until now, the priests had paid no attention to any talking, but at this one of them touched the Codfish Duke on the shoulder, shaking his head as he did so.

They went up the stairs, which led to the roof of the building. There was no coping to the roof, but around the edges, on all sides except the far side, there stood a three-deep row of the big priests. On the far side, on a stone base about six feet high, there sat an idol. The idol was made of copper, or what looked like copper in the light of the gas flames that shot up from little holes here and there in the ground. The image was the figure of a man, sitting down, his hands resting on his knees. He was about a third larger than a well built human being.

In front of the idol there stood five of the big priests with robes heavily decorated in gold. But what drew Jimmie Cordie's eyes and the eyes of the other adventurers were the objects that were placed in front of the five priests. On the stone floor stood five frameworks of wood, built in the form of a triangle, and each about six feet high. From a cross beam hung two iron rings. There was another ring where the two sides came to a point on the floor. And from each ring dangled short ropes. Beside each triangle there sat a tray of knives.

"Holy mackinaw!" Jimmie Cordie said in a low whisper. "Flaying!—Get set, you apes. We'll try for the knives."

"Steady, Jimmie!" Grigsby interrupted calmly. "We'll be led up closer. Then when the halt comes we'll try for it."

One of the priests at the idol called out, and the priests motioned the robed prisoners forward. No attempt was made to guard them closely. It was as if the priests had the uttermost contempt for these men who were to be skinned alive.

The line went forward up to the triangles. Now it was a straight, one-man line, company front. The priests were about ten feet behind them. As they got close, a priest stepped forward and held up his hand. The line halted.

"Duck soup!" Jimmie said softly, with a grin. "I can reach my knives from here. All set?"

THE PRIEST said something, and the soldiers of fortune heard the other priests closing up behind them.

Jimmie had drawn his breath to shout when—the idol spoke! Sonorous words issued out of the metal lips in a snarl of command.

On the priests' faces, those that could be seen, there suddenly appeared an expression of utter astonishment and fear.

Then, as the idol spoke again, every priest in the room went to the floor, face to the ground.

"What the hell?" whispered Red. "Jimmie, what's comin' off?"

"How do I know? Anyway, we're getting some kind of a break. Stand perfectly still, old kid!"

Once more the voice came from the idol, and the priests rose and ran for the stone stairs. As the last one disappeared, the head of the idol rose from the shoulders, and in its place there appeared the head of the Fighting Yid.

"For the love ave all—!" Red yelled.

"Kvick!" the Yid interrupted. "Up here, back of de idol. Make it snappy! Maybe I didn't make it stick.—Hurry up, Irish bummer, or I sic dem on you!"

Jimmie Cordie, in passing a tray of knives, stooped and picked up the biggest one. Red saw him do it, and he picked another up. "Now we will have something to play wid—"

The *bang-bang-bang!* of a .45 Colt interrupted him. He looked up, to see the Fighting Yid beside the idol, firing at the priests who had begun to return to the roof. One of them, having looked back, had evidently seen what was happening to the men who were to have been flayed and had also seen the Yid.

"Give 'em hell, ye Hester Street scut!" yelled Red, perfectly happy once more.

Jimmie and Red climbed upon the base of the idol and went around behind it, the Yid's gun roaring over their heads as they climbed.

Back of the idol a flight of stone steps led from the roof down to the ground. About fifteen or twenty feet away from the bottom of the steps there began a gentle slope that led up to what looked like the side of a canon. Ten feet up the slope was a square opening, about three feet in diameter.

"Go to the hole und in it," shouted the Yid. "I hold dem back."

"Nothing doing!" Jimmie said. "Come on, Yid. We'll all hold them back, once we're in that hole."

As they went into the hole the Boston Bean said to Red, "Down—then up—and now down again. Life is a sad puzzle, isn't it, Mr. Dolan?"

"How do I know? Wan thing is sure, and that is ye are goofy as hell—all the time."

The Yid, once they were all inside the opening, fired up at the priests, who had begun to come down the steps. Then he slammed a heavy metal door shut. The door opened inward, and on the ground was a heavy log that evidently was used to brace it, once it was shut. The Yid set the log in place, one end in a small hole in the ground, the other end against the door, under a metal strap.

"**TRY UND** kick it dot in," he said cheerfully.

"Where does this tunnel lead to?" Jimmie asked as they started down.

The hole—it could hardly be called a tunnel—slanted sharply down, and was unpaved.

"All de vay out into a ravine. My, dere is svell vater dere, und—"

"Ye say it!" Red interrupted, firmly. "Ye say it, I double dare ye to say it. Wan word about water from ye, and I'll kill all the Yid-cat lives ave ye!"

"Und vot de hell a Yid-cat is, I don't know. Take it hold of poppa, little von, und poppa vill—"

"Less talk, Yid," Grigsby said quietly. "Get us to water as soon as possible."

The Yid handed Jimmie Cordie a belt in which there were a few cartridges and the Colt .45. "I go ahead, Jimmie. You be de rear guard."

"I'll go wid ye, Abie," Red announced. He wanted to hear what had happened to the Yid.

The tunnel was just big enough to allow the passage of one man, if he kept his head and shoulders bowed. The Yid went first, and Red, bent almost double, followed. For all the discomfort of this position, Red began asking questions. "What happened to ye, ye Yid monkey?"

"Oi, vot didn't? I vas valkin' along, carryin' George, an' singin' mit contentment, und all of a sudden over de mouth dere came a big hand, und right after dere came vot felt like a blanket. Und den George was lifted avay from me, und I vas lifted up und carried myself. I heard it some guy say, 'Dis is de von of—' "

"Ye heard some one say that? Well, ye di-ert-ty Yid liar! Ye heard and understood—"

"Get a move on," Jimmie called from the rear. "They've got around the door. I'll—"

The .45 began issuing orders to the priests to halt. *Bang—Bang—Bang—Bang!*

"That'll be all for a few minutes," Jimmie said. "Until they drag out the wounded. How long is this gopher hole, Yid?"

"About a mile," the Yid called back.

"Yeah?—Step on the gas, then!"

"I am going as fast as I can did it now," the Yid said, loud enough for Red to hear. "Vot am I supposed to did, fly through de—"

"Do as Jimmie says, ye gibbon. Get a move on ye! I—holy cow! I stepped on a sharp wan!—The toe ave me is gone intirely."

"I thought it dot all de Irish had it hoofs like mules, und—"

"Oh, ye did? Listen to me, ye Yid beneath notice. The Irish had feet and toes on the feet long before the Yid—By the black curse ave Antrim, I have stepped on another!

"Go on, tell me! 'Twill take the mind ave me off the pain. Tell me, and tell the truth if ye do be able, which I misdoubt."

"Vat a time to esk it! Vell, I understood vat dey vos sayin', because dey talked it in Hebrew. De old-time Hebrew dot my poppa, who vos a rabbi, taught me mit de aid of sixty-nine broom handles."

"Your poppa was a pink-tailed gorilla, ye mean," Red said. He had just stepped on another sharp one.

"Just for dot, I von't tell it you nothink. I tell it to Jimmie."

"Aw, hell, I was only kiddin' ye, Abie. Go on, tell me. An'

bedam', if I scrape the elbow ave me wan more time it's mad I'll be gettin'!"

AGAIN THERE came crashing reports from the Colt. And afterwards, Jimmie's voice:

"Get going up there! I've only got six shells left!"

"Go faster, ye Yid-cat. And while ye are doin' it, tell me what happened."

"Vait till we get it out. My, such a place to tell it a story!"

"Maybe we won't get out at all. Tell me now!" Red was a firm believer in bringing everything up to date.

The Yid told him—part of it, anyway. For he was interrupted whenever Red refused to believe him, or whenever Red stepped on a sharp rock. Summed up, what the Yid told Red was that the priest who had carried him had separated from the rest on an order. The Yid waited until they got to a dark place, and then, with a jujutsu hold, he had killed the priest and put on his robe.

He had hunted around after that, in the dark, and looking for traces of Grigsby and the others. Finally—how long after that he did not know—he met a lone priest back of the stone house. He jumped this priest and got a hold on him that made the priest talk. The priest told of the tunnel that led to the surface, and he explained several other things.

The mountain was practically hollow, due to volcanic action, hundreds of years ago. The priests and their wives and children lived on top of the mountain next to it, and they had several ways of getting into the great caves without appearing on top of the ground.

When the Yid got that far, Red demanded, "Why the hell didn't they get the treasure and stay outta the damn place altogether?"

"Vot treasure? Dere is no treasure dere. It is the tomb of von of de favorites of Timur i Leng. She died while on the march mit him. Some voman, I forgot the name. It vos something like—"

"What the hell do I care what her name was? Get on with it."

"On vhere, Mistaire Dolan? De priest dot I had, tried it at last to yell und—"

"Did he?"

"No. Den I vent in de tunnel, und all the vay out—den back in again to look for de gang."

"What are a lot ave Yids guarding a tomb for?"

"Vell, it seems dot von time, a long time ago, dis guy Timur caught a lot of Hebrews goin' somevere. He vos goin' to kill dem all, ven just at dot time, his voman died. He got it de idea dot he vould put dem und deir descendants forever, guardin' her last restin' place. So he made it dem svear an oath dot dey vould. Dese priests are de descendants of de first bunch. Now you know all about it."

"I do like hell! How did ye get into—?"

There came the sound of four fast reports, then two more, slower.

"That's all!" Jimmie called. "Drop back here with me, Red. Bring your bread knife along."

"Vait," the Yid shouted. "I see it de opening."

"Come on, Jimmie," Red yelled. "Jimmie, are ye comin', ye shrimp?"

"As fast as I can, you big ape," Jimmie answered from the darkness.

THE YID led the way up a steep incline and then pushed aside what looked to be a wall of tree branches. "Here ve are. Climb it down de tree, un den dere is vater und—"

"Go ahead and do it," commanded Jimmie Cordie, who had come up.

One by one, the Yid first, they parted the branches and climbed down a good-sized tree. In doing so they lost most of their respective nightgowns—Red especially. His caught on a branch, and when his feet landed on the ground he was almost in the same condition as when Jimmie had awakened back in the underground room.

There was a spring near the base of the tree, and the first thing they all did—all except the Yid, that is—was to limp over and bury their faces in the cold water, drinking as much as they dared to.

"I hope to high heavens," Jimmie said, as he stood up, "that our persistent little playmates won't insist on hanging around with—"

"Take a look up at the opening, Jeems," the Boston Bean said, calmly.

They all looked up. There was the head and shoulders of one of the big priests showing in it.

"Holy cats!" Jimmie said. "We're worse off here than in the tunnel. I guess it's a case of back to back until—"

"Over dere iss rocks on top of de knoll. I can see it dem from here." The Yid pointed at a little knoll about twenty or thirty feet away. "Up dere ve can rock dem."

Jimmie Cordie looked at the knoll, which appeared to be more or less covered with rocks about the size of a fist. He laughed. "What could be sweeter? Come on!"

By the time they had reached the top of the knoll, four priests were on the ground, and others were coming down the tree and out of the opening. Those on the ground made no attempt to rush the knoll. It was evident that they were waiting for something. In the end, about thirty of them had arrived on the ground.

"They've heard of your ability as a pitcher, Mr. Dolan," the Bean said, as the soldiers of fortune stood up, each with a little pile of rocks at his feet, "and they are waiting for their whole ball team to get here."

"I'll bounce some rocks off the heads ave them, the big scuts! Pitcher or no pitcher," declared Red.

They all laughed, and Carewe said, "Yid, how did you arrive in the giddy old joss? My sainted Aunt Maria! I was surprised when the head of that idol lifted and your classic map appeared."

"I was foolink around, und I vent up de steps. Dere vos de old boy sittin' dere. I took it de look at him, und I found dot he had it a kind of door in de back."

"You mean a door anyone could see?" asked Jimmie Cordie.

"No, Jimmie. I had it a hand on his knee, und all of a sudden I heard it something in de back. I vent around, und dere vos de open place. I got in, und found dot de head lifted up so dot a man's head could come up from de shoulders, und den the head could come down over. So I thinks, vell, votever comes off, if any of you vos left alive, it comes off in front of de god, or vot de hell ever he—"

"Stop usin' them words together like that, ye heathen Yid," commanded Red, virtuously.

"Vot vords?—Den I got in und stayed in until—"

"Supposin' a priest had come along and found ye there?"

"Vell, I vas in, und he vould be out. He vould have had to get me out, vouldn't he?—Supposin' dot you had been born vhile travelin' mit your aunt on de ocean, Irish loafer? No von came, und—"

"Here comes the umpire," the Bean interrupted. "Better get in the box, Mr. Pitcher."

A priest whose robe was covered with symbols worked in gold was now coming down the tree.

"Oi," the Yid mourned. "Vot could it I do mit a .45 right now! I bet I could knock it dot yellow-hammer out of de tree mit the eyes shut."

"Try it with a rock," the Boston Bean suggested. "You ought to be able to throw that far."

"Better save your ammunition, Yid," Grigsby said. "You'll need all you've collected before—Here they come."

CHAPTER V

THE GREAT WOLF'S DESCENDANT

TWO URYANKHES TARTARS who rode in advance of a patrol of some twenty more, got off their horses and climbed upon a rock from which they could see a good deal of the surrounding country. One was about sixteen; a slim, fierce-eyed hawk-nosed boy, the son of Sahet Khan, who ruled five thousand of the most dreaded fighters in the hills. The other was a man of about forty-five or fifty, a noted leader of forays.

"What do you see, son of Sahet Khan?"

"Nothing of interest, Vyatka. There is no—Wait!" The boy's eyes, in vision equal almost to those of an eagle, tightened a little as he looked at the base of a hill far below. "I see—there are men near the hill.—Now they are advancing. Toward a knoll. At the top of the knoll there are—apes, I think. Although they look white in the sun. They are—It is an attack."

Vyatka laughed. "Truly your eyes will soon equal those of your father, O Zagatai. You are right. Except that the apes are naked men. The attackers are the bearded slaves of Timur who live on top of the mountain of the chasm. They burrow into the ground like moles, and seldom are seen."

"What? Those dirt-eaters—sons of unspeakable mothers!—that I have heard talk about? Now is our chance to slay some of them. Back, Vyatka! We will leave the horses and go down by the spring path. Look! Those on the knoll are trying to beat off the attack by throwing rocks. If we can only get between the moles and their mountain hole, we will have them."

On the way down, Zagatai asked, "Why has not my father destroyed them and their kennel before now?"

"Because, O descendant of the Great Wolf, Jenghiz Khan," Vyatka answered, "it is impossible to get at either them or their kennel. It is only when some of them are caught in the open that we are able to slay them. The mountain top on which they live, and which they farm enough to give them food for themselves and their sheep and cattle, is like the seat of a camp stool. To climb to the seat is impossible, save on one side; and there, as the level land begins, there is a chasm many thousands of feet deep. That is why the mountain is called the mountain of the chasm.

"The dogs have a wooden bridge across the chasm which they can raise and lower by ropes. Always, there are some of them on guard at the bridge. For hundreds of years, they have lived there, men, women and children."

"Do they never leave the top of the mountain?" Zagatai asked, as he slid down the side of a rock.

"Not many at a time. It is told around the campfires that they guard something underground. This much I know: they pop into a hole like a long-eared rabbit; and once in, if pursued, they have some way of caving in the hole behind them. The Uryankhes have caught many of them before they could get to a hole, however," he added, with a grim smile.

"Are they fighters?"

"Yes, O Khan-to-be of all the Uryankhes, they are fighters. Learn this, eaglet. All Jews are fighters, and will fight to the death. But generally they are untrained in the arts of war—. Turn here. We are close to the big bowlder that marks the—"

"I know where we are," interrupted Zagatai, haughtily. "Once we reach the base of the hill, we will get between them and the hole they came out of. Then we will form a circle around them and let our swords sink deep."

Vyatka, who had led the Uryankhes in battle even before Zagatai was born, concealed a smile as he answered, "As you order, mighty one."

THE PRIESTS advanced slowly up the knoll. Their approach reminded Jimmie Cordie of a steam roller going up a steep grade of road. No attempt was made to surround the knoll and come up on all sides. It was as if the priests were sure of their victims; and as a matter of fact, they were.

The soldiers of fortune stood there, their lean, tanned, hard-bitten faces impassive, their eyes cold. All knew that they did not have one chance in a million to beat off the attack, and that once taken prisoners again, they would face the flaying triangles, this time without chance of rescue. Yet there was no show of nerves or fear.

The priests, as they came closer, spread out a little, two or three together, so as to offer as small a target as possible for the rocks.

"About time to try to stop 'em, Jimmie," Grigsby said.

"I guess it is. Well, we've all had a nice time at the party, and if we get—Let's go!"

It was fast, hard, accurate throwing; but all it did was to knock seven or eight priests over before the rest closed in.

This time, it was not as easy for the priests as it had been in the first tunnel, and in the room. The Yid fought like a wounded grizzly bear, and as he was still wearing his clothes and his heavy boots, more than one priest reeled back from the Fighting Yid, who was living up to his name.

The Yid had two rocks, one in each hand, and he cracked heads and ribs with them and his kicks had the force of mules' kicks. He butted with his head, bit with his teeth, and all in all, acted like a Fighting Yid who has gone crazy. The priests were trying to take their former captives alive; hence they were handicapped.

Jimmie Cordie and the Bean, after the first contact, found themselves back to back. The Bean was a clean fighter; but having served in the Legion, he knew several things that could be done in a fight when odds were great. Jimmie Cordie was like a lean wolverine in the northern woods—and there is no better scrapper in the world, weight for weight, than the wolverine.

The first priest who reached him, Red smacked over the head with a big rock, after dodging his outstretched hands; and big as the priest was, he went down, his head crushed in like an eggshell. The next moment, Red saw Carewe go down, after trying bravely to stop the charge of another priest almost twice as big as he was. Carewe met the rush without giving an inch, but sheer weight and momentum downed him, with the priest on top. Red jumped, looking a lot like a big white-skinned, red-haired gorilla, and he landed on the priest's back. A second later he had killed the priest with the rock. Then two more priests lifted him off.

Carewe had been almost knocked out by his fall, and Red's landing on top of the priest had completed the job, as far as Carewe was concerned. He passed out of the picture.

Red, as he was lifted, went berserk. He had been manhandled once before by these priests, something which seldom happened to him. This time he became a sort of animated pinwheel crossed with a skyrocket, plus a strain of cannon cracker filled with T.N.T.

Grigsby fought as he always fought, with a cold little smile on his lips and in his eyes. Like the Bean, under ordinary circumstances, he was a clean fighter; but now he used every trick he knew to disable.

THE FIGHT resolved itself into six little groups. Four or five priests on the outside, and at the center a man who was fighting to the death, if possible. The Bean and Jimmie Cordie had been separated.

They fought, each according to his nature, and all silently—except the Yid, who always talked a blue streak when he was fighting. "Oi! Let it go of me! Take dot—und dot—und von for you. Oi, such a business!—Oh, you vould! Take dot!—Let it go de neck! How you like dot, Mistaire?"

One by one, they went down. First the Bean, then the Fighting Yid, then Grigsby. Red next; and at last, Jimmie Cordie, down under two or three priests. However, there were more than a few priests down also.

The priest in the gold-worked robe, who had been standing a little to one side, gave an order; and the other priests started to pick up the men whom they had finally pulled down. As they did so, another priest shouted something and pointed. The rest of them looked in the direction in which the priest was pointing, and those who had hold of the captives, suddenly let go.

They had good cause to let go, too. For between them and the tree there stood five Uryankhes Tartars, their swords resting easily across their left forearms, with pleased smiles on their dark, high-cheekboned faces. Advancing up the knoll on all sides were eighteen or twenty more of the merciless Uryankhes.

The priests were unarmed, and to the last one, they knew that they could expect no mercy. They and their ancestors never had received any mercy from the hill tribes, especially not from the Uryankhes, on the border of whose territory the mountain stood. The priests knew they were cut off from any refuge, and that they were about to die, and yet they showed no fear.

The priest who had issued the first order issued another. Ten of his followers ran to him, forming a wedge, with him in the middle. Then they started down the knoll toward the tree, full speed ahead. The remaining priests formed a circle, their captives in the center, and waited for the Tartars.

The wedge broke the Tartar circle, but it lost four priests as the two Tartars nearest went down. Closing up again, however, the priests kept right on toward the tree. The five Uryankhes stationed there spread out a little, and crouched, their swords ready. When the wedge arrived it widened out and every priest in it, save the one in the center with the gaudy robe, literally flung himself at a Tartar. With that the robed priest sprang for the tree, reached it and swarmed up it like a big cat—up and into the hole. The five Tartars partially evaded the priests, or received them on sword-point. But before the Tartars could disengage themselves, the leader of the priests had gotten back into the hole.

The five Tartars, snarling like cats, ran to get into the massacre up on the hill. It could hardly be called a fight. The weight and strength of the priests did them no good now—not against the swords of these savage Tartars.

Red, as soon as he was turned loose, tried to get up, but he could not. He managed to sit up, however, and as he did so, he saw the slim, boyish Zagatai, who was within ten feet of a big priest.

"E—eeeee yah! Zagatai, ye little divil! Go get 'em, ye fightin' cock ave the North!"

Zagatai flashed a glance at Red, grinned and then leaped at the priest, his sword ready to deal the slashing cut of the Uryankhes.

Jimmie Cordie raised himself on an elbow. "What the heck are you—? For Pete's sake! How did the Uryan—? Look at the hill!"

THE MOUNTAIN back of the tree was slowly sinking in, for a space of about twenty feet on each side of the tree and above the hole for some fifty feet. As it settled, there came a landslide that first snapped the tree off near the ground and then covered it.

Jimmie called out, "The old boy went in and pulled the mountain in after him."

Zagatai shouted an order, which was repeated by the Tartars near him. It was to the effect that the naked white men were not to be touched. He was afraid that some of the Uryankhes, in their eagerness to slay, might not stop long enough to recognize that these naked men were Captain Cordie and his war brothers.

Jimmie Cordie was on his feet by the time Zagatai and Vyatka came up to him.

"You, Captain Cordie!" Zagatai said in Pushtu. "You—the blood-brother of my mighty father, and standing there naked? Where are your clothes?—There also is the Lord Red, and—"

Jimmie, who had known Zagatai since Zagatai was a baby, grinned as he answered, "I'll tell you all about it later, O son of my blood brother. Now I desire food, and clothes for us all."

RED DOLAN sat down beside the Fighting Yid in the main encampment of the Uryankhes.

"How are Beany and Carewe getting along?" asked the Yid, lazily.

"Both ave them scuts is sitting up. From the way they do be eatin', they're all right. Where is Jimmie?"

"Mit Sahet Khan and George. My, de old gent thinks it a lot of Jimmie, don't he?"

"Why shouldn't he? Jimmie saved the life ave him when some Chinks were going to cut the head off him. Didn't ye know that, ye ignoranneymus? He and Jimmie went through the blood brother rites—Holy mackinaw, the feet ave me is still sore!"

"Tell you vat, Irisher. Go back to de priests and get it some of dot salve vot dey rubbed in Beany und George. Dey give it you some, if you ask dem."

"I'll do that little thing some day, and I'll offer to swap them a Yid monkey for it.—What the hell are ye lookin' at?"

The Yid held up a little statue which was covered with mold and crusted dirt.

"It's a image of Buddha. It vas on de lap of de big idol, und I slipped it in de pocket ven I vas monkeyin' around."

"Maybe it's gold. Scrape that dirt off it."

"Vot mit? I ain't got it de knife, nit-wit."

"Take the fingernail ave ye. Here, give it to me."

Red scraped, and after a minute he announced, " 'Tis green underneath. Like a glass—'Tis an emerald that I'm scratching on!"

Jimmie Cordie came out of Sahet Khan's tent at that moment and walked, over to the other two.

"Jimmie, the Yid robber stole this at the tomb. See, 'tis set wid an emerald."

Jimmie Cordie grinned. "The Yid ought to be ashamed of himself, Mr. Dolan. We wouldn't do such a thing, would we? At least, not more than—Let me see it, Red.—Holy cats! If it is—"

Sahet Khan, in addition to giving Jimmie an outfit of clothes, had insisted on Jimmie's wearing one of his belts, from which hung a sword. Jimmie drew the sword and began scraping the statue.

He cleaned off the dirt, and then held the object up. He looked at it a moment, then he handed it back to the Yid.

"Take good care of it, Yid," he said. "Know what you've got? That is one of the famous lost statues of Chaung Tzu. It's cut from a single emerald. Timur i Leng must have got it in some loot. He left it at the tomb of his sweetie. The priests didn't dare touch anything of his, after their oath, I guess."

"How much is it vorth?" asked the Yid.

"Worth? Darn near all the money in China, boy! Listen, there were three of these, made from three emeralds. That was about the year two hundred and ten, B.C. Two of them were lost. You have in your hand one of the lost ones."

"No kidding, Jimmie? Vot is it vorth in real money?"

"I'm not kidding. Any mandarin or War Lord in China would gladly pay you a hundred thousand for it, to say nothing of what some museum might offer you. Yen Yuan will pay that much for it, I know.—That's one real emerald, Mr. Cohen; and its historical value is—"

"Vait a minute, Jimmie! You said, 'pay me.'—Is dot right, Jimmie?"

"Why, the— Oh, I see. Pardon me, Yid. I should have said, 'pay us.'"

"I forgive it dis von time, but not again!"

"And who the hell do ye think ye are, to be forgivin' any wan, ye flat-faced duck? Wan word outta ye, and I'll—"

Jimmie Cordie laughed. "Listen, Red. Get something else to call him. That flat-faced duck thing brings up unpleasant memories of old man Timur."

"Jimmie, I've just thought ave something. Let's go back and open up the damn hill. Maybe we can find another wan. This time, we will go wid plenty in the hands ave us to settle the hash of any ave the big scuts that do be left."

"Not me, old kid! Personally, I think I'm darn good and lucky to be packing my skin around, instead of having it made up into a belt."

"I guess, it's right ye are, Jimmie! Lucky for us this Yid ape could speak the lingo, ain't it?"

"Yeah, boy! We ride for the Big Swords in the morning, gents.—Better get some sleep."

ABOUT THE AUTHOR

ANOTHER WRITER WHO makes his bow to readers is W. Wirt—a man whose life has been packed with adventures. We asked Mr. Wirt to stand up and introduce himself so that we can all get some idea of what sort of hombre can spin a salty yarn such as this. Mr. Wirt has the floor:

Born—Boston, Massachusetts, 1876.

People on both sides hard-boiled Maine and Massachusetts Presbyterians of strictly English descent. All but one—but that one was a direct descendant of one of Sir Francis Drake's captains. The King of Spain had a standing offer of one thousand golden crowns to the hombre that would present him with "That pirate devil's head." Every once in a while one of the elect breaks out. The rest of the family at once put it down to the old pirate.

My late pa was one of them, all right. I think he had more than his share of the blood. He was a special agent and one of the very few Americans who served in the Secret Service of foreign countries. He went here and there, all over the world, in the oddest places, from northern China to the South Sea Islands, from there to Alaska and way points. Sometimes for Uncle Sam in the Post Office Department; other times for other people.

My education and experience? They are part and part. If there ever was a scrambled one I had it. When I wasn't much bigger than knee-high to a grasshopper my pa began taking me along with him, whenever he could do so safely. I remem-

W. Wirt

ber military, private, public and every other kind of school in a dim way. He'd leave me in one somewhere, go and attend to his knitting, then come back and get me, and away we'd go again. But the constant education I received from him regarding the conduct of "an officer and a gentleman" under any and all circumstance still remains vivid in my mind. One month we'd be in England, evening clothes after six as regular as clockwork, down at one of the big estates for the week-ends, then, in a month or a darn sight less, we'd be in some "flop house" as poor broken-down bums—I acting the part of the devoted son who wouldn't leave his poor old ex-con father, and so forth.

After I reached eighteen I worked with him for a good many years, and when he was called to join his venerable ancestors I carried on alone. No matter where I was, in the Orient or anywhere else, I missed him—with his cool laugh in the face of death and his never failing, slow, amused drawl. His favorite weapon was a sawed-off shotgun carrying buckshot. This, of course, was for use in the places where the little yellow and black brothers congregate mostly. I miss him yet, and always will—and that's that.

I have been behind a badge for Uncle Sam some little time and at present am still special agenting, but on my own, seldom going out of the States and not hunting for any trouble at all, having more than my share already. I've had my gun in the ribs and ears of a few jaspers and used to say "Put 'em up!" so darn often that my longhaired partner—now bobbed haired—every once in a while wakes me up with a demand to know if I have any good reason for poking my finger in her side and hollering at her in the middle of the night.

Then there have been many times when the reverse English was in force and I did the reaching for the blue sky, promptly and in haste. All in all, I lived and rambled when things were wide open, no blue laws or anything, just help yourself to the mustard if you wanted any. And I am darn glad I did. Man, howdy, you could go over the mountain, in "them" days and see things—and do 'em likewise, if you wanted to.

I and Schley whipped the Spanish fleet together, I as a volunteer and Schley as a regular. There were a few others present, but we did most of it. In the late argument I did some "hush, hush" stuff.

My present standing? Well, been married seventeen years; have two children, boy and girl. Have an old place in Maryland near Washington, a police dog, three or twenty-six kittens and cats, an old "colored lady" named Medora to make the corn bread, plenty good old corn lick—I mean corn licorice—to drink and am "out of commission."

A lot of my old buddies drift through, hang their hats up behind the door and drink my said good old yellow-with-age corn licorice, eat some fried chicken and curse me in all the living and dead languages because I won't let go all holds and go wild-catting over the hills once more. They don't get a rise out of me at all. I'm like the colored man who, when asked if he wanted to make a quarter, replied: "No, suh, I done got me a quarter." All I want is peace and quiet.

www.ingramcontent.com/pod-product-compliance
Lightning Source LLC
Chambersburg PA
CBHW030534030726
47495CB00004B/992

9781618276339